MW01492302

TINY WILD THINGS

DANIELLE M. WONG

Storm
PUBLISHING

This is a work of fiction. Names, characters, businesses, places, events and incidents are either the products of the author's imagination or used in a fictitious manner. Any resemblance to actual persons, living or dead, or actual events is purely coincidental.

Copyright © Danielle M. Wong, 2025

The moral right of the author has been asserted.

All rights reserved. No part of this book may be reproduced or used in any manner without the prior written permission of the copyright owner. This prohibition includes, but is not limited to, any reproduction or use for the purpose of training artificial intelligence technologies or systems.

To request permissions, contact the publisher at rights@stormpublishing.co

Ebook ISBN: 978-1-83700-079-1
Paperback ISBN: 978-1-83700-080-7

Cover design: Blacksheep
Cover images: Depositphotos, Shutterstock

Published by Storm Publishing.
For further information, visit:
www.stormpublishing.co

ALSO BY DANIELLE M. WONG

Last Liar Standing

Swearing Off Stars

For Mom—for believing

PROLOGUE

So this is how it ends—with me standing over a corpse. Dirt wedged beneath my nails, blood caked onto my palms. Body fraught with tension. Heart thudding uncontrollably. Hands trembling, limbs stiff like the lifeless ones beneath me.

The sky shifts above as I bristle from the cold. From the shock, the truth, the knowing. I freeze for a moment—paralyzed by each drop of fear multiplying inside my gut. Succumbing to paranoia. *What happens now?*

Hypotheticals run through my psyche's labyrinth, possibilities lost in the fray. My head clouds before instinct finally takes over. *Movement beats inertia.* I have to go. I need to get the hell out of this place.

Adrenaline courses through me as I snap into action. Bury the evidence, burn the remains. Get rid of the body. *The body.*

I screw my gaze shut, recalling everything that happened just moments before. I still see the light fading from both eyes... the life bleeding out in slow motion. I remember it like a film, the footage rolling across a screen at the forefront of my brain. I can't stop it.

I feel a tightness in my chest. Is it sadness, regret, or something else altogether? Perhaps it's just the disbelief catching up to me. The swell of emotions continues circulating in my veins. Sensations mount, threatening to burst right through my flesh.

My breath is ragged as I unfurl my fingers—still balled into a fist—and cast my stare downwards. Only one of us will make it out alive. I realize that now. Only one of us can survive.

Just then, there is a foreign sound behind me. I whip around to identify the source. *Nothing.* My vision blurs slightly, making me doubt everything I see. But it was more than a crunch of leaves. I am sure of it. Bile rises to the back of my throat as I take another look. I have the strange sense that something—or someone—is watching me.

Night will arrive soon, cloaking these surroundings in a blanket of blackness. The air has a tangible charge that tells me it is about to storm. Birds loom overhead—lurking like giant gray omens. In this moment, I am both predator and prey. The wind snaps violently against my body as I step further into the woods. It is time to leave.

I work quickly, erasing any and all signs of my presence. *What will the police think? Will they believe me?* As I go, my mind begins to spin a tale. A convincing story that explains everything, with no detail left unaccounted for.

When I am finished, there are no more traces in sight. Not a single inkling or clue left behind. It's almost like I have disappeared entirely—from place, from memory. Like I was never even here at all.

ONE

I have always been drawn to tiny, wild things. *Feral creatures.* As a child, I would chase rabbits across our lawn and track fledglings while they prepared for first flight. I'd watch them flap their wings violently, feathers shuddering in a frenzied midair dance. More often than not, the birds would fall to the ground within seconds. *Tragic beauty in my eight-year-old eyes.* Every so often, though, there would be an outlier: a little turtle-dove gliding exultantly above the treetops. What started as a ferocious quiver rapidly morphed into a gallant flight. Those were the moments that made my heart race. I would run beyond the confines of our yard—deep into the forest—and follow. Gaze forever fixed on the sky. Those were the moments I felt free.

* * *

The past and present are inextricable. I know that better than most people. Occasionally, I catch myself obsessing over previous events until they threaten to derail me completely. Vicious tears spring forth as a painful memory takes hold. Disturbing recollections play out on the film screen in my mind's eye, progressing until I descend into a perilous spiral. There is only one way to escape.

My heavy stare lands on the cluttered desk in front of me. I drum three fingers against its tight-grained surface and try to shift my focus. Although ample panic recedes, the stubborn knots in my shoulders refuse to budge. I gradually roll my head from left to right, stretching each side of my trapezius until the muscle loosens.

The article draft I printed out is far rougher than I would like—more scribbles than anything else. My notebook overflows with fragmentary sentences and half-hearted annotations. I am currently tasked with profiling trendy skincare regimens and evaluating their efficacy. The regrettable fact that none of them work, however, is complicating matters slightly.

I write for *SYNC*, a popular lifestyle magazine with national circulation. Our target demographic continues to broaden, so it is not uncommon to spot a wide range of people clutching the unmistakably sleek cover. *SYNC* has the polished appeal of *Vogue* with the story range of *Vanity Fair*. That is what I love about the magazine: it delves into myriad topics, from fashion and health to politics and music.

Ever since declaring journalism as my major, I have dreamed of covering significant events and pushing boundaries through my work. Unfortunately, I have also been stuck with the same beat for about two years: my entire span of employment at *SYNC*. Instead of investigating and producing politically charged content, I am consistently assigned fluff pieces.

I anticipated having to prove myself early on—everyone knows that new staff writers do the grunt work—but I am starting to doubt that things will change anytime soon. An abundant list of beauty trends stares back at me menacingly. As much as I would love to outsource this assignment to a makeup junkie or skincare-obsessed intern, I always write my own articles, no matter how tedious.

* * *

The phone rings around midnight. I have just finished pouring myself a sizeable bowl of cereal: my makeshift dinner. Show me a writer who does not keep odd hours, and I will raise you ten sleep-deprived, caffeine-fueled staffers. I am surprised to receive the call, since most of my friends adhere to a more reasonable schedule than I do.

Edna Pryce. The name flashes across my phone screen, sending a jolt of panic through me. I clear my throat and attempt to camouflage any reluctance before I answer.

"Francine."

I stiffen at the sound of my editor's voice. "Hi, Edna."

"Are you busy? It's late."

Her question is rhetorical. Still, the thought of telling Edna Pryce that I am too busy to take her call is enough to make me lose my appetite.

"Not at all—I'm wide awake." The last part is a flagrant lie, but she is probably none the wiser. My unwavering insomnia renders me fatigued yet restless on a regular basis. I have not mentioned this to anyone at work, least of all Edna.

"Good. I have a scoop for you."

I swallow a burgeoning groan and brace myself for another trivial assignment. I have inherited several bottom-of-the-barrel pieces during the past few months, thanks largely in part to my lingering newbie reporter status.

"It's an interview," Edna continues. "This is big."

I perk up at her words. As long as this is not a spring fashion feature, color me interested. "Who's the interview with?" I wonder aloud.

Edna pauses before answering. "Jonathan Kramer."

My stomach drops.

"Are you still there?"

I draw in a quick breath. "Jonathan Kramer as in... the famous artist?"

"Yes." For the first time ever, Edna actually sounds surprised too. "*The* Jonathan Kramer."

"Oh my God." I feel the corners of my mouth rising as elation supersedes disbelief.

"I know you've been itching to tackle a serious assignment, so consider this your big opportunity."

"Edna... this is incredible. Thank you!" I do not bother concealing the emotion in my voice.

"Yes, well," she responds inscrutably, reverting to her signature flat tone. "It's my pleasure."

"I'm stunned," I tell her. "I've been following Jonathan Kramer for years."

"Haven't we all."

"But he always declines interview requests," I say. "So, why is he willing to speak with us now?"

"I wish I knew the answer," Edna says. "But I haven't even told you the greatest part. This is his last interview—ever."

I try to visualize the bold type: JONATHAN KRAMER'S FINAL INTERVIEW.

"I'll have an assistant send you additional details later. The transportation circumstances are a little odd, but nothing about this situation is normal."

"What kind of transportation circum—"

"Our lawyers are still working on it."

"Okay. Can I email you later with some potential angles for the article?"

"Sure." Edna's replies are terse at best.

"Thanks!" I fidget with my phone, resisting a mounting urge to ask any of the other hundred questions racing through my head.

"I don't need to tell you how colossal this is," she adds. "Don't screw it up."

I hear a click and realize that our conversation is over. Edna's personality is like a forced sip of iced coffee: cold and bitter. At least that is how everyone describes her. I have not even been at SYNC long enough to land on her bad side, much less her radar. According to my coworkers, Edna ignores you persistently until you have earned a few precious minutes of her time. New writers are essentially invisible, which is why this phone call is more than shocking.

I am always skipped or dismissed during pitch meetings. Still, I make sure to arrive armed with engaging ideas every week. There was one instance when my #MeToo angle caught Edna's attention, but she handed the assignment to a senior writer instead. Any reason why she would let me handle a story this significant eludes me. It just doesn't add up.

I disregard the untouched bowl of cereal and reopen my laptop. The battery has deteriorated so much that I resort to keeping it permanently plugged in. My fingers fly across the keyboard, composing a short follow-up email to Edna.

I may not fully understand why she trusts me, but I do know this: Jonathan Kramer is a private man. I can count on one hand the number of interviews he has given over the duration of his career. Four journalists total have had the privilege of speaking with Kramer, and not for a lack of trying on everyone else's part. The artist is nearly impossible to get ahold of—with no publicist or agent in tow—and declines almost every request sent his way. This evasiveness has only served to elevate his prestige over the years.

The fact that this assignment could launch my career is not lost on me. It is time to learn everything I can about Jonathan Kramer, because one thing is for sure. I have to nail this interview like my life depends on it. I need to write the hell out of this article—spin gold from any impending material and turn dialogue into diamonds. I cannot afford to mess this up.

TWO

I am standing behind my childhood house when I notice a wild rabbit across the lawn. I stare for the longest time, watching its little nose twitch as storm clouds shift overhead. When light beads of rain start to fall, the rabbit takes off. I chase it across the grass and into the forest—far beyond the borders of our backyard. There I am, running clumsily in the frilly lavender dress Mom insisted upon.

The storm picks up quickly, soaking my braids like a dunk in the pool. One of my shoes comes off along the way: a lonely, patent-leather Mary Jane, stuck in the mud. I don't even bother picking it up, because the rabbit is almost out of sight. Rainwater stings my eyes as I continue chasing it through the woods. Oaks tower over me and dense shrubs line the sodden ground.

A few moments later, I trip on a fallen branch. The entire thing happens in slow motion: tumbling headfirst along the uneven forest floor. There's a small hill, and I can feel myself descending as my body picks up momentum. But all I can think about is the rabbit. *I've lost it.*

I wake up breathless as my dream ends. It's one that I have had many times. I always come to right before I reach the bottom of the hill. I awaken while moving—forever falling and never stopping. The lack of conclusion used to be frustrating, but I have learned to expect it.

I rip off the bedcovers and walk into my tiny kitchen. The dark gray walls have always bothered me, though I've never gotten around to repainting them. Maybe I will finally go to the hardware store after I return from my interview. *Doubtful.* I flip on the coffee maker and tap my fingers against the counter while it brews. Then I take a few scalding sips before resuming my packing efforts from last night.

I kneel next to my suitcase and try hastily to cram an extra pair of boots inside. I always pride myself on being a minimalist packer, but that skill is usually predicated on prior knowledge about my destination. At this point, I am attempting to prepare for every type of climate I can think of. Attempting and failing.

I am rolling my favorite sweater into a tight cylinder when I hear the knock. *His* knock. I have been so caught up in prepping for this interview that I forgot about our plans. I stand up and brush off my jeans.

"Just a second!"

I hurry to the entryway and pause before proceeding. One deep breath to calm my nerves, one more to steady myself. Then I reach out tentatively and turn the knob.

The door creaks open to reveal Liam. All six feet of him: hazel eyes, lean muscles, and an adorable set of dimples. I sense a familiar flutter in my core as he smiles—that same butterfly feeling I used to turn up my nose at. The one I got when we first met. The one I still have whenever he is nearby.

Liam speaks first. "Hey, you."

"Hi," I say softly. "Come in."

Having him back here feels like everything at once—strange yet comfortable, scary but exhilarating. I walk to the sofa and grab a heavy banker's box. It is overflowing with Liam's things: albums and clothes that I finally rounded up.

"Thanks," he says, setting the box on the counter. "I was starting to miss my favorite flannel."

I laugh, because we both know that he hates wearing anything besides T-shirts. "Let me know if there's something else that you think of," I say quietly. "I tried to find it all, but..."

"A lot of our stuff is mixed together," he offers.

"Yeah." I half-smile. "Exactly."

There is an awkward pause—the inevitable void that prolonged distance creates. A tender silence. I want to fill it, but I don't know what to say.

"So," Liam says. "What have you been up to?"

I didn't plan on telling him about my newest assignment, but he catches a glimpse of my suitcase before I can change the subject.

"I'm just doing laundry and packing. Boring stuff."

He raises an eyebrow. "Going on vacation?"

"Not exactly..." I tell him about the interview opportunity, along with my travel plans.

"Wow." Liam's eyes widen. "That's incredible, Fran."

I can't help but grin. "Thanks."

"What a great opportunity for you! It sounds amazing." He reaches out to touch my arm, but I jerk it away. "Sorry." Liam looks down and runs a hand through his hair.

"It's okay." My voice rises. "I'm leaving tomorrow, so I have to finish packing for the trip."

We are caught in the clutches of another long, discomfiting pause.

"Fran," he says gently, "I don't want to pry... but are you sure this is a good idea given everything that happened?"

I look up until we lock eyes, visceral sensations taking hold. A stubborn lump manifests in my throat as Liam averts his gaze. I start to feel that same overwhelming lure, the one that often gets me into trouble. For a moment, I think I might suggest that we get back together, that we give ourselves another chance.

"I miss you," Liam says, inching closer.

My heart quickens. "I miss you too."

"Fran," he whispers.

I feel myself moving towards him, the only man I have ever really loved. But before I can take another step, something within me alters. A pivotal shift.

"What is it?" Liam asks as I pull away.

"I—I'm sorry," I tell him. "I think you should go."

"Fran," he protests softly.

"Please, Liam. Just go."

After he leaves, I wonder if I made the right decision. Not just today, but every choice I have ever made regarding our relationship. *Especially the one to end it.* Part of me believes it was all a mistake, the heartbreaking finality of a once-beautiful connection. Maybe we should have continued living as a couple.

It is not until I turn around that I come to my senses. As I walk away from the door, something catches my eye, a spectacle that I have tried desperately to hide—to fix, cover up, and obliterate from my memory. I even moved a media stand front and center, piling books high around the television in a desperate attempt to create any physical barrier possible. I do my best to ignore the area, but I inexorably obsess over it, fixating on its mere presence. *The spectacle exists.* Dark and deep, rough at the edges. A large hole: punched straight through the living room wall.

THREE

When Edna told me that the transport arrangements would be odd, she was not exaggerating. I expected a lengthy flight or inconvenient train ride—the kind where I would be crammed between two oversized passengers en route to some tiny southern stopover. *But this?* This is unprecedented.

I glance through my travel packet one more time, noting the scarcity of its contents. Normally, there would be tickets, press passes, and meal vouchers. But there is nothing more than an assignment brief and a brochure about Kramer's early work. This man's desire for confidentiality knows no bounds. I even had to sign a verbose nondisclosure agreement in order to confirm our interview. The NDA was obviously approved by SYNC's legal department before reaching me, but I still have a few misgivings.

I am currently on my way to board a *private* jet parked at a *private* airport: not exactly my typical scene. The most unusual part of this entire situation, however, is that I have no idea where I am going. Not one clue. According to Edna, SYNC's lawyers contested a significant amount of the conditions listed in Kramer's contract. Each of their concerns was then met with ardent—and tenacious—pushback from the artist's team.

This tiny airstrip is nothing like the JFK runways I am accustomed to. I have never set foot on a private jet before, so I must physically restrain myself from oohing and ahhing at every opulent detail. I feel like a freshly cast actress waiting for the director to yell, "*Cut!*" My idea of extravagance is sitting in the exit row with an empty middle seat, so this is an entirely new level of indulgence. I catch glimpses of a marble and glass bar, a large flat-screen television, and surrealist artwork hanging on the walls. A flight attendant shows me to a leather seat about twice the size of what I expect before offering me a snack.

"Champagne and chocolate strawberries?"

I politely decline the drink and opt for tea instead. Despite the luxury of my surroundings, I am technically working. This commute is nothing like the sort I am used to, though. Being the only passenger on an airplane is at once intoxicating and extremely strange. I see a pilot talking to the flight attendant, offering an awkward wave while they smile at me in unison.

I lean back as bullets of rain whip past my window. After glancing around to make sure no one is looking, I exhale and fog up the bottom corner. I draw a little heart with my pinky—just like Mom and I used to do. It fades quicker than I expect, but the memory still manages to leave a grin on my face. I am fondly reminded of our first family vacation to California.

I stiffen when I notice the flight attendant's sudden reflection. *He is standing right behind me.* I turn around to face him, along with a woman who I definitely did not see.

"Sorry to startle you," he says apologetically. "This is Bette, another flight attendant."

"Hello." She smiles down at me, her voice lyrical.

"Hello," I chime back.

"Here's your tea." Bette removes a tiny porcelain cup from

the silver tray in her hands and places it on a scalloped doily in front of me.

"Thank you."

The two flight attendants hover nearby, watching my every move. I glance in their direction before they withdraw their stares and return to the back of the plane.

"Good morning," the pilot's voice blares through a tiny speaker. "We'll be taking off soon."

The sudden sound makes me bristle. I still have no idea where this plane is flying to, or where I am headed once it lands. Privacy is apparently Jonathan Kramer's lifeblood. Even after the assignment concludes, I can never reveal where he lives. It was all listed in the NDA—obligatory, according to Kramer's lawyers.

The original contract stipulated that I travel without a phone. *Period.* Obviously, SYNC's legal team had a field day with that. After successfully combatting said requirement, the lawyers chipped away at Kramer's demands until reaching a reasonable compromise.

I bring the warm cup of herbal tea to my lips and take a calming sip.

Bette returns to collect it on cue. "Sit back and relax," she adds before walking away. "Let me know if you need anything else."

My hands are empty and idle, and I feel even more restless than I was before. This is undoubtedly the strangest assignment I have ever received. I pull out my phone and scroll through Edna's recent email, reminding myself that this scoop is categorically worth it. *Jonathan Kramer's Final Interview.* The headline boldens and expands—broadening until the words canvass every inch of my brain.

The sheer gravity of this project begins to engulf me, draining every ounce of energy I have left. Chamomile mitigates any remaining apprehension coursing through my veins.

Sleep deprivation—a regrettable byproduct of staying up late last night—renders me extremely tired. My eyelids hang heavy as we taxi to the runway, closing against my will until everything is a blurred mess of fractured light and distorted objects. I do not fight it. *I cannot fight it.* After a fleeting moment, there is only darkness.

* * *

Turbulence jolts me awake. My head moves back and forth as we hit a pocket of rough air, but I still feel too drowsy to sit up straighter. I peel my eyelids open and turn to look out the window. My stomach rolls—not from turbulence, but from shock.

We are no longer flying through the sky. A hard—and abrupt—landing places us firmly on the ground. The plane halts to a jarring stop as I wonder how long I was asleep. A double ding sounds from the speaker, with Bette reappearing shortly after.

"We are here," she says.

I return her smile, although I have no idea where *here* is.

"Right this way." She ushers me through the open aircraft door and down a flight of stairs.

I look in both directions, but the runway stretches on before disappearing into a blur of haze. This must be some sort of private airstrip. I'm used to walking through terminals and waiting to pluck my bags off of the frequently delayed carousels found at commercial airports. I would normally hail a cab or call an Uber or a Lyft.

Here, everything is different. Foreign... shrouded in mystery. There are no signs to clue me in to my location. This nondescript weather doesn't help much either—crisp air with a drizzle.

"There's your ride." Bette leads me to a black van idling in the distance. "The driver will take you to Mr. Kramer's main residence."

I wait for a driver to appear, but the trunk pops open instead. Bette looks at me expectantly and gestures to my bag. Surprised, I grab the handle and load it into the back.

"Have a safe journey," she says, giving me a quick wave.

"Thank you." My spirits lift as she begins walking away.

I open the car door and climb inside. Next thing I know, I am buckled into the back row of a moving van. I strain against my seatbelt to look out the windows ahead. It is raining harder now, and the terrain mainly consists of fields and shallow hills. There are no recognizable landmarks that might give away a location. Is this all part of Kramer's property?

My immediate instinct is to check my phone. I pull it out of my bag, heart sinking at the dearth of tiny bars. *No signal.* I restart it, hoping that reception might improve along the way. But I cannot manage to get a signal as we barrel along this unknown road. My maps application still thinks I'm in New York.

To make matters worse, I cannot even see my driver. The front seat is separated by a partition—sort of like the setup inside a limousine. Only this is no limousine. I think about calling up front and asking how much longer we have en route, but swiftly decide against it. I tell myself that there is no need to panic. *Everything will be okay.* I repeat the phrase until I actually begin to internalize it.

The reality of this undertaking is drastically more unnerving than what I anticipated when I signed on the dotted line. My imagination conjured up images of being privy to exclusive intel while Kramer's private security team escorted me around. I could never have imagined how this was actually going to feel.

The situation is almost as crazy as it sounds, but I am just desperate enough to do it. I am also sane enough to appreciate how incredible this opportunity is, and humble enough to recognize my shortcomings. I am not in any position to turn down a career-making assignment—especially when it's Jonathan Kramer's last interview.

With every wind of the road, I become more aware of a growing remoteness. The wheels roll onward—gripping increasingly rough terrain with each rotation. Although my view is hindered, there is a knowing in my gut. Any pulse of city life has dulled to a quiet hum, undetectable if not nonexistent. I am headed straight for abject isolation.

Unease bubbles up until I feel sick to my stomach. Between that and the continuous bumps that a backrow seat affords, I am growing more nauseous by the minute. *Queasier than I felt on an ocean cruise last summer.* I close my eyes and try to deep breathe like the captain suggested. It doesn't work.

I inhale slowly through my nose before choking down vomit. Predictably, the rancid taste lingers in my mouth long after. I feel the van slow to a sluggish pace about fifteen painstaking minutes later. We make a slight turn, continuing along what feels like unpaved, pebbly ground. I am relieved to finally feel the car come to a halt.

My view is hindered, so I still have no idea where we are. The abrupt sound of a slammed door cues me to unbuckle my seatbelt and run a hand through my matted hair. The back door opens suddenly to reveal my driver: a portly middle-aged man clothed in a wrinkled navy suit.

"Welcome to Mr. Kramer's estate," he says in an indecipherable accent.

I tentatively hunch my way over to the door.

"Here you go." He offers a hand.

I accept it, wondering if he is also briefed on the contract I signed. The thought nauseates me all over again. "Thanks," I say, stepping out of the car and taking in my first unobstructed look at the Kramer residence. The sight is nothing short of staggering.

FOUR

This property is undeniably breathtaking, reminiscent of another era. I am in the prestigious presence of an early twentieth-century, Gatsby-esque, colonial-style mansion. There are fountains and marble sculptures—catching the scattered sunlight—along with terraced gardens on the opposite side of the drive. A series of artistically manicured hedges lines the perimeter of the grounds, though Kramer's land seems to extend well beyond any visual limit. This estate occupies the elusive space between refined and ostentatious.

My first thought is that royalty must live here. *Art world royalty*. I would put good money on an appraisal of sixty million or more, just for this palatial home. And that doesn't even take the property's acreage—or other features—into account. I marvel at how much land Kramer probably owns.

"Miss?" the driver prompts.

I hurry around the van to pick up my bag.

He gestures to a landscaped walkway leading up to the front door. "They'll be waiting for you."

I thank him and turn back towards Kramer's estate. During

my walk, I notice a cottage across the vast lawn. I wonder if anyone lives there before shifting my attention to the pavement beneath my feet: uneven and full of fractures. Despite its lavishness, the property appears substantially worn down. *Decrepit.* This architecture is old-fashioned, but it also seems like the place has not been touched or tended to in years.

I hear a faint hum behind me—the car's engine. I glance over my shoulder to see the driver pulling away. As I watch him disappear into the distance, reality hits me harder than it did before. I have absolutely no idea where I am.

I have not yet reached the front door when it whips open to reveal a tall middle-aged woman wearing a wool turtleneck. Her hair is piled high in a prim bun, while her lips purse into a tiny line that emphasizes her pointed chin. I pause—expecting a cold exchange—but the woman's demeanor transforms before I can even open my mouth.

"Hello there," she greets me with a warm smile. "We've been expecting you."

I walk up to the doorstep and return her expression. "Hi, I'm Fran."

She hurries me inside and sets my bag on an entryway table. "I'm Laurel, Mr. Kramer's housekeeper. Can I take your coat?"

"Oh, thank you." I shrug off my parka and hand it to her.

"Mr. Kramer is working in his studio and should be back soon." Laurel hangs my coat in a large closet and gestures to the staircase. "May I show you to your room?"

"That would be great," I say, grabbing my duffel bag.

"You'll be staying upstairs in the main wing."

I still cannot quite fathom the fact that I get to stay in Jonathan Kramer's home. I follow Laurel and steal a few glances of the property's interior. My writer brain chronicles any detail it can get ahold of. *Blue glass knobs on a hutch near the front door, burnished wood along the banister, and a porcelain candle sconce that looks like a French antique.*

I notice some white frames scattered across an otherwise bare wall while we ascend the staircase. Most of them house photographs of Jonathan and his late wife, Jane. I recognize her from an obituary I found in the library archives. She was gorgeous—dark hair, full lips, and deep brown eyes. Laurel whips around to see me lingering a few steps below.

"Jane was really something," she says knowingly. There's an air of something else too, but I can't quite identify it.

"She looks so happy," I respond quietly. "What happened to her is awful."

Laurel nods solemnly.

"Did you know her?" I ask.

"No." She shakes her head. "I didn't start working for Mr. Kramer until after his wife passed."

My heart sinks a little. I was hoping to ask Laurel some questions about Jane before Jonathan got back.

"He used to reminisce a lot, though." Laurel looks at the frames, reliving a memory. "This wall of photographs was a lot when I first moved in."

"He took some of them down?"

She nods. "They were all over the house. But I think it was too difficult to see Jane's face everywhere... not just in his mind's eye, but on the walls too. He wanted to have a fresh start."

"That makes sense. Did he—"

"We should probably get you settled before he returns," Laurel cuts in.

I think about asking her another question but decide against it. Instead, I follow her down a narrow hallway once we reach the landing.

"I'm looking forward to speaking with Mr. Kramer," I say.

"I'm sure you are." Laurel pauses outside of a closed door. "My advice is to let *him* bring her up. Trust me. If Jonathan wants to discuss Jane, he will."

* * *

This room will take some getting used to. It is more than sizeable, but the furniture is organized into an odd arrangement that gives me pause. A significant amount of floorspace is impeded by clusters of unused pieces. There are two tapestry rugs crammed into the far corner, with faded patterns and knotted tassels on the ends.

I set my bag on a wide dresser and assess the layout. *Has this always been a guest room, or was it repurposed for storage?* There is a handsome—albeit dust-laden—armoire blocking three tall bookcases. Everything appears to be antique, complete with distressed wood and old-fashioned hardware. I peer down at the armoire's ceramic knobs and briefly wonder how old they are. Each surface is chipped sporadically, lined with pale mauve dots.

My eyes drift upwards until they land on a decorated ceiling. I examine the Victorian paper pastiche, noting its classical motifs and a series of multihued flowers on the edges. The center is adorned with a hand-painted mural. It depicts a clear blue sky—complete with flying doves and red rosebuds. There are also a few cherubs hovering above the fluffy clouds, with wings that remind me of the birds I watched as a child. This entire ceiling is like another world: a place I could get lost in.

I break my stare, returning my attention to the furniture in front of me. I have to be careful not to zone out too much. My doctor used to tell me that. After an unsettling childhood incident, my mother practically forced me to see a psychologist.

I haven't spoken with him in a while—though recent events have certainly made me consider booking an appointment. I have started to dial his office number on more than one occasion, but I always hang up before it rings.

A series of visits could potentially alleviate—or even cure—

my ongoing insomnia. Maybe a few sessions would ease my nerves about what happened with Liam. Maybe a trained professional could help me forget about that night entirely, erasing it from my memory like pressing *delete* on a keyboard.

FIVE

I continue pacing around the room, realizing that something about it feels familiar. I run my fingers along the chenille bedspread and stare at its floral pattern. The style reminds me of another print—something from my youth. That's it: the pink wallpaper inside my childhood bedroom.

I turn up my nose at the image before softening gently. It brings back sweet memories of my mother, Mary. She was always so chic and sophisticated—from her waist-length brunette curls to her taste in design. I never once saw Mom looking anything less than impeccably dressed, even on lazy weekend mornings. She probably hoped that I would follow suit.

When I was little, she tried to tempt me with themed tea parties, sewing sessions, and bouquet-arrangement classes. Much to her chagrin, I never really showed any interest, consistently eschewing refined activities in favor of outdoor hobbies. The forest behind our house was my preferred playground. I would arrive home with muddy shoes and skinned knees, nose burnt from a day of backyard adventures. Always alone and never with friends.

Mom set me up on play dates every so often before taking stock of her wasted efforts. She understood that I was a bit peculiar, and she adored me anyway. Sometimes I would return from school crying because I failed to get on well with the other kids. I remember seeing Mom's face fall, bright eyes marked by sorrow. She would take me into her arms and tell me how loved I was. *My sweet, beautiful girl.* I can still hear her voice.

What would she think of me now? Not much has changed since then. I am still the odd one out... the recluse who doesn't quite fit in. Sure, I can force small talk and make acquaintances. But my truest self—my essence—only comes out when I am alone.

Sometimes, I think I have thrown myself into work as a coping mechanism. Pinned my self-image entirely to my career success... or lack thereof. That's part of why this assignment is so important to me. My job is all that I have.

The realization makes me stiffen. It only emphasizes the internal stress that I feel, the mounting pressure from Edna to knock this interview out of the park. *What if all these years have been for naught?* What if I botch this project and get fired? Then I really will have nothing to show for myself...

Hunger pangs eventually pull me from my spiral. I walk over to the dresser and fish through my bag for a 5th Avenue bar: Liam's favorite candy. I travel with one everywhere I go. I developed the habit when we were first dating, mainly because it reminded me of him.

We were in that early stage of our relationship when we couldn't stand to be apart. We could barely keep our hands off of each other, but our bond transcended the physical. Liam was the first person to really encourage me to pursue writing as a career. He read my work, urged me to follow my journalistic passion.

Obviously, toting around sugar pales in comparison to being with him. I would much rather go back to the way things were before—the way they used to be. When life was freer and less complex. *When trust was fully intact.* I'd trade everything and more to go back in time. Still, this silly candy ritual comforts me in a sense—especially when I am so far from home.

It suddenly dawns on me that I might not be far from home at all. I might, in fact, be standing in New York right now. *What if the plane was just a decoy?* A calculated trick to make me think I was flying across the country. My inquiring mind weighs the possibility as my stomach gurgles in protest.

I unwrap my 5th Avenue bar and sit on the bed's edge. What if Kramer's property is just a stone's throw from Brooklyn? *What if he's been hiding in plain sight all along?* A chunk of crunchy peanut butter wedges itself between my teeth as I consider the idea.

I pull out my phone expectantly, only to discover that it still shows zero bars. I pace around the room with my eyes glued to the screen, hoping to detect even the slightest variation in reception. Twenty minutes flash by without success. Despite standing on the bed, waving my phone around slowly, and lifting it as close to the ceiling as my outstretched arm could manage, I am no closer to finding a decent signal than I was when I first arrived. I set my phone on the nightstand and resolve to resume my efforts later.

I walk over to my bag and consider unpacking. Unfortunately, we have yet to clarify exactly how long I will be visiting this property. SYNC's legal team negotiated heavily before I finally agreed to a vague length of stay. *A couple weeks at most.* Being notoriously finnicky, Kramer was unwilling to commit to a definitive timeframe for this interview. I am hoping that he might be able to at least provide a ballpark estimate once I meet him.

I unzip my bag and pull open the armoire doors, inadvertently disturbing a thick patina of dust in the process. The precarious structure sways as its hinges creak shrilly. I steady it

—between coughs—and close the doors as slowly as possible. Living out of my suitcase for the time being suddenly seems like the wisest choice.

I chew on my bottom lip and silently pray for a Wi-Fi connection. *No such luck.* I will have to ask Kramer if he has an encrypted network and explain that I need access for work. Honestly, the artist is already starting to get on my nerves. His incessant need for privacy is beyond irritating—not mention the bane of my current situation.

How am I supposed to check emails and message Edna? She will have my head if I don't contact her soon. I was also planning to brush up on a few succinct Internet biographies before our conversation, but it looks like that won't be happening either.

At least I did a fair amount of research about Kramer beforehand: his early life, career boom, and public exhibits. I have my summary notes written down on paper, along with an entire host of questions floating through my head. The combination should make for a groundbreaking interview. Now all I need is the artist himself.

* * *

To merely say that Kramer is famous would do a disservice to his worldwide reputation, not to mention his talent. *He is the art world's Mozart*—that is the precise compliment that one journalist gave him early on. The comparison obviously stuck. Critics have varied interpretations when it comes to the meaning of Kramer's work, but they all agree about one thing: the man is a genius.

SYNC—along with every other publication and news outlet —sends regular letters and emails to the only addresses we have on file for Kramer. The information is likely expired, or was never even his to begin with. We writers have a running joke that the day Kramer returns one of our inquiries will be the day that pigs fly. I admittedly stole a quick glance outside after Edna called me about the assignment.

Kramer wasn't always this private, though. His first pieces went public in the late seventies—amidst a politically charged and turbulent landscape. He was a well-known activist who supported anti-war protests and participated in women's rights marches. He has experimented with multiple mediums, but his vibrant, hand-blown-glass sculptures are by far his most popular. Kramer's work swept the awards circuit within two years, garnering him international fame. Critics and buyers everywhere flocked to his shows to gaze at—and get their hands on—his coveted art. To own a Kramer is to own a piece of history.

He frequently attributed his success to his wife and longtime muse, Jane. Kramer called her his constant source of inspiration, earning the couple even more admiration from adoring fans. He and Jane sold their large Midwestern farmhouse in the nineties and moved to an undisclosed location that they built themselves. Tragically, she ended up passing away from lung cancer shortly thereafter. Kramer was justifiably beside himself. *Then he went dark.* No one has seen a new piece for the past two decades.

Kramer's sudden withdrawal from the public eye caused understandable panic amongst critics and consumers alike. There is a prevalent rumor that he now lives in a private residence in Connecticut, but it has never been proven. Kramer's pieces have increased immeasurably in value over time, selling at auctions for millions of dollars. Some people think that Jane's death caused an irrevocable shift in him—a void so large that he might never be able to create again. The writer in me hopes that there is more to the story... an unexpected twist that no one sees coming.

SIX

I blink in the darkness and take a deep breath. *Where am I?* The sharp stream of air stings my lungs as I inhale again. *What time is it?* I must have dozed off. It is pitch black in this room, so my eyes cannot make anything out. I sit up quickly and reach around for my phone.

I am not afraid of many things, but I absolutely hate the dark. *Always have.* I start to panic when I cannot find my phone. My fingers reach around the floral comforter, but all I grab are empty handfuls. I feel my heart race while I frantically inch towards the edge of the bed. I am about to stand up when I finally see a tiny illuminated screen.

My phone vibrates once from the floor: a text message. I lean down and stretch out my arm, but I cannot reach it. I fall face first onto the polished hardwood instead, a loud thud sounding as I hit the ground. My shoulder absorbs most of the shock, so I wince while trying to sit up and steady myself. I grab my phone and turn on the flashlight, aiming it erratically at the wall until I find the switch plate.

My heart begins to calm once the lights are on. I glance

around the room, refamiliarizing myself with the awkward furniture arrangement. This layout feels as off-putting as the frigid temperature does. I am about to search for a warmer comforter when my phone buzzes once again with a text from Liam.

> Hey Fran. Just wanted to make sure you got in okay. How was the flight?

I have a rule for myself when it comes to texting Liam: wait at least one hour before responding. I created it right after we split up. Despite a few close calls, I have never broken my self-imposed mandate. It exists for a principal reason. The waiting period forces me to think before I reply, preventing any impulsive reactions. Part of me is still worried that I will agree to get back together with him, and I would be lying if I said I have not come close.

Liam will always worry about me, regardless of our current relationship status. Not because I'm a woman, and not because I am his ex-girlfriend. He will worry simply because that's the kind of person he is. He cares about everyone in his circle—genuinely wants the best for all of us. Despite everything that happened, he still has a heart of solid gold. Which only complicates matters further...

I take a deep breath and stick my phone inside my pocket. Then I gather my pajamas and toothbrush to wash up. The bedroom door creaks when I open it, revealing the long hallway I saw earlier. This darkness looks like it could swallow me whole. I think about turning a light on, but I'm worried about waking someone up.

I wonder if Kramer is sleeping in a nearby room. I would hate to disturb him and make a bad impression, especially on my first night here. I turn on my phone light instead and tiptoe down the hall. I glance around to find the bathroom, but all of the doors are closed. I cannot remember which one Laurel pointed out earlier. At the moment, they all look the same to me.

After turning a few different locked handles, I am finally successful. I flip on the bathroom light and shut the door quietly behind me. Everything is stark white: the minute console sink, noisy porcelain toilet, and sizeable clawfoot tub. A fluorescent bulb flickers overhead as I turn on the faucet. Two tiny windows hover above the showerhead, but I cannot see anything outside because of the late hour. There is nothing more than a swirl of inky blackness beyond the pane.

I brush my teeth slowly, relishing the feeling of minty paste against my gums. My jaw cracks as I swish: a nagging reminder of the incessant grinding issue I developed months earlier. I turn on the shower and undress, tensing slightly at the cold. Considering its age and appearance, this property might be devoid of any heating system whatsoever. I give the knob another generous crank and silently pray for warm water. After waiting for about five minutes, I give up.

If it were any other day, I would just skip my shower altogether. But I have been traveling by plane and sitting inside a strange van. Given my damp armpits and oily scalp, I am craving a decent wash. The icy water sends me shivering the moment it hits my body. *Holy hell.* I shower as quickly as I can, globbing shampoo onto my strands and smearing soap across my forehead. It finally warms up just before I finish.

Frigid air meets my wet skin as I step out of the shower, somehow managing to make me even colder than I was before. I grab a terrycloth towel off the rack and wrap it tightly around my shoulders. The mirror is partially fogged up, with condensation bleeding around the edges. I reach out and swipe across its damp surface.

I remove my hand to reveal a patch of unsullied reflection. I stare at it intently, studying the nooks and crannies of my young but aging complexion. Parts of it vex me more than others: the emerging lines on my forehead and a stubborn freckle beneath my left brow. Wrinkles and texture dominate what was once taut, creamy skin.

The beauty-centric articles I write only serve to heighten my awareness of all things superficial. Researching products, trends, and treatments has rendered me hyper-conscious when it comes to my own imperfections. Although this initially spurred a makeup obsession, it was ultimately short-lived. My hapa skin tone is surprisingly difficult—read *impossible*—to find decent color matches for.

After searching tirelessly for the perfect foundation, I finally gave up. Then I started focusing on skincare instead. While I've exerted a fair amount of effort establishing a solid multi-step regimen, I haven't exactly achieved the results I was hoping for. I've lost hours scrutinizing the nondescript features staring back at me. Other than a pair of almond-shaped hazel eyes, there is nothing particularly distinctive about my face.

Liam once said that they were so luminous he could see his reflection inside. If memory serves, I pretended to gag after his compliment. I smirk at the fleeting recollection and pull myself away from the mirror. After throwing on some flannel pajamas, I finger-comb my hair and switch off the light.

Once I make my way back to the bedroom, I am surprised to see a white envelope lying on the floor. Someone must have slipped it underneath the door. *Was it there before I left?* I reach down and pick it up, feeling the weight of heavy paper in my palm. Then I open the envelope to find a piece of cardstock with scrawled writing.

Sorry we missed each other today. I got back late from the studio and didn't want to bother you. I look forward to meeting you tomorrow.

—J. Kramer

My stomach drops as I set the note down. I open my suitcase and silently curse my limited energy stores for letting me nap earlier. Kramer must have heard me snoring through the door: an impeccable first impression. I grab my phone charger and find an outlet next to the bed. Then I plug it in and set three alarms—beginning at 6 a.m.—for good measure. I need to guarantee that I wake up early for our interview. I would much rather be waiting for Jonathan Kramer than have him waiting for me.

I crawl into bed and check the timestamp on Liam's text. It has been well over an hour since he sent the message. I compose a quick reply, but my text refuses to send. *No service.* I try a few more times, but I cannot manage to find a signal anywhere. *Zero bars.* The reception here is definitely spotty, but the fact that I received Liam's message gives me hope. There is probably a better area of the house or even a Wi-Fi network I can access tomorrow.

I am still thinking about Liam long after I shut my eyes. Given our tumultuous history, it's virtually impossible not to. He is still my best friend. My *only* true friend. That's how we first began—as mates.

We met at a stereotypical college frat party. The kind you only attend because you think you're *supposed* to be there. I remember convincing myself that those gatherings were formative. Believing that if I didn't show up, I would be missing out on a pivotal part of the university experience.

That changed when I met Liam. I ducked out early with the sole intention of walking back to my dorm. But just as I was leaving, we collided. *Literally.* There was nothing cute about our meeting, but something sparked between us that night. It's been burning ever since. So even if we cannot sustain a romantic relationship, I need Liam in my life in some way, shape, or form.

Unremitting thoughts plague my head as I struggle to keep still. This mattress is rigid and uneven, and my feet have nearly gone numb from the cold. I fluff my pillow and writhe around in a desperate attempt to find some sort of comfortable position. After an hour of turning over to no avail, my body only winds up tenser than it was before. Despite it all, I eventually manage a fitful sleep.

* * *

It is still dark outside when my phone alarm beeps the next morning. I sit up straight and rub my eyes, light beads of rain tapping the windowpane as I crawl out of bed. Any dreams elude me—forever lost to the previous night. After securing my toiletry kit and selecting some clothes, I crack open the bedroom door and brave the hallway.

Everything is more obscure than it was yesterday, but I do not even bother using my phone light. I know exactly where the bathroom is: the third door on the left. My mind wanders as I tread past the other closed doors, wondering what lies behind them. I imagine unlocking each one, rotating every brass knob and peering inside. *What secrets do they hold?* Yet another question to ask Jonathan Kramer.

I splash water on my face and forgo makeup this morning. After running a brush through my dark hair, I gargle with spearmint mouthwash and hightail it back to the bedroom. Then I change into a cream-colored blouse and pull on my favorite pair of skinny jeans. The house remains frigid, rendering my thin sweater virtually ineffectual. I search for a jacket before remembering that my parka is hanging in the downstairs coat closet.

I lay out a selection of interview equipment: one thick spiral notebook, two ballpoint pens, and my trusty recorder. While I normally work on my laptop, I have a nagging feeling that Kramer will be more comfortable with me using paper. I scoop up my supplies and step into a pair of boots before leaving the room.

This time, I *do* need a flashlight. I pull out my phone to illuminate a pathway while navigating the hall. Then I approach the staircase tentatively, attempting to minimize any racket. My effort is wasted as the wood creaks beneath my boots. I descend the remaining stretch, slowing my pace even further before reaching the bottom.

My eyes blink in the continual darkness. I hover my tiny phone light around the vicinity, wondering where to begin. The lower level of the house is so massive that it is impossible not to get lost. I wander, noting the presence of an old hearth that leaves me with the abrupt desire for a roaring fire. Its mantelpiece is covered in unopened matchbooks. I imagine myself warmed by the glowing coals, feeling flooding back into my limbs.

I eventually make my way into what appears to be a living room. There is a long sofa on one side, adorned with leather upholstery and velvet throw pillows. Several chairs are spaced evenly around a coffee table with a large centerpiece in the middle. It must be one of Kramer's sculptures. I lean over the table to take a closer look, straining my neck to examine the piece. *From an early oeuvre.* It is absolutely magnificent, with thick layers of red and purple blown glass crafted into an amorphous shape.

I consider sitting in one of the chairs, but they appear to be impeccably undisturbed. Everything looks so perfect—from the crown molding to the antique bolection mantel. It seems like nobody has used this room in years. I decide to explore more of the house instead, at least until Kramer wakes up. Rain continues to sprinkle outside as I move into another room. This is clearly the kitchen, which I assume is unrenovated, given the rustic stove and laminate countertops.

Just then, a text notification flashes across my screen.

Jonathan Kramer is lying to you. Get out while you can.

SEVEN

The message stops me in my tracks. I read the words again and stare at them in disbelief.

> Jonathan Kramer is lying to you. Get out while you can.

I immediately unlock my phone and look at the sender's contact information: unknown. My eyes scan the text a few more times. *Who sent this?* How did they get my number? A muffled sound steals my attention. I think it's coming from upstairs, but I cannot be sure. *Is it Kramer?* I exit out of my messages and keep moving through the house.

The next room is large and windowless. I almost stumble over a thick rug as I enter, but quickly appreciate how it muffles the sound of my steps. I wave my phone around and clutch my notebook tightly against my chest. For someone who hates the dark, I am really being tested right now. There are stacks of bookcases and a few large armchairs facing the wall. The room is so big that I have to illuminate it in sections, like piecing together a puzzle. I run my phone light along the next area, noting an oil painting and a trinket cabinet of sorts. *Then I hear a voice.*

"Good morning," says a raspy male tone.

I drop my phone and freeze. The light lands face down, so I'm left standing in total darkness. My heart thuds against my chest as the voice speaks again.

"I didn't mean to startle you, Miss Hendrix."

I hear a slight screeching sound coming from behind me. It grows louder, and so does the voice.

"I prefer the darkness, you see. I do my best thinking before the sun rises."

I whip around to see the outline of a figure headed towards me. My eyes haven't fully adjusted, but I can make out a rough shape. When my limbs finally regain feeling, I reach down quickly and grab my phone. Then I aim the light directly in front of me. I see an old man in a wheelchair. *Kramer?*

"Oh my, that is extremely bright." He squints and holds up his hands.

"Sorry!" I say, moving my phone away. "I didn't realize anyone was in here."

"That's all right," he says. "My apologies for scaring you."

This man must be Jonathan Kramer. *Who else would he be?* What an odd and uncomfortable way to meet.

"Shall I turn on a light?" he suggests.

"Yes, please."

A few moments later, I'm standing across from a world-renowned artist. He sits in an electric wheelchair, slightly hunched over. Kramer is unlike anything I imagined. He's diminutive in appearance, a trait exaggerated by his quiet, strained voice. But despite this fact, meeting him exceeds my greatest expectations.

Bright blue eyes belie Kramer's worn features. There are deep crinkles around them, perhaps accumulated from years of stolen smiles and raucous laughter. The artist wears khaki slacks and a dark sweater that emphasizes the whiteness of his wiry hair.

I step closer and extend a hand. "Nice to meet you, Mr. Kramer."

"Now, now. None of that," he says with a grin. "It's *Jonathan*. Something about Mr. Kramer being my father, and all that jazz." He waves a palm through the air.

We both laugh, and I feel myself relax a little.

"Well, if you're *Jonathan*," I reciprocate, "then I'm Fran."

"It's great to finally meet you, Fran," he says as we shake hands.

I flinch at the ice-cold temperature of Kramer's fingers and hope that he doesn't notice.

"This is a really nice space," I say, gesturing to the overflowing bookcases and cozy reading nook. In the light, this room is much less frightening and a lot more impressive.

"Just my little library." He smiles. "I've spent years amassing every first edition I could get my hands on. Please, see for yourself."

"Those are first editions?" I ask in disbelief.

"Most of them."

I walk over to the shelves and feel my eyes widen as I take a closer look. Kramer must own hundreds of first-edition classics. I reach out on impulse, but quickly pull my hand away.

"Go ahead," Kramer urges. "Open one."

I tentatively run my finger along a ribbed brown spine. I gently pull it out of the bookcase and peel open the cover. *Travels into Several Remote Nations of the World.*

"Ah," Kramer says. "That's a special one."

"*Gulliver's Travels*," I whisper, delicately palming the novel.

"Impressive," he says after a moment. "How did you know that?"

I look up and smile. "I'm a voracious reader—always have been."

"Wonderful," he muses as I slide the book back in.

My eyes scan the remaining shelves, searching for other recognizable titles. I want to see them all.

"How do you like the rest of the house?" Kramer asks me. "I trust that your room is comfortable enough?"

I don't have the heart to tell him that his furniture arrangement is confusing, or that the room is freezing. "It's perfect," I lie.

"And you've taken a thorough look around?" he asks, pointing to my phone light, which is still turned on.

"Oh"—I shake my head and turn it off—"I actually haven't. *Not yet.* I really just unpacked my things and slept yesterday." I shrug. "I would love to see more, though. You have quite a massive property."

"Yes, well." He nods. "There'll be time for all that. But for now, I suggest we have some breakfast. Are you hungry?"

"Starving," I say as a nearby light flicks on.

Kramer chuckles at my puzzled expression. "That's just Laurel," he explains. "Waking up the house, right on cue."

I nod as several other lights follow suit. Before I know it, the entire place is filled with a much welcome brightness. I literally feel the tension leaving my shoulders. Kramer moves over to the doorway, and I follow him out of the library.

I steal glimpses of the lower level as we make our way to the kitchen. Every wall is filled with colorful paintings and photographs. I see a few of Kramer's most famous sculptures along the way. There's a fiery orange one—large and vibrant— sitting atop a modest end table. I instantly recognize it as one of the first pieces he ever sold. If memory serves, he made hundreds of thousands of dollars from that sculpture alone, only to buy it back years later as a gift to his wife.

"Have a seat." Kramer gestures to a breakfast nook opposite the kitchen.

I scoot into a padded leather booth that reminds me of something found in an old-fashioned diner. There are vintage metal ads on the walls and white doilies on the table. I lay a napkin in my lap and set my pens, notebook, and recorder beside me.

"Good morning," Laurel chirps from the kitchen. She's wearing another wool turtleneck—a lighter gray this time—and a pair of brown loafers. Her hair is woven into the same high style as before. Laurel's bun is so tight that the corners of her face appear to be lifted by at least a couple inches.

"Morning to you," Kramer says with a nod. "What's on the menu today, my dear?"

"Same thing as *every* morning." Laurel shakes her head and lets out a laugh. "Crispy bacon and poached eggs."

"Sounds delightful," he chimes back.

My stomach grumbles as the delicious smell wafts in.

"Laurel makes the best bacon," Kramer tells me. "You're not a vegetarian, are you?"

"Definitely not. Unless you count that failed attempt in college..."

"Well," he chuckles. "At least you came to your senses eventually. I've never trusted non-meat-eaters."

"I think you'd perish without your daily dose of bacon," Laurel says as she sets two steaming plates on the table. "What would you like to drink, Fran?"

"Just water, please."

She nods and opens a wooden cabinet.

"Thank you," I say as she hands me a full glass. "Everything looks great."

"Enjoy, you two. Just holler if you need anything." Laurel smiles warmly and leaves the room. I notice her limping slightly on the way out, but I can't tell if it's just part of her gait. This is the first time I've really paid much attention.

"Mmm," Kramer hums over his food.

I cut into my egg and watch its bright yellow yolk spill out. I've never been a big breakfast person, but who am I to turn down a home-cooked meal with an eminent artist?

"Laurel is wonderful," he says between tiny bites. "She's always been a big help."

I glance up and notice Kramer's shaky hand clutching the fork as he struggles to stab an egg white.

"She seems very nice," I agree. "How long has she been working for you?"

"About fifteen years," he says.

"That's great. You two seem pretty close."

"Oh, yes. Laurel is like family."

I have the sudden urge to ask Kramer to elaborate, but I fight it.

"She's been here through thick and thin," he adds. "A true-blue companion."

It sounds like he's talking about more than a housekeeper. *Are they genuine friends?* I make a mental note to dig deeper.

"How was your flight over?" he asks casually.

I wonder if I should even broach the subject of his bizarre contract.

"Was everything all right?" Kramer prompts.

"Um," I hesitate. "It was fine, just different."

His face is expressionless as he chews on a piece of crispy bacon.

"It was a little unnerving, to tell you the truth. I've never boarded a plane without knowing my final destination."

He continues to look at me impassively.

As our shared silence approaches the threshold of incredibly awkward territory, I decide to double down on my curiosity.

"Can you give me a little hint as to where we are? I swear not to tell a soul..."

There's another long pause, and I wonder if I've gone too far. *This man is impossible to read.*

But Kramer's look changes in a flash. "Oh, Fran," he says with a twinkle in his eye. "I know what you're doing."

My stomach tightens.

"Let's hold off on the questions for now, shall we? It's just breakfast."

Kramer says everything lightheartedly, but I suddenly feel like a chastised child. I nod and take another bite of food.

"I'm looking forward to showing you the rest of the property," he continues. "I think you'll find it quite interesting. There's so much to see here—lots of rich history."

"I'm looking forward to that too," I say. "How old is this house?"

"Oh, maybe a hundred years, give or take."

"That's amazing," I tell him. "I love old architecture."

"The previous owners made some renovations in the sixties and seventies," Kramer says. "You may have noticed an eclectic mix of design and décor," he adds with a wink.

"I like it," I lie again. "You've done a great job of blending everything together."

"I guess I'm trying to maintain some of the property's integrity." He laughs. "If that's even possible at this point."

After we finish the meal, I try to shift our conversation towards the interview. "So, what type of timeframe were you envisioning for this visit?"

"Well," Kramer says, throwing up his hands. "However long it takes, I suppose."

I wait for a wink or some sort of grin, but it never comes. *I'm on a deadline.* As much as I want to respect his time, my job is at stake here.

"You can't rush these things," he adds with a shrug.

I clear my throat and try a different approach.

"I was thinking we could start the interview today and probably finish up by the end of the week. Does that work for you?"

"We'll see," he says noncommittally.

I swallow back my response. Edna will want a quick turnaround, and I dread the idea of asking her for a hypothetical extension.

Kramer regards me silently, seeming to sense my discomfort.

I decide to change the subject. "I wanted to ask you about cellular service. I can't seem to get a signal up in my room."

He looks confused.

"It's just that I need to check email and connect with my editor at some point..."

Kramer folds his napkin and sets it neatly on the table. "I'm afraid that there's spotty reception throughout the entire property. You might have more luck in a different area of the house."

"Okay, I'll try that. Do you have a Wi-Fi network that I might be able to use?"

"I'm afraid not, Fran," Kramer says. "I don't even have a landline." He flashes me a regretful look and shrugs. "Never really had much use for a phone."

I give him a convincing smile and silently hope that I'm able to find an area with decent reception. A few minutes later, Laurel comes back in and pours us each a coffee. I'm surprised that Kramer takes his with extra cream and sugar.

"Makes the caffeine go down easier," he says.

I take a long sip and watch Laurel from across the room. Her steps are fluid this time—no limp in sight. If I had to guess, I'd say that she's around forty years old. She's tall and slender, and the flawless bun on top of her head further emphasizes her height. She has dark brown hair with scattered strands of gray peeking out from behind her ears.

As Laurel pauses to adjust her turtleneck, I wonder how

irritating the material must be. Just looking at it makes me itchy. The garment's light gray color reminds me of our overcast skies back home. Laurel's plain clothes only work to emphasize her understated beauty. Despite her minimalist style, she possesses an attractive face and figure—rosy cheeks, long legs, and a pretty smile.

Kramer grabs my attention with a comment about the weather. The sun rises without me realizing, barely brightening the sky as it goes. I briefly glance out the large kitchen window to see gray masses of storm clouds hovering over the house. They look like heavy clumps of wool hanging in midair.

"It's really coming down out there," Kramer says.

I listen to the loud rainfall and clutch my steamy mug tighter.

"Cold?" he asks.

"A little. I tend to get cold easily."

"You and I are similar," he says with a smile. "I'll have Laurel put a heated blanket in your room."

"That would be great." I nod between drinks. "Thank you."

Kramer explains that there's a coal furnace in the basement, but he doesn't think it's still safe to use. According to him, fires, whiskey, and hot tea are the best ways to stay warm during the winter months. "I love this house, but it's too old for its own good," he says with a wry smile. "Just like me."

I can't help but smile at his witty demeanor. Looks really *can* be incredibly deceiving. The man appears to be folding in on himself, but he's as sharp as ever.

"Would you like more coffee, Fran?"

"Oh, no thanks." I am dying to start this interview—the sole reason I'm here—but I don't want to push him too hard. When there's a long pause in our conversation, I decide to give it another attempt.

"Was is strange to get used to a new home after living in your old one for so long?"

He shoots me a confused look.

"I would imagine there was an adjustment period," I prompt.

"I've lived here for ages," Kramer says firmly.

I look down, wondering how I can clarify my question in a sensitive manner.

"I'm not sure what you mean, Fran." He drains the last of his coffee and chases it with a swig of water.

"Before your wife passed," I begin gently. "What was it like to uproot everything and move?"

"Jane loved the outdoors," he says wistfully. "She was all about nature—everything green, green, green."

I try rephrasing my question. "What made you decide to leave your farmhouse?"

Kramer purses his lips and looks away.

"I really don't mean to pry, it's just that I was wondering—"

"Our interview hasn't even started yet," he says resolutely.

I nod and back off a bit. I have no intention of offending him.

"It's only your first day here."

"I know," I concur.

Kramer mutters something inaudible to himself.

"There's no rush," I say gently. "But when do you think you might like to begin?"

"Not yet!" He raises his voice. "I'm not ready."

I apologize and push my interview supplies further into the booth. *This is going to be even harder than I thought.* Kramer has no qualms about calling me out.

"I'm not ready," he repeats. "I need more time."

We sit in stillness for what feels like ages. Surprisingly, it's not as uncomfortable as I would have imagined. Maybe I went too far by mentioning his late wife, Jane. After all, Laurel *did* warn me to wait until Kramer brought her up. But I sense that there is something here—a romantic angle that will provide the scoop so many other journalists have failed to get. That could really elevate this piece to new heights. Still, I probably should have listened.

I take a deep breath and look out the window. It's raining even harder now than it was earlier. I can see the guesthouse from here, though it's partially obscured by a patch of trees. Their leaves rustle in the wind as water droplets bleed onto the ground.

Kramer leans back in his wheelchair and sighs. "I'm sorry for raising my voice," he says quietly. "That was inappropriate."

"It's okay. I didn't mean to upset you."

There's another lengthy pause before he finally speaks again. "I miss my wife ferociously."

"I understand. I'm so sorry." I feel awful for aggravating Kramer before we even start this interview.

"Have you ever lost someone close to you, Fran?"

The directness of his question throws me off. Kramer stares at me intently, blue eyes bright and blazing.

"Yes," I tell him. "I have."

He parts his lips, gaze unwavering. The silence booms between us as I look away. For a moment, I think Kramer is going to ask me to elaborate. *To tell him about my loss.* But instead, he simply nods and says, "I'm sorry."

I exhale in relief. He clearly isn't ready to share everything about his past, and neither am I.

EIGHT

After breakfast, Kramer and I return to the library. He asks if I want to look through more of his first-edition collection. I happily oblige, especially since it's the coziest space I've been in so far. The entire room looks completely different in the light. It's like a blend of two worlds—old and new. *Regal yet charming.* It's a place where I could spend hours on end and lose track of time.

As I glance around, I realize that this library reminds me of something straight out of an Agatha Christie novel. The oil paintings, crystal chandelier, and marble fireplace conjure up a certain Victorian elegance. Between the luxurious materials and Kramer's first editions, the objects in this room must be worth a fortune. I didn't realize it was possible to cram so much wealth into one space.

I peel my eyes from the embellished ceiling to look at Kramer. We sit opposite each other—him in a wheelchair, and me on a leather sofa. There's a polished mahogany table between us, piled high with books: stacks of Austen and piles of Hemingway. Kramer even plugs in a space heater, and my toes actually begin to defrost. I silently thank the heavens for electricity and modern appliances.

This is admittedly my ideal way to spend a rainy day—nestled in with classic novels. If I didn't know any better, I would think I was dreaming. *Especially since I'm in the presence of Jonathan Kramer.* As much as I want to sit back and indulge in some midmorning reading, I have a job to do. I'm here in a strictly professional capacity.

Given his mild outburst earlier, I decide to take a different approach with Kramer—a more cautious one. I won't push him to answer questions unless he starts volunteering information. Even during periods of silence, there's still plenty to observe. The way his hands shake when he opens a dusty hardcover. The occasional throaty chuckle that escapes his mouth. The unmistakable twinkle in his eye while he reads lines of Shakespeare.

"I must be honest, Fran," Kramer says suddenly. "I don't want this to be a normal interview."

I tilt my head, wondering exactly what he means.

"You know," he continues. "Simple question-and-answer format... all that nonsense."

I nod, though I'm not sure where he's going with this.

"I believe that answers so often get misconstrued during interviews. At least that's what I would imagine."

"Mr. Kramer, I—"

"Jonathan," he corrects.

"*Jonathan,*" I begin again. "I promise to do my very best to clarify everything during our conversations. I'm not looking for any skeletons in the closet, if that's what you're thinking."

"Oh, no," he says with a subtle smile. "I don't think you're at all ill-intentioned. That's not what I'm implying."

I sit up straighter and wait for him to explain.

"I just feel like the best way to get to know me is through shared experience."

This time, I can't hide my confounded expression.

"What I'd like is for us to partake in various activities together during this coming week." Kramer folds his hands neatly in his lap. "Visiting the studio, taking a stroll around the property, maybe even hunting if the rain lets up. We can pepper in some interview segments as well, but that would be the best way for you to really understand who I am."

I consider what he's saying for a moment. *Shared experiences.* He has an interesting point. Plus, I'd really get to observe Kramer in his element if we went to the studio.

"What do you say, Fran?" he asks hopefully.

Some people feel extremely uncomfortable during interviews, and Kramer definitely seems to fall into that category. Maybe this would be a better way of getting to know him. "That sounds like a great idea," I agree. "What would you like to do first?"

When there's a welcome break in the rain, we decide to take a walk around the estate. I'm eager to see more of his property and get a glimpse of the yard. Contemplating the acreage of these sizeable grounds, though, I don't think we will cover very much territory.

"I'll just be a minute," I call back as I run upstairs to drop off my notebook and recorder. Judging by Kramer's response so far, I doubt I'll need them during our stroll. I set everything back inside my suitcase and glance at my phone. *No new messages.* I vow to check again later and head back down.

When I reach the entryway, I find Kramer bundled up in a peacoat and argyle scarf. He's sitting in a different chair this time—one that looks considerably more old-fashioned.

"I'm just going to grab my parka from the front closet," I say, pulling on my boots.

"Are you more of an optimist or a pessimist?" he asks from his chair.

I look up to see the artist wielding an umbrella with a grin on his face.

"Perennial optimist," I lie.

"Me too." Kramer winks and sets the umbrella on a side table.

Minutes later, we find ourselves beneath a heavy overcast sky. The threat of more rain hangs in the air as a moderate breeze rustles my blouse. I pull my coat tighter around me and stick my hands into the deep pockets.

The exterior's historic appearance instantly wins my attention. It's magnificent, ancient, and eye-catching—all at once. I'm struck again by the worn-down look of the ground beneath my feet. A mass of cracks and fractures mars its paved surface. I wonder how often Kramer actually ventures outside.

We haven't made much progress when I notice him falling behind. I immediately pause and try to slow down my pace.

"I have to warn you," he says apologetically. "I move like a snail in this thing."

"No worries," I respond quickly, watching as he struggles to navigate the uneven terrain. The sight tugs on my heart. "Would you like me to push you?" I offer.

"No, no. That's all right. Thank you, Fran."

"Well, I'm in no rush," I say with a smile. "Take your time." When I steal another glance at Kramer's wheelchair, he seems to notice.

"This old thing is almost as primeval as it looks," he tells me. "My other chair is charging."

I nod, attempting to slow my pace even more without offending him.

We continue in silence for a while until he speaks again. "I can tell that you're a very kind person."

The directness of his compliment surprises me, especially because we've known each other for less than two hours. "Thank you," I say sweetly as we keep going.

When we reach the end of the front walkway, Kramer gestures to the left. I follow him quietly and take in the view: verdant hedges and towering trees abound. The foliage almost feels like a makeshift border or fence around the property. It also renders it difficult to see beyond the horizon.

When we clear one of the hedges, an even more impressive landscape comes into view. I can't help but pause to admire its beauty. An array of cobblestone paths winds around a large ivory fountain. Just beyond, a vibrant patch of trees stretches on for what looks like miles. Fall drenches each leaf with rich, vibrant colors. The whole thing is like something from a painting. Gold, scarlet, and deep orange hues saturate the striking scene and leave me near breathless.

"Beautiful, isn't it?" Kramer asks.

"Gorgeous. You would never even know it was here..."

"Exactly," he says. "Concealed splendor is the best kind."

Something about the way he speaks gives me pause. The words feel oddly cryptic.

"Shall we continue, Fran?" he prompts. "There's a good spot up ahead."

We eventually stop at a marble bench near the fountain. I take a seat and relish the rhythmic sound of flowing water.

"I like to come out here to think," he says, untying his scarf.

I smile and imagine Kramer staring at the trees, deep in thought. There's an undeniable softness about him that eases my nerves.

"I feel her presence so strongly, sometimes," he continues.

I perk up and assume he's referring to Jane, but I don't want to pry.

"Like she's here with me," Kramer whispers and closes his eyes.

I wait for a moment before speaking. "You said that your wife loved the outdoors. Did you enjoy spending time in nature together?"

He nods, eyes still closed.

"That's lovely," I say gently. "Was there a spot like this at your previous home?"

He's silent.

"I bet it was—"

"You mentioned that you've lost someone too," Kramer says suddenly.

I look at the fountain and nod. I knew it was only a matter of time until he would broach the issue again.

"What was it like?" he asks me.

I take a deep breath as flashes of the funeral play over in my head. "*Hard*. Very hard."

Kramer fidgets with his scarf and changes the subject. "How long have you been a writer?"

"A few years," I tell him.

"Still a nascent career, then." He smiles.

"Definitely," I agree. "But I've always loved to write. I still have a large stack of notebooks filled with childhood stories."

He nods and opens his mouth to ask another question.

"Have you always wanted to be an artist?" I preempt him.

Kramer shrugs. "More or less. I could never express myself properly through any other medium. Art is the only thing that ever made sense."

I instantly wish I was recording this conversation. I repeat his quote back in my head so I remember to use it in my final story.

"How did you first get into it? Did your parents encourage you?"

Kramer cocks his head. "Not exactly." There's a slight bitterness in his raspy voice. "My father abhorred self-expression, and my mother wasn't really the creative type."

I listen to his loaded answer and wonder what his dad was like.

"Were your parents artistic, Fran?"

"Not really. But I was always encouraged to read anything and everything."

"Ah," Kramer says. "Hence your affinity for the written word."

"Exactly. My mom had this huge shelf filled with paperback novels. I remember begging her to let me read them the second I got tired of picture books."

He lets out a short laugh.

"It wasn't anything compared to your mammoth library," I continue with a grin. "But to me, it was bliss."

"I have no doubt. Do you have a favorite novel?"

I think for a second. "Probably *The Great Gatsby*."

"Fitzgerald fan, are you?"

"Very much so."

Kramer's face lights up. "I have an interesting bit of trivia for you," he says.

I lean in a bit, wondering what he's going to tell me.

"Did you know that the book almost had a completely different title?"

I shake my head.

"Several, in fact. Fitzgerald was considering about five or six others shortly before publication. *Among Ash-Heaps and Millionaires*; *On the Road to West Egg*; *The Red, White, and Blue...*" He trails off for a moment. "The remaining ones escape me right now."

"I had no idea," I say honestly. "I just love that story so much. And *Gatsby*. I guess I find it all sort of endearing... the way he was so deeply misunderstood."

Kramer stares at me with an impenetrable expression.

"Anyway." I shrug. "That's probably my number one choice. Your house kind of reminds me of his."

"Does it, now?" He raises a brow. "How so?"

We talk for a while longer before I fully understand what he's doing. To say that Jonathan Kramer is evasive would be the understatement of the century. He's an expert at dodging questions, and shifts our conversation with a deft ease that I should have picked up on sooner. He has me blabbing on and on about myself instead of asking him even a fraction of the questions I prepared. *Exactly who is interviewing whom, here?*

NINE

Our interview progresses at a snail's pace. Kramer continues to dodge my questions and sidetrack me with his own queries. When I cannot stand it anymore, I think back to my previous assignments and resolve to regain the reins of this conversation.

My job is on the line, here. So is my journalistic reputation —or at least my budding image. Edna is not easily impressed, but she *is* easily disappointed. The possibility of letting her down doesn't sit well with me. Getting fired from SYNC would be awful for several reasons, many of which extend far beyond anything superficial. I have bills to pay... rent to make... expenses to handle. I don't have a safety net.

"So," I begin, attempting a firmer tone. "Are you still producing as much work as you used to?"

"Oh, Fran," Kramer says admonishingly. "If you've done your research, you know that I haven't sold a piece in years."

"I do know that," I respond without missing a beat. "But I also know that you can create without creating for the public eye."

He smiles, revealing a set of near-perfect teeth. *Are they dentures?*

"So," I try again. "Are you still producing as much work as you used to? Or even a fraction of that?"

Kramer is quiet for a while, intermittently sighing and tapping a finger to his lips. *What is he thinking?* The clouds shift overhead, and it seems like time is running out. Our precious little break in the rain might finally be coming to an end.

"You don't have to answer," I tell him. "I understand."

Then he speaks. "Not as much as I used to, but more than you'd expect for a staid old man like myself."

"Well," I say doubtfully. "You don't exactly strike me as *staid*." There's a self-deprecating quality about Kramer that I find fascinating.

"I'm glad to hear that my secret hasn't gotten out." He raises a gray eyebrow. "But in reality, I'm just a boring codger with some fancy art supplies."

"You're definitely selling yourself short," I counter. Kramer is subverting my expectations in every way. *What was I expecting, unrelenting pride?*

He chuckles. "I may be a longtime creative, but I assure you that I'm pretty set in my ways. Most of my days are routine and quite monotonous."

I nod, hoping that he will continue.

"Anyway, I don't produce art because I want to... I create because I *must*. I have to."

This is the most he's elaborated since we started talking. These sound bites are interview gold. *If only I was recording.*

"Do you know what that's like, Fran?"

I refuse to fall into his trap again, so I keep my response simple. "I'm not sure." Then I ask another question before he can do the same. "What does it feel like? Can you describe it for me?"

He stares off into the richly colored forest, lost in thought.

"It's like a force. A force that needs to come out—something much stronger than myself."

"That sounds intense," I say quietly. "Is the feeling just as powerful as it used to be?"

"Stronger," he answers quickly. "Though I can't work as quickly as I could before. Everything takes longer, these days. My latest project has proven that, time and time again. It's humbled me in a sense... my final act." He turns back to look at me.

"Your *final act*?" I can't hide the surprise in my voice.

"Yes. I've never been one to rest on my laurels."

One last project? Kramer is definitely getting older, but he still has a lot of life left in him. *What isn't he telling me?*

"The piece is going to be unprecedented," he continues. "It'll blow everyone away."

"Is it going to be another glass sculpture, or are you envisioning a different medium?"

Kramer leans back and flashes me a skeptical look. "You're asking a lot of questions, Fran."

"Well," I counter. "This is an interview, isn't it?"

"We're just getting started," he says mercurially.

It starts to rain before I can respond. *Just my luck.* I reach out slowly and feel light water droplets tickling my palm. But what starts as a drizzle quickly turns into a heavy downpour.

"Ah," Kramer says with a twinkle in his eye. "I guess the pessimists won out today."

* * *

The day's events leave me in a state of exhaustion. Something about being in an unknown place drains what little energy I have left. That, in addition to a few more hours of attempting and *failing* to interview Kramer once we got back to the house. Every question was either evaded or met with a vague and unusable response. I politely decline his dinner invitation and tell him that I would like to turn in early. He understands, and we plan to resume tomorrow.

Back in the safety of my room, I reread the mysterious text from earlier.

> Jonathan Kramer is lying to you. Get out while you can.

The message intrigued me before, but this has to be a scam. It is probably just someone trying to disparage Kramer's name. That often happens with celebrities and the famous elite. For every admirer, there is a skeptic. But how does this person know that I am interviewing him? How did they get my number?

I rack my brain for answers. Maybe it's someone from SYNC. A senior writer trying to mess with me, or someone who is feeling jealous that Edna gave me this assignment. *That's probably it.* Still, I cannot help myself from responding. I keep my reply short and to the point.

> Who is this? What is Kramer lying about?

I wait for a few moments as the message tries to send, but give up after a while. Then I shower quickly before shivering into pajamas and returning to my room. I'm relieved to see that Laurel left a thick comforter on top of the bed, along with a few fleece blankets. Between my exhaustion and the extra layers of warmth, I have a feeling I will sleep much better tonight. I even find a nightlight in one of the dresser drawers—the perfect remedy for my aversion to dark spaces.

I set my alarm, flip off the main light, and get into bed. But a text comes through right as I am about to fall asleep. The sudden buzz excites me, since I still haven't found a good area of the house for cell reception. *Is it from the mysterious texter?* I immediately reach over and grab my phone. It's another text from Liam.

> Wow, so you still have no idea where you are?
> That's Cheetos. How's the interview going
> so far?

I feel myself smile at his reference. We used to babysit Liam's little cousins together, and *Cheetos* was our codeword for *bullshit*. We had so much fun running around the backyard with them, playing tag and waging water-gun wars. Sometimes it feels like those memories are lost in an alternate dimension.

I was another version of myself back then—a totally different person. I miss that period of time more than I care to admit. The easy days before everything got so complicated. I miss who I was... who *he* was. I miss who we could have been.

I think back to the moment that everything changed. *The night of the incident.* I open my eyes and take a deep breath. It's too painful to remember, and too difficult to consider right now. I don't want to get worked up, but maybe it is too late. All I can think about now is what happened that night.

If it weren't for the incident, Liam and I would still be together. Everything would be better—close to perfect—and we would be happy. I glance at my phone again before setting it back on the nightstand. Then I take a deep breath and try to pull myself out of a hypothetical spiral.

I may have been tired before, but I feel completely wired now. I toss and turn for what seems like an hour, maybe longer. Then I can't take it anymore. After a heated mental debate, I peel back the covers and walk over to my suitcase.

I rummage through it in the lowlight and find what I am looking for: a tiny bottle of medication. I twist it open and dump the contents into my palm. Then I stick the rest away and stand still– frozen. I stare at the pill for a moment, wondering if I really need it.

I eventually decide that I do, so I bring it to my lips and dry swallow. I feel it slide down my throat as I get back into bed. The sensation used to be painful, but I've gotten used to it. *The brief burn.* Sometimes, it's cathartic to let go and lose myself in the darkness. But other times—like right now—it's not. I lay my head back and pull the blankets over my body. The heaviness is oddly soothing, or maybe it's just the medicine. Then I close my eyes and let sleep overcome me.

TEN

Despite the medication, I'm able to wake up earlier than I did yesterday. The house is dark and quiet as I tiptoe downstairs with my phone light. I'm careful not to make a sound, but I hear occasional creaks as I go. Oddly enough, they continue long after I've stopped moving. The noises give me pause, but I chalk them up to settling cracks since Kramer's place is so old.

I reach the lower landing and retrace my steps from before. My main goal is to find decent cell reception. I've been without communication for longer than I'd like, and I need to contact Edna as soon as possible. She's most likely wondering if I've dropped off the face of the Earth. *I basically have.* She'll undoubtedly want to know which city I ended up in, so I'll have to be honest and tell her: I have no clue.

The strange creaking noises continue as I make my way down the hall. The last thing I want to do is disturb Kramer, though the thought that he might already be awake crosses my mind several times. Maybe he's sitting in that pitch-black library again. He caught me off guard yesterday, so I'm prepared for him to pop out at any given moment.

The library door is cracked open, giving way to more darkness. I reach out tentatively and push it forward. Part of me expects Kramer to say *Good morning*, but the air is stiff and silent. My phone light reveals an empty room with no lurking artists in sight. I realize that he must still be resting, though I have no idea where he sleeps.

I switch on an overhead light and take a seat near the bookshelves. My phone has two bars in this spot, which is the best reception I've gotten so far. *By a landslide.* I swipe the screen hopefully and open my mail app. After a few moments, it updates with twenty-three new messages. One email from Edna stands out among the rest. I'm not surprised to see a very short, to-the-point message staring back at me.

Francine,

Where the hell are you and why haven't you answered your phone?

Edna

Almost right on cue, my phone vibrates with a new notification: ten missed calls. All but one of them are from Edna. *The last one is from Liam.* My stomach does a backflip when I think about us together. The recent memories are painful, but I can't just ignore him. He's probably wondering why I never texted him back.

After sending a slightly less direct—but just as succinct—message to Edna, I reread Liam's text. He wants to know how the interview is going, but I don't know what to say. *Is it even happening?* I'd like to be honest, but I don't even have the words to explain how inscrutable Kramer is.

I hover my thumbs over the screen, wondering how to

respond to Liam. Something about being here—far away from normalcy—makes me miss him even more. I haven't felt this conflicted since we first separated. Maybe I've just been too distracted.

Just then, a voicemail notification pops up. I settle back into Kramer's armchair and press the phone to my ear. Liam's voice floods my head all at once.

"Fran, it's me. Haven't heard from you in a bit, so I'm just calling to make sure everything is okay. It's weird not knowing where you are... I guess you could be anywhere right now. So, at the risk of sounding like a broken record, I miss you."

The sound of his voice instantly pulls me into an unwanted memory. *The night I lost control.* I feel myself succumbing to it, letting the recollection slowly overpower my better judgment. I turn it over in my mind until I recall a sudden change. *The flip of a switch.*

I still don't remember exactly how it happened—how everything became so violent. Liam and I were supposed to meet for a late dinner downtown. I spent the hour before strolling through our city, relishing its vacant Tuesday night streets. In the dim light, I noticed a man walking his dog: a small terrier of some sort. He yanked on the leash, swearing loudly when his pet didn't comply. Then he kicked the dog. *Again and again.*

I think we both yelped at the same time. On pure impulse, I ran towards the man. That's the last thing I remember before blacking out. When I finally came to, I felt like a witness observing a crime scene. He was sprawled out on the ground— face covered in blood—still breathing, but badly injured. The dog was gone.

I stood there frozen—*horrified*. I couldn't breathe. I was choking on my own fear, unable to piece together exactly what happened. I glanced anxiously around before hurrying in the opposite direction. After clearing several blocks, I called Liam with a shaky voice.

Of course he was shocked when he saw me. *Confused and scared.* He started asking questions that I couldn't answer—so many questions. I continue to relive that night again and again, regardless of how badly I try to forget it. Even now, it's like I'm sitting in the car with Liam, driving home with bloodstains on my hands.

"Fran," he says desperately. "You need to talk to me!"

I stare out the window as we pass by bars and city lights.

"Baby," he prompts again. "Did someone hurt you?" I feel him reach across the seat and touch my arm.

"Stop, Liam," I say, shoving him away. I don't want to talk about it.

"Please, Fran," he begs. "I just need to know what happened."

I shake my head. I can't talk about it. Not yet. Maybe never.

But Liam keeps pushing me—harder and harder. By the time we get back to our apartment, I've had enough. The incident plays in my head like a nightmare on repeat. The more he pushes, the more upset I get. Like stoking a fire. There's this overwhelming anger inside of me that I can't contain anymore. It needs to escape. I feel it burst out of me: blood gushing from an open wound.

The change is instantaneous, imperceptible to anyone but me. It's dark and wild—purely carnal. A detachment. Not a choice, but a reaction. Suddenly I'm holding the baseball bat I keep near my front door. The one I bought in case of intruders. The slugger feels cool against my palm: titanium on pale skin.

I take the bat to my dining table. It crashes into the centerpiece first, piercing blue glass. Shards fly through the air in a slow motion only I can see. The release is disturbingly euphoric. It's terrifying and exhilarating. An electric bolt.

My knuckles turn white as I grip the bat tighter. What's next? My body reacts before I can think. I turn towards the *kitchen and smash everything in sight. Bowls, glasses, and stacks of plates explode before my eyes.*

I've lost track of Liam, who probably fled the apartment in horror. His voice is nothing but a hushed background noise at this point—secondary to my uncontrollable impulse. I make my way into the living room, smashing the coffee table, bookcases, and flat-screen TV as I go. Then I turn towards the wall. I swing, and I don't miss.

Liam disappeared for a few days. It took me a few more to even process what happened. It had been so long since one of my *incidents*. Several years, actually. I was so diligent about taking my medication and doing my exercises. I wrote in my journal every day and never missed a dose. I even meditated regularly and practiced relaxing breathing routines. But preventative measures only go so far.

My psychologist showed me how to control the episodes. His techniques helped for a while, but apparently, they weren't strong enough. That night—the night of the incident—was the first time that Liam found out. *The first time he'd ever seen me like that.* For years, I worked so hard to compartmentalize that aspect of myself. To shove it down deep and hide it like a secret.

That night changed everything. Who knows what could have happened if Liam had never left? I might have hurt him. *Or worse.* Besides, things could never be the same between us once he saw me like that. So I did what I had to do: I broke it off.

For weeks, he pleaded with me. He tried to convince me to change my mind. Liam wanted to know more—to truly understand what happened that night. But I refused to talk about it. I was embarrassed... ashamed. The sad part is, Liam did absolutely nothing wrong. The fault was mine, and mine alone.

A distant gunshot jerks me out of my memory. I sit up straight and look around the room. My heart races and I get up and move cautiously towards the doorway. I'm still the only one here, and there are no lights on anywhere else downstairs. I walk back into the library and take the same seat as before.

The gunshot echoes in my head. Kramer mentioned something about us hunting together, though the image of him wheeling around the forest is an anomalous one. Maybe he's outside practicing right now. That's probably what the noise was. Still, I feel an odd sense of impending danger. I imagine the sound of my mother's soothing voice—the things she would say if she could see me now. *Sweetie, why did you agree to this assignment? You're all alone, and you don't even know where you are...*

I wish more than anything that I could call her. She would know exactly what to do. About Liam, Kramer, and everything else cluttering my mind. It's always been that way, ever since I was a child—an awkward little girl. I would get myself into some sort of pathetic mess, and she would swoop right in and save the day.

My mom always said that I wasn't like other kids because I was special. She'd often tell me this when I came home from elementary school in tears, wondering why I couldn't get along with my classmates. *You're just different, sweetie. You're special.* At the time, I took immense comfort in her words. But looking back, I realize that she was obviously just trying to make me feel better. Mom knew I was a strange girl, but she was too nice to say so.

I always had a hard time relating to other children. It wasn't until I got older that I learned how to act. How to behave so that people would accept me. *How to be someone else.* I think that's why I loved playing in the woods so much. It was my only escape.

Another gunshot makes me jump. *What the hell?* It's still so early in the morning—dark and foggy outside. I sit up straighter in my chair and listen expectantly. My knuckles turn white as I grip both armrests simultaneously. I wait for another loud sound, but it's silent. Even the creaking in the house has subsided.

I glance at my phone and check the time: 6 a.m. on the dot. My sleeping medication usually renders me lethargic the next morning, but I'm full of energy. *Still no gunshots or creaking sounds.* The silence rings in my ears and starts to make me restless. It feels like only a matter of time before something—or someone—else startles me.

My mind files through creative ways to figure out my whereabouts. Unfortunately, the blocker Kramer's staff installed is impenetrable. I still have service, though, so I must be someplace within the continental United States. *But where exactly?* There are undoubtedly other ways to figure this out. Instead of wasting time, I need to avail myself of every opportunity that this situation presents. Maybe something in this house will give me a clue.

I decide that I should explore more of the first floor. My curiosity about this property is unquenchable, especially given Kramer's evasiveness whenever I ask questions. This is the perfect opportunity to get a better lay of the land. I turn on my phone light once again and walk quietly out of the library.

I make my way down the hall until I'm standing back near the staircase. This entryway reminds me of an over-cluttered foyer I once saw in a design magazine. Everything looks haphazardly placed, but also positioned with intention. Almost like the space is trying too hard to appear a certain way.

I find myself lingering by the large wall of photographs. There are dozens of whitewashed frames, filled with sepia pictures of Kramer and Jane. Most of them are of her, though. She had striking features and a gorgeous figure. One of the photos shows her strolling along the beach, long hair billowing in all directions.

After scanning more of the pictures, I notice something

strange about Jane. *She's not smiling in any of them.* Instead, an indecipherable expression stares back at the camera. Her dark eyes seem to be looking through the frame, watching me. It's completely unnerving.

I suddenly feel like furtive messages are looming over me—lurking around corners and hiding in the walls. Secrets I'm not supposed to know about. This house is equal parts beautiful and mysterious, much like Kramer's late wife.

"Good morning, Fran," says a hoarse voice.

I whip around to see Kramer. He's a mere four feet away from me, sitting in his chair with a smile on his face.

"Hi," I say, trying to swallow the shock in my voice.

"Scared you again, didn't I?" he asks with a raised eyebrow. I can't tell if his tone is jovial or contrite.

"No," I lie. "I was just admiring these photographs."

"I see," he whispers. "Portraits of my Jane."

I nod and inch toward the wall. It's dark, so I can barely make out Kramer's expression.

"Hmm." He sits still for a moment. "What do you think?"

"Of the photos?"

He nods.

"They're lovely," I say quickly. "She's—she was gorgeous..."

"Yes."

"When were these taken?"

"Oh, at various times," he says vaguely.

"I noticed that she—"

Kramer suddenly flips on the lights.

Momentarily blinded, I flinch and instinctively cover my eyes.

"How about a quick breakfast?" he asks without missing a beat. "Laurel can whip something up in a flash. Would you like eggs and bacon?"

"Okay," I agree, though my stomach is still clenched. Kramer is nothing if not unpredictable. I want to ask him what he was doing earlier this morning. *Was he hunting in the forest? Where did he come from?* So many questions race through my mind, but I am hesitant to ask any of them. As a journalist, I am used to prying for information. I do it for a living. Still, there is something about Jonathan Kramer that puts me on tilt like nothing else.

ELEVEN

"I thought we could spend some more time outside today," Kramer says after we finish eating. "Especially since the rain cut our little chat short."

"That sounds good to me." I drain my juice glass and smile.

"No chance of a drizzle this morning," he adds. "I can feel the sun in my bones."

"Sun would be wonderful," I say as I clear our plates. Laurel is nowhere in sight, and I don't want to leave a mess for her to clean up.

Kramer sits back in his chair and sighs. "Warm weather is rare this time of year," he says sadly. "So we must take advantage of it today."

We lock eyes for a second, and he can ostensibly tell that I'm sorting through potential locations in my head.

"Doesn't narrow things down too much," he says with a grin. "Maybe I'm just messing with you... hmm?" He winks, though it looks more like an inadvertent eye twitch.

"I'll figure it out eventually," I say playfully.

Kramer shrugs his thin shoulders.

"I just have to get something," I tell him. "Be back down in a second."

I race up the stairs and grab my writing supplies for good measure. Maybe he'll actually let me record our conversation today. Kramer may be the one in control here, but he *did* grant SYNC an interview. Hopefully Edna will read my email and understand any foreseeable delays. After all, I can't produce a draft until I have the chance to conduct this interview.

I throw everything into a slim tote bag and toss it over my shoulder. Kramer is waiting near the door when I reach the bottom of the stairs.

"Ready?" he asks as I pull my parka out of the closet.

"Just about. Where are we headed today?"

"Follow me," he says, opening the front door.

There's a slate-gray ramp connecting the home's entrance to the front walkway—the same one Kramer used yesterday to bypass the steps. We start by taking a similar route as before, but make an unexpected left turn near the hedges.

"Not too much further," he says after a few minutes. "Almost there."

I follow slowly behind him, taking in anything I can get my eyes on. The winding cobblestone paths, quick glimpses of the guesthouse, and shadows cast on the cracked pavement beneath my feet. The sun is shy this morning, peeking out hesitantly from behind a thick mass of clouds.

Kramer stops at an iron gate several feet ahead. It's covered with ivy and patches of rust. I close the gap between us and peer through the bars.

"Here we are," he says. "Will you do the honors?"

I reach out and push the gate open, wincing at the shrill creak it makes.

"Thank you, Fran." Kramer wheels past and gestures for me to follow suit.

Beyond the gate is a tiny, sheltered courtyard. The space is so tucked away that you wouldn't even know it was here. I smile and shut the gate behind me, admiring all of the little details: climbing vines, bright string lights, and overgrown wildflowers. This place reminds me of a dreamy secret garden.

Kramer is stationed in the far corner, next to a wooden bench. I join him and take a seat between two vibrant English rose bushes.

"This courtyard is so pretty," I say.

"You like it, do you?"

I nod and take another look around. At first glance, this beautiful space completely contrasts with the man beside me. His diminutive appearance looks entirely out of place in this magnificent garden. The multicolored flowers are abundant and brushed with dewdrops. I wonder how they've stayed so effervescent, despite this cold weather.

"It's like a fantasy," I muse.

Kramer smiles and looks down at his feet. "I created it for *her*," he says after a moment. "For my Jane."

Her name sets an alarm off inside my head. *Jane.* He's finally ready to talk about her. I'm dying to ask more questions, but I don't want to overwhelm Kramer.

"She loved things like that," he continues, gesturing overhead.

"String lights?" I offer tentatively.

He nods. "Anything that twinkled."

We sit in silence until he speaks again. "I usually spend time out here when I need a good respite."

I reach slowly into my bag and feel around for my interview supplies. My finger catches on my spiral notebook, but that's not what I'm aiming for.

"That's fine, Fran," Kramer says without even looking at my bag. "You can record this."

I relax slightly and find my recorder. Maybe he's starting to realize that I don't have a hidden agenda. *I just want to tell his story.*

"I trust you," he adds with a subtle smile.

"I'm glad," I say softly. "Thanks again for talking to me."

He laughs as I turn on the recorder. "Living alone has its perks, but there are plenty of times I miss having normal conversations."

"You have Laurel," I suggest. "She seems really nice."

"Yes, of course," he agrees. "But I try not to bother her with my boring stories. She doesn't want to listen to an old man ramble on about life."

I shake my head. "I think you're being too hard on yourself."

Kramer shrugs and laughs again. "I can assure you, I'm really not much fun to be around these days."

"Well"—I change the subject—"why don't you tell me what you were like when you were younger?"

He tilts his head and thinks for a moment.

"What were you like when you first met Jane?"

Kramer is silent.

For a moment, I think I've gone too far. I've triggered something, maybe even offended him.

"I was smitten. Absolutely head over heels for her." Kramer has a far-off look in his eye, almost like he's reliving the memory.

"How did you two meet?"

"She came to one of my shows," he says. "One of my early ones, before I was famous. It was held in a rundown campus basement, complete with cheap lighting and mold between the floorboards."

"Was it love at first sight?" I venture.

"Oh, yes." Kramer continues to stare off into the distance. "Without a doubt."

I'm about to ask another question, but he has more to say.

"I can still see her standing beneath those basement fluorescents. No one looks good in that type of lighting. *No one.* But

Jane just glowed... she was an absolute vision." Kramer breaks his stare and looks back at me. A slight breeze rustles the wispy hair on his head.

I can't help but smile. "That's very sweet."

"Look at me waxing nostalgic," he says, waving a hand through the air. "Yesteryear and whatnot."

"It's great," I encourage him. "You've said before that Jane was your biggest source of inspiration."

He adjusts his coat and nods.

"Does that still hold true after all these years?"

"Yes," he says firmly. "She was, and will always be my muse."

"Can you describe what the inspiration feels like?" I ask him. Kramer's quotes are great, but I need more vivid details and elaboration to really make this interview pop.

He parts his lips to answer, but stops short. "Jane..."

Just then, a loud sound reverberates through the courtyard. I flinch at the suddenness of it. *Was that a gunshot?* I whip around to see Kramer, completely unfazed.

"What was that?" I ask him.

"Nothing to be worried about," he says, waving me off.

I'm wary, and he knows it.

"Sometimes," Kramer continues, "local guys like to hunt in the forest. Mostly deer and easier game: birds, squirrels, and rabbits."

The last word sends a chill through me. *Rabbits.*

Kramer seems to sense this. "Don't be scared, Fran. It's perfectly safe."

I feel myself stiffen as the thought of nearby shooting sets in. Now it's *me* who feels lost in a memory.

"Fran?" Kramer's voice quickly pulls me out of it. "Are you all right?"

"Yeah," I lie. "I'm fine."

He seems unconvinced.

"It just startled me," I tell him. "That's all."

"Have you ever been hunting?"

"No." I'm not sure if it's a lie or more of a half-truth.

"Well," Kramer says, "it's perfectly normal, and quite common in many parts of the country. Many areas of the world, I should say."

His comment reminds me of the most pressing question on my mind.

"People *everywhere* hunt," Kramer continues.

I can't swallow the words forming in my mouth.

"It really is a universal—"

"Where are we?" I finally blurt out.

He looks utterly taken aback.

"I *really* need to know. It's just that—"

"Let's get back to our previous discussion," he interrupts.

"Please," I try again. "Why can't you just tell me?"

In response, Kramer reaches across the bench and turns off my recorder.

I pick it up and look at him quizzically.

"You're not following the rules, Fran," he scolds.

"Look," I explain. "You have to understand how hard it is to have no clue which state I'm sleeping in. Can't you at least narrow it down for me?"

"That wasn't part of our agreement."

Apparently, Kramer is truly as enigmatic as his public persona lets on.

"Okay," I agree reluctantly. "I understand."

There's a long pause as he looks down at the cobblestone ground.

"Let's rewind a bit. Can you tell me more about Jane?"

"Like what?"

"Let's see," I say, scanning my memory. "What was she like before you started a family together?"

"She was... *light*."

What does that mean?

"Carefree, spontaneous..." He pauses. "Happy all the time."

Did that change once she had children? *Or maybe after she got sick?* I struggle to formulate the question in a sensitive manner. "Did Jane—"

"That's enough," Kramer says resolutely. "I think we're finished for today."

"Wait," I counter. "I promise not to ask about my whereabouts anymore. I won't even record the rest of this conversation."

But he is already halfway to the iron gate.

TWELVE

I spend the afternoon transcribing notes and trying to get another signal from my room. It's impossible. Liam hasn't texted me back since yesterday, and I have no confirmation that Edna even received my email. She'll understand everything after this is all over—once I get home and explain how bizarre Kramer really is.

His hot-and-cold persona reveals itself again. Despite a tense ending to our little outing earlier, Kramer invites me for dinner in the dining room. Of course I agree, though I'm nervous that he's just going to admonish me for my *offensive* question.

I change into a clean sweater and make my way downstairs around 6 p.m. Kramer is waiting for me at the head of the table with a smile on his face. At least he's back in good spirits.

"Good evening, Fran," he says as I take the seat across from him.

"Good evening."

"How are you feeling?"

"Great," I respond in the most even tone I can manage. "How are you?"

"Wonderful."

Laurel emerges from the kitchen carrying our dinner. *Where has she been all day?* She is wearing yet another turtle-neck tonight, although this one is a deep shade of green. I notice that she mainly seems to dress in earth tones, like gray, taupe, and brown.

"Mmm," Kramer hums as a delectable smell wafts in.

"Here you go," she says, setting down two buffet-sized platters of food on the table. "Enjoy."

We both thank Laurel and feast our eyes on the meal she prepared. Carved turkey, roasted squash, and buttered green beans overflow from the piping hot dishes in front of us.

"Just call if you need anything," she says before disappearing through the swing door.

"Bon appétit." Kramer starts cutting into a thick slice of turkey.

We eat in silence for a while, mouths occupied by food and drink. *Is it too soon to resume the interview?*

"Haven't had this dish in a long time," he finally says. "It's delicious." Kramer pauses and stabs a green bean with his fork. "Jane loved these things."

"They're amazing." I do my best to refrain from asking any questions about her.

There's more silence as we finish our meals. Laurel returns from the kitchen with tea and shortbread. Part of me believes that she's a mind reader.

Kramer sips some Earl Grey and stuffs a cookie into his mouth. He has an insatiable appetite for a septuagenarian.

"I noticed the guesthouse when we were walking around earlier," I say between bites. "Does anyone live there?"

"Yes." He nods quickly. "That's Laurel's place."

"Has she been there for a long time?"

"Several years. She's been living in that house ever since she started working here."

I nod as the buttery shortbread slides down my throat.

"Laurel is a great help," he adds.

"It's nice that you two get along so well."

"It is," he agrees. "I'm not a very easy person to get on with."

I look at him in disbelief. He may be finicky about interview questions, but Kramer seems like a fairly down-to-earth man.

"It's true," he says. "I know I'm not everyone's cup of tea, but I've always been a bit quirky—a little *different*."

I smile and take a sip of water.

"I'm sure you already assumed this," he adds with a chuckle. "But I was never the popular kid in school."

"Neither was I," I tell him.

"Really?" He raises an eyebrow. "I would have guessed differently."

I let out a measured laugh. "Quite the opposite."

"Did it bother you?"

"Um, a little bit. More than I wish it did."

Kramer is still for a moment. "I always liked being an outcast," he says quietly. "It was more fun that way."

I try to imagine him as an awkward teenager. *The image is fitting.* Just then, I feel my phone vibrate and instinctively press my hand to my pocket. It's probably a message from Liam or Edna.

"You can answer it if you want to," Kramer says without looking up from his tea.

I pause, wondering how he even realized that my phone buzzed. The notification was so quick and quiet.

"It's these hearing aids," he tells me. "They pick up *everything*."

"I'll check it later," I say. "No worries."

"Boyfriend?"

I'm surprised at how forward he's being.

"If it is, you should really check it. He's probably wondering if you're okay."

I smile slightly and take another sip.

"Ex-boyfriend?" he pries.

I sigh and decide to borrow the biggest cliché in the history of clichés. "It's complicated."

Kramer laughs. "I may be old, but I haven't lost all my faculties yet. I bet I'll be able to understand."

I can't help but laugh.

"Oh, c'mon," he urges. "I reminisced about my Jane today. Now it's your turn."

"I've known him since college," I start. "We got together sophomore year."

"Ah," Kramer says with a twinkle in his eye. "A young romance."

I nod. "Everything was always so easy with us."

"*Was?*"

"*Is*," I say quickly, catching myself.

"Oh, Fran," Kramer chides. "I'm getting the sense that you're not being entirely truthful."

I stare at the table, avoiding his eye line. There's an uncomfortable moment of silence before he asks another question.

"Is he a nice guy?"

"Yes," I answer a little too firmly. "Liam is the best." I instantly wish I hadn't said his name out loud.

Kramer nods, though I detect disbelief in his expression. Another quiet pause prompts me to clarify.

"We got into a fight," I explain. "A bad fight."

Kramer sits up a little straighter.

"All couples fight," I add. "It's normal."

"And what spurred this fight?"

"We just..." I trail off.

Kramer appears to be hanging onto my every word. But the sight of him stops me from elaborating. I take a breath and remind myself that this is a work assignment. We're not two friends reminiscing about old flames. This is my job.

* * *

Hours after dinner ends, I am wide awake with no sleep in sight. My phone vibration turned out to be another text from the unknown sender.

> For your eyes only. Jonathan Kramer isn't who he says he is. A master of deception? MAYBE. But it's only a matter of time until the truth comes out. Don't believe me? Find out for yourself.

I stare back at the message. *This has to be a joke.* There's no detail or proof—no evidence to back these claims up. I let out a breath and decide to ignore the text. Still, it's irritating to think that someone out there is messing with me.

I have zero new messages from Liam, but he's on my mind now more than ever. I regret mentioning our relationship to Kramer earlier—a careless mistake. *I'm* interviewing *him*, not the other way around. Damn that artist and his inquisitive nature.

It feels bizarre to talk about Liam. To taste his name on my tongue. I think of him often, but usually confine any feelings to my head. Especially those concerning our relationship. Thanks to Kramer, my focus is now completely fixed on my ex, along with the reason we broke up in the first place. If things were different, we would still be together. *Of course we would.* But I can't forget about that night.

I remember it all too well: the blackout and the blinding rage. I close my eyes and rub my temples, wishing I could massage those thoughts away. I would erase all the bad memories and replace them with copacetic ones. I'd delete everything from that night—the one I might not ever get over.

I blink back tears and try to switch off the horrible memory before it overcomes me. *But it's too late.* Everything plays back like a movie scene: an awful sequence I can't look away from. My chest tightens as the dog's yelping echoes through my head. It's like I'm back on that empty sidewalk, running towards a stranger as the darkness consumes me.

Recalling Liam's reaction makes my heart pound even harder. His million questions and concerns. *His fear.* I wanted so badly to be alone after that incident. To retreat... to seal myself away in a necessary bubble of solitude. But then Liam actually left—he disappeared.

I asked him to, didn't I? The details warp and blur around me. In this moment, I am pulled back to the crushing low I felt. I am buried beneath the shame, the guilt. Overpowered by anger and pain. Suffocated by the sheer weight of emotions I still cannot understand.

THIRTEEN

Cracks of sunlight hit my face until I wake with a start. *What time is it?* I've gotten so used to getting up before dawn and rising when the house is still dark. I like having a head start on my morning to prepare for the day ahead. Today is a very different story, though. I didn't even remember to set my alarm last night.

I jump out of bed and decide against a shower. Instead, I throw on some clothes and race downstairs. The first floor is illuminated with lights flipped on and curtains drawn.

"Good morning," Laurel chimes from behind me. She's wearing a black turtleneck and slim khakis.

"Hi," I reply quickly, still looking around for Kramer.

"He's in the library," she says.

"Oh." I nod and notice her signature hairstyle. I swear that Laurel's twisted bun is higher and tighter every time I see her. It must be painful. I run a hand through my own hair and wince at the thought.

"Can I fix you something for breakfast?" she asks.

It's the first time I've noticed her heady floral perfume. Rose, just like my mom used to wear.

"That's okay," I decline. "Thank you, Laurel."

She nods and gestures towards the library. "He'll be expecting you."

I smile and hurry to meet him.

"Well, hello," he says when I walk in. "You're up late this morning." Kramer is sitting in his favorite chair, reading an old copy of an unidentifiable book.

"Yes—sorry," I apologize. "Slept through my alarm."

"You look tired, Fran," he observes. "Did you sleep all right?"

"I'm fine," I assure him.

"If you say so," he says after snapping the book shut.

This interview is different from any other I've done in every single way. Normally, there's a scheduled phone call, or a meeting with a specified start and end time. But this one just goes on and on with no true break. *How can I speed things up?*

I'm still on a deadline, and Edna hates excuses. I doubt she'd appreciate the peculiarity of my current circumstances. It's strange to be staying in the same area as your subject, let alone sleeping in the same house.

I think back to challenging interviews I have conducted in the past. *They weren't all straightforward, were they?* Surely, I have had to think outside the box while dealing with certain subjects. I run through a few previous examples, remembering a particularly finicky opera singer I spoke with last year. He was reticent to answer any of my questions, choosing instead to break into song before I could even get the words out.

On the opposite side of the coin, there was that up-and-coming party planner who couldn't stop blabbing on about her skills. Listening to the recording and transcribing our conversation took literal days. Just like the musical piece, I ran myself ragged mining for gems—glimmers to set the articles apart. Somehow, both of them were hits. Despite getting through those difficult assignments, though, this one still poses a veritable challenge. I get the sense that Kramer is sizing me up and analyzing my every move. I hate it.

"Would you like something to eat?" he asks. "Laurel can brew a pot of coffee or whip up some eggs and—"

"That's okay," I tell him. "I saw her in the hall, but I'm not very hungry."

Kramer mutters something inaudible and sets his book down.

I feel my phone buzz and fight the urge to take a peek. I swear that this library is the only spot in the entire house with any sort of reception.

"You might get hungry while we're out today," he says. "I'll have Laurel fix a basket of food."

"Where are we going?"

"I thought we could take a visit to my studio."

I perk up at his words. It'll be great to finally get off of this property. *Maybe I'll even figure out where we are.* There are bound to be street signs along the way.

"Or we can visit a different day," he continues. "It's perfect weather for hunting..."

"The studio sounds great!" I say enthusiastically. "Let me just gather my supplies."

Part of me thinks that Kramer is going to object—tell me not to even bother bringing my notebook and recorder. But he just smiles and says to meet him in the entryway.

I check my phone as soon as I get upstairs. It's a message from Edna.

> Got your email. Call when you get a chance.

I shake my head and stick my cell away. Didn't she read my message? I don't even have enough reception to text her in real time, much less to make a phone call. Then again, I might be able to sneak away for a quick conversation today. There's probably decent coverage near Kramer's studio.

"Is Laurel driving today?" I ask after heading back downstairs. "Or is a car picking us up?"

"Neither," he says while I pull on my boots.

I stare out the window and glance around for our ride.

"A car won't be necessary," Kramer clarifies.

I shoot him a curious look and crack open the door.

"The studio is reasonably close—about a ten-minute walk."

I feel my shoulders slump. *Of course.* The studio is located on his property. I assumed that we would finally be venturing off of Kramer's estate, but I should be so lucky.

"Can you lock up?" he asks, handing me a clunky ring of keys.

"Sure," I say, wondering why we haven't bothered locking up any of the other times we've left the house.

"Thanks, Fran."

I hand the ring back to him and steal a glance at the other keys. *What do they unlock?*

"Follow me," Kramer says, wheeling himself along.

Neither of us is bundled up today, given the sunnier skies. I look around the property and take in the serenity of it. This is such a large, quiet plot of land. *Save for the occasional gunshots.* It's hard to imagine living—and working—in an indisputably secluded area. Kramer has essentially sealed himself off from the rest of the world.

"My studio is just past those hedges," he tells me.

The walk is even shorter than he estimated. No more than five minutes at a snail's pace.

"One moment," he says, fishing around the same key ring.

I notice that this building resembles the guesthouse. Both are painted the same ochre shade, with navy blue awnings and two single-pane windows on either side. It's hard not to get them mixed up, especially given their proximity to each other.

"Darn thing," Kramer mutters as he jiggles an old brass key. "Hold on, Fran."

"No worries," I say, taking another quick look around. The similarity of the buildings continues to amuse me. Then I spot the most obvious difference between the guesthouse and this studio. *There's no ramp leading up to the former.* That makes a lot of sense, considering the fact that Laurel lives in the guesthouse. Kramer would have no reason to access the building.

"Here we are," he says victoriously. "Come in!"

I follow him inside and shut the door behind me. It's old, so I have to force it. An overwhelming paint smell floods my nose as I take in the space. The aesthetic is even more overpowering than its distinct scent. My gaze feasts upon a wall of artistic jewels created by the man in front of me.

Vibrant pops of color compete for attention as my eyes dart around the room. *Cerulean hues, rich emerald paint, and magenta blown glass.* Kramer's studio showcases projects I've never seen—majestic sculptures and *sui generis* pieces of art. His work leaves me entirely speechless. It's stunning.

There's a tall worktable pushed up against one of the walls. Its laminate surface has scratches and dents, probably from so many years of use. There's a thick pad of paper in the center, along with a mug of pencils and ballpoint pens. I imagine Kramer hovering over the table while sketching out his designs.

The mysterious text from earlier comes rushing into my head. *It has to be a scam.* There's no way that someone could just make all of this up. The art is real, and so is the artist. There's nothing fraudulent going on here.

After I finish staring at more of the space, Kramer gestures to a pair of wooden chairs across the room. We unpack the basket Laurel sent—turkey sandwiches and fruit slices—and start eating. Kramer chews ravenously before finally coming up for air.

"I wanted to apologize for yesterday," he says after a while. "I didn't mean to push you."

It takes me a moment to figure out what he's referring to. Then I remember: I told him about Liam last night.

"Sometimes, I tend to intrude a little more than I should."

I consider this for a moment, wondering who he really talks to on a regular basis other than Laurel.

"It's just an innate sense of curiosity," he continues. "That's all."

I swallow a small bite of my sandwich and wave off Kramer's concern. "Really," I reassure him. "You don't need to apologize."

The silence that follows has me thinking of Liam again. I wonder if he's responded to my last text. *He probably has.* Not that I'd have any way of knowing, given the fact that I'm stuck in the middle of nowhere. An anonymous setting with an equally mysterious subject. All the more reason to finish this interview as soon as possible.

I try to steer the conversation back to Kramer's studio and his future art.

"My next work will be unprecedented," he tells me.

I make sure that my recorder is switched on. "What will the theme of your next piece be?"

"It's going to shock the world," he whispers.

I nod, remembering that Kramer referred to his *final act* in one of our earlier conversations.

"Will it be glass, just like your previous sculptures?"

"It's going to blow everyone away."

I sigh and try a more direct approach. "Is this your last piece ever?"

"It will be brilliant," he says with a distant look in his eyes.

"Can you tell me *anything* about your next project?" I ask, trying to conceal my irritation.

Kramer puts a shaky finger to his lips. "Not yet," he says.

I feel my shoulders collapse. *This is going nowhere.* The second I start to feel like we're actually making headway, the rug is pulled out from under me.

"You'll get your answers soon enough," he adds cryptically. "Sooner than you realize."

* * *

After an uneventful dinner, I shower and get ready for bed. My phone has no new messages or texts. I set it on the nightstand and get under the covers. Even with several extra blankets from Laurel, this room still feels frigid. My body is nothing if not tired and knotted. I'm exhausted from our day at the studio. It was neat seeing some of Kramer's pieces, but trying to get him to answer questions is absolutely draining.

I close my eyes, hoping for a night of easy sleep. *Of course it's not that simple.* A series of creaks and strange noises start to emanate from the walls the second I turn the lights off. I roll my eyes at my own trepidation. After all, this is an old house. I'm probably just hearing settling cracks. Still, the consistency of the sounds is enough to render me wide awake.

An hour later, I turn over and grab my phone. There are still no messages. I clearly don't have any service in this room, so I open my camera app and scroll through old photos. Each one jogs a different memory—mostly good, some bad. I let myself linger on the ones of Liam, but only for a moment. *Another self-imposed rule.*

Then I get to a series of pictures that I should have deleted long ago. *Why do I even keep them on here?* It's completely stupid. An undeniable—and possibly avoidable—trigger. But before I can stop myself, I start to look at them. Grainy images of Liam and I before we broke up. As I look at the blurry photos, I feel nothing but anger. It's overwhelming and irrefutable. It's like my wound has healed, leaving nothing but a rancorous scar in its place. Where there was once pain and tenderness, there's now an inexorable rage.

I think about the man who kicked his dog. Then I dream about hurting him. *More than I already did that night.* Instead of fleeing once I came to my senses, I could have stayed. I could have beaten his body until he couldn't take any more punches. *Kicks to his chest and blows to his head.* Taken his thick neck between my hands and squeezed. *Choked the life out of him.*

In my dream, the man struggles beneath me—thrashing violently around on the filthy ground. I squeeze harder, and I don't stop until he goes limp. *Completely still.* Then I stand up and hover over his dead body. I stare at the corpse until I feel the edges of my mouth pulling upwards into a budding grin. I glance in a store window and look at myself, hair disheveled and shirt marred by bloodstains. *Then I laugh.*

In the morning, I wake with a faint smile on my face.

FOURTEEN

Kramer suggests a day of hunting in the forest. Well, he decides on hunting more than suggests it. I'm not exactly given a say in the matter. To be honest, it's not really my top choice. It's not even on my list. In fact, we would steer clear of anything even remotely related to hunting if it was up to me. *The lengths I'm going to for this interview.*

"So you've really never gone hunting, huh, Fran?" he asks after we leave the house.

"Never."

"*Really?*" He's back in his motorized—and fully charged—chair today.

"Really."

Kramer wears an amused expression as we round the driveway. There's ample cloud cover this morning, with bits of sun peeking through the gray. The weather changes on a dime here, wherever *here* actually is.

"Well," he finally says. "You're in luck, Fran. You're going to learn from the best." He's dressed in all brown, with denim pants and leather boots. A camouflaged baseball hat completes the ensemble.

"Is it difficult?" I ask him.

"Not if you know what you're doing."

We stop in front of a small storage shed.

"Is this where you keep your supplies?"

Kramer nods. "Can you open it up?" He produces the same clunky key ring from yesterday. "It's that tiny silver one in the middle."

I unlock the shed and push its creaky door forward. A large cobweb hangs from the frame, making me wonder how often he really uses this equipment.

"When's the last time you went hunting?"

Kramer raises his eyebrows. "It's been a while," he admits. "Longer than I'd like."

We enter the shed slowly, me trailing cautiously behind Kramer. He flips a switch and illuminates the small space. A fluorescent bulb flickers overhead as I look around. There's not much to see, save for a worktable, two fold-up chairs, and a dusty curtain. I watch as he travels across the shed. Then he pulls back the curtain, revealing a wall of weapons and ammunition. I feel my jaw drop.

"I'm going to take my trusty favorite," Kramer says as he reaches for a gun.

I watch him pick it up with ease and store it in a holster on the side of his chair. *Was that there before?*

"Now we have to choose one for you," he says, tapping a finger to his lips. He stares me up and down with an unreadable expression.

"I'm fine just watching you hunt," I say quickly. "*Really*. I don't need a gun—"

"Let's try this Remington 572," Kramer says, gesturing to a rifle at the end of the top row.

I accept the gun reluctantly and hold it at arm's length. Just being in proximity to these weapons makes me uncomfortable.

"Don't worry, Fran," he says with a chuckle. "It's not loaded."

We grab a few rounds of bullets and leave the shed. I lock up and hand the ring back to Kramer, who places it in a zipper pouch on his chair. I'm left wondering what those other keys unlock.

"Hunting is pretty simple," he tells me. "But there are a few rules we have to abide by."

"Can I record this?" I ask hopefully.

"Sure." He nods as we head towards the tree line.

I reach into my pocket and flip on the recorder, hoping to get some quality content during today's lesson.

"Rule number one," Kramer says. "Safety." He stops moving and reaches for my rifle. "Never point this at anything you don't intend to shoot."

"Got it."

"Same goes for the trigger," he continues. "Don't press it until you're ready to fire."

Kramer shows me how to turn the safety on and off. I watch him load and cock the gun, then I do it myself.

"Very good," he approves. "Let's keep moving."

We clear the hedges and reach the edge of the forest. The sky has already shifted in the short time we've been outside. I squint as a bright ray of sun hits my eyes.

Kramer pauses and gestures to my gun. "Rule number two. Stance is extremely important."

I point the rifle towards the ground and hand it to him.

"Hold the weapon like *this*," he instructs.

I take the gun back and try to copy his position. As I thread my arm through the opening and above the sling, I feel completely out of my depth. He waits patiently while I adjust my grip.

"Perfect." He smiles and starts moving again. Kramer's motorized chair is surprisingly fast.

"Really?" I ask, hurrying to catch up.

"For a beginner," he says playfully. "Ideally, we would take some practice shots first, but something tells me you want to jump right in."

That couldn't be further from the truth. *I'd rather do anything else.* I consider correcting him, but it seems counterproductive. I'd rather just get this over with.

"Rule three," Kramer says. "Eyes on the prize."

I expect him to slow down or stop again, but we keep moving quickly.

"Right behind you," I reply, hastening my pace. But the gap between us is growing.

"C'mon, Fran," he calls back. "Don't fall behind!"

Kramer somehow makes traversing the uneven terrain look easy. The wheels on his chair are thicker and more rugged than any I've ever seen. It's strange to watch him move through the forest so effortlessly. It must be an uber-expensive, custom chair.

"How long have you been doing this?" I wonder aloud.

"Oh, I've been hunting for years." Kramer smiles. "Probably longer than you've been alive," he adds with a wink.

We continue moving through the woods as I take in a vibrant array of fall colors. Honey-hued plants contrast the verdant shrubs and deep brown patches of dirt. A rich maple towers overhead, with leaves so red it looks like a burst of blood against the sky.

"Eyes on the prize," Kramer says. "Remember, Fran. It's best to steer clear of distractions and unimportant details."

"I'm a writer," I counter. "Details are my bread and butter."

Kramer just laughs and shakes his head.

I steal more curious glances as we go. This place reminds me of something from a fairy tale, with a peaceful landscape untouched by time and civilization. My breathing is shallow when we approach another cluster of trees.

"What exactly are we looking for?" I ask him.

Just then, a rabbit scurries across our path. I watch its tail fly through the air like a tiny polka dot.

"Ask and you shall receive," Kramer says quietly.

My shoulders instantly tense. The thought of hurting an innocent animal makes me nervous.

"Keep still," he whispers, fingers moving deftly towards the side of his chair. But before he can reach his gun, the rabbit scampers away. "Damn it."

I start walking again, keeping an eye out for any wildlife. Maybe my clumsy steps will scare them all away. Kramer is shockingly stealthy—quiet even as he rolls over the crunchy leaves. He moves like a trained soldier. Then, somewhere along the way, he starts tracking a deer—a large buck with a striking spread of antlers. We follow him for what feels like half an hour, over bumpy terrain and underneath a moody sky.

"We're old friends," Kramer tells me. "I've tracked him before."

We eventually approach a crystal lake. It's so clear that I can see my reflection perfectly until little fish bubbles spoil the still water. I'm about to dip my fingers in when Kramer's voice stops me.

"Don't move, Fran." He sounds equal parts frustrated and focused. "He's close. I can feel it."

We stay still for a long time—long enough for me to wonder if Kramer is just messing with me. Then I see the deer peek his head out from behind a thick oak trunk, several yards away.

"Found you," Kramer whispers.

The whole thing happens so quickly. I notice him shift ever so slightly, barely moving at all. Then there's a gunshot.

"No!" I hear the scream before I feel it leave my mouth. It's more of a cry than anything—a pained wail that echoes through the woods.

Kramer seems surprised at my reaction, but looks unfazed as he wheels himself over to the wounded animal, whose leg twitches briefly before going still. He sighs, then whips a knife out of his pocket.

"Wait," I protest. "You're not going to do that now, are you?"

His only response is an unnerving chuckle. Kramer leans down and reaches for the buck, lifting his motionless head from the muddy ground.

The sight of it is too much. Something bitter churns inside my gut. I feel it crawl up my insides until I'm left with a rancid, acidic taste in my mouth. *Vomit.* I'm going to be sick. I immediately rip my eyes away from the dead creature and turn to face the lake. But it's too late. I throw up all over the forest floor.

* * *

My body aches from crouching down all day. *How does Kramer do it?* Even sitting in his chair must get uncomfortable from time to time. I wipe mud and puke off the bottom of my boots and go upstairs for a hot shower. To my relief, the water pressure cooperates this time. It's strong enough to ease the knots out of my muscles. Now my limbs are tender, my mind is exhausted, and my body needs to rest.

I try my best to empty my thoughts—to let them sink into the pillow beneath my head. It's a futile effort at first, but not for long. Once I stop trying altogether, I fall asleep surprisingly quickly. My recurring dream welcomes me with open arms: just like an old friend. And suddenly, there I am, standing outside of my childhood house.

I see a wild rabbit run across the grass. Its tiny nose twitches as I watch from a distance. Heavy storm clouds hover over the yard and rain droplets descend. The rabbit stops momentarily, only to take off again. I chase it across the lawn and into the forest, far beyond the confines of our backyard.

The brewing storm escalates rapidly. Thunder rolls in my

ears while I run through the woods, losing a shoe along the way. Beads of rain sting my eyes as I continue chasing the rabbit. It's almost gone—nearly out of sight. My lungs expand against my tiny rib cage until my breathing grows ragged.

Then I trip on a rogue branch. The entire thing happens in slow motion: tumbling headfirst along the uneven forest floor. There's a small hill, and I can feel myself descending as my body picks up momentum. But all I can think about is the rabbit. *I've lost it.*

I wake up gasping for air. The dark room slowly comes back into focus as I calm myself down. *It's just a nightmare.* I repeat those four words until I eventually drift off again. This time, I do not remember my dreams. Or maybe I don't dream at all.

* * *

I started seeing a child psychologist when I was seven years old. *Not by choice.* His name was Dr. Frederick Mueller, and his office smelled like peanuts and hand sanitizer. I remember staring at the wall during our first session. *So many awards and accolades.* He even had toys on his desk for me to play with.

I eventually thought of Dr. M as my friend. Lord knows I didn't have enough my own age. He was patient, kindhearted, and funny—catnip for a lonely, misunderstood girl. I didn't even start questioning why I was there until I got older. Old enough to realize that our *hangouts* weren't purely social.

I recall asking my mom why I was talking to a psychologist in the first place. She was elusive and vague, doling out generalizations. *It's normal, sweetie. I'm sure plenty of young people see therapists.* Her responses worked until I hit middle school. That's when she was forced to tell me the truth—the real reason she first sought out help.

I remember watching the lines on her face as she spoke. They deepened with each word, growing more exaggerated with every syllable. *You were playing in the yard as a child, and I couldn't find you. You never came home. It was raining so hard—storming, really. I was scared. I went to look for you, worrying you'd hurt yourself or skinned a knee.*

Then my mom fell silent. It was like she was reliving the memory, experiencing it again while she recounted it to me. I noticed her eyes watering, her voice wavering as she continued. *I looked everywhere. Then I finally found you. Deep in the woods, rain-soaked and crying. Your dress was muddy, and you were missing a shoe. I ran to you before I spotted something else. You were standing over this tiny, mauled animal—all guts and blood. I think it was a rabbit.*

Her final words stunned me. *But, sweetie, the scariest part was this.* My mom drew in a sharp breath. *When I asked you what happened, you couldn't even tell me. You had no memory of the incident.*

FIFTEEN

Today is the sixth day I have been here. *Stuck on Jonathan Kramer's property.* What initially sounded like a dream opportunity now feels more like unwarranted punishment. So far, my interview attempts have proven futile. Turns out, the artist is an awful subject. Regardless, I'm still on a deadline. A fast-approaching one at that. I'm rapidly losing hope that I'll be able to produce an impressive—or even decently written—piece for SYNC.

As of now, the only recordings I have are bits and pieces of broken conversations. Sure, I've spent a considerable amount of time observing Kramer and trying to ask him questions. I need more responses, though. I think about broaching the subject with him during breakfast, but he beats me to the punch.

"I'd like to rectify something," Kramer says resolutely.

I swallow a chunk of toast and wince as the burnt edges scratch my throat.

"I owe you a proper interview."

I wonder if I'm actually hearing him correctly.

"You've been patient with me these past few days," he continues. "Now it's time for me to return the favor."

"You're up for that?" I ask him hopefully.

"I think I finally am."

I take a sip of water and return his smile. "We can ease into it. You know, start with easy questions and work our way to more complex ones," I suggest.

"Thank you, Fran. I'll try to answer as many of them as honestly as I can."

One hour later, we meet back up in the living room. Kramer wears navy corduroy pants and a tight-knit sweater. He wanted to stay in today, given the inclement weather. Wind whistles loudly outside and rain taps against the large pane windows. I'm sitting across from him, nursing a steaming mug of black tea. When he finally gives me the okay, I press *record* and start the interview.

"When you look back on your career, is there one moment that stands out more than all the rest?"

Kramer thinks for a moment. "Probably my first show. Not that tacky one in the university basement, but my first *real* show."

"Where was it?"

"New York City. My agent flew me out there and set me up with this great gallery space in Chelsea."

I think of the various art shows I've covered for SYNC. "Was it a temporary exhibit?"

Kramer nods. "Just for the week. But what a week it was."

"Did you sell a lot of pieces?"

"At that time, I barely had anything to sell. I was still so new. But my agent wanted exposure for the few pieces I had mastered—some of my early blown-glass sculptures."

"I read that you were commissioned very early on."

"I was lucky," he says. "Several people who visited that show wanted me to create one-of-a-kind art for them. *Pieces of my choosing.* And they were willing to pay big bucks." His blue eyes light up as he speaks.

"You became well known pretty quickly, especially for a young artist..."

"That's true," Kramer says, taking a swig of coffee. "I was lucky to gain traction early on."

"How did you metabolize the sudden fame?"

"I was a cocky kid," he says with a shrug. "So much of it went straight to my head."

"That's understandable."

"I learned fairly quickly that humility is the greatest quality an artist can have."

The rain picks up outside, drawing our collective attention to the window. It seems like a storm is brewing. After a long pause, I decide to shift topics.

"Are you comfortable speaking more about Jane?" I ask gently.

Kramer looks down at the hardwood floor.

"We don't have to," I add. "I have plenty of additional questions about your early career and how you—"

"That's all right, Fran. We can talk about her."

I feel a wave of relief wash over me. *Now we're really getting somewhere.*

"You said that she came to your first show?"

"Yes." He grins. "The tacky one."

"Did she champion your art from the very beginning?"

"Oh, yes. Jane was by far my biggest supporter. She believed in me more than I believed in myself, and that continued throughout my entire career."

Maybe that's why he's been unable to create like he used to.

"What was your life like together once your career took off?"

"We spent all of our free time in the same place," he gushes. "Couldn't keep our hands off of each other. She was all I cared about."

I'm about to ask another question when he continues.

"It wasn't always that simple, though. Things really picked up after the first couple years. I had to travel a lot for gallery openings and award shows."

"Did she join you on those trips?"

"Sometimes, but she couldn't always come with me."

"It must have been hard to be apart," I venture.

"It was. But Jane was very understanding. She was always more of a homebody, anyway."

"What did she do before you two got together?"

"Well, she was a student when we first met."

"What did she study in college?"

"I believe she double majored in psychology and anthropology."

"That's neat," I say.

"My Jane loved her studies. She was so fascinated by people and their odd behaviors. Always wanted to know about the reasoning behind things. She was a brilliant young mind."

I contemplate asking additional questions about Jane. I still want to know more about her personality pre- and post-motherhood. But I don't want to push my luck. *All in good time.* Kramer tells me more about the early part of his career: the growing passion to create inimitable sculptures and his quick rise to fame.

"I don't want to disappoint you, Fran," he says after a lengthy answer. "But I'm getting a bit tired." He rubs his right eye and stifles a yawn. "Might even go take a nap."

"Of course," I say. "Please don't worry about it. This was a great session!"

Kramer beams at my burst of optimism. "I quite enjoyed our conversation," he tells me.

"Me too," I agree. Just then, I feel my phone vibrate. I glance down at it while he switches on his chair motor.

> For your eyes only. Jonathan says that his wife
> died from cancer, but he's lying. Don't believe
> me? Find out for yourself.

I stare at the cryptic text. For some reason, this one sends a chill through me. *Lying about Jane's death?* This information carries a lot more weight than the previous messages about Kramer. I look up and stop him just before he leaves. "Can I ask you one more thing?"

"Of course," he says blithely, turning back to face me.

"How do you respond to people who imply that you're a fraud?" The directness of my question makes me flinch.

Something flickers across Kramer's face—an indecipherable expression.

"Critics," I clarify. "Just people who claim that—"

"Who claim that *what*?" His voice is taut.

I reply nervously. "That you have a secret."

"I didn't realize anyone thought that," he muses with a quiet laugh. "But I suppose everyone has secrets." And with that, Kramer leaves the room.

I sit still, deeply regretting the last question that slipped from my lips. *How could I ask him that?* It's a whole lot better than prying about his wife's death, but it's still too bold. After mentally beating myself up for several minutes, I think about Kramer's strange response. It wasn't defensive at all, but it wasn't an answer either.

I spend the next few hours transcribing my recordings in the library. I even search for reception at multiple points, but am proven unsuccessful. Edna's head is probably about to explode from our lack of communication. My looming deadline hangs over me like the heavy clouds above.

The storm intensifies quickly. Bullets of rain pound the foggy windows as wind whistles outside. Kramer's house is otherwise quiet and devoid of creaks—a welcome change from the past few days. There's also a possibility that I just can't hear them over the sound of the storm.

The rest of the afternoon brings an odd feeling that I can't quite describe. I'm obviously relieved that the interview is progressing. After today, I almost have enough material to write a solid draft—one that Edna won't immediately turn up her nose at. But besides my assignment, not much else progressed. I still have no idea where I am. I could be halfway across the country. I still have zero cellular service. No new messages or texts. More than anything, I still feel completely out of my element. The truth is, I'm desperate to finish this assignment and get the hell out of here.

Kramer and I have a slow dinner together before parting ways once again. Laurel makes a delicious meat casserole with whipped potatoes and sautéed greens on the side. We don't talk much during the meal, and our shared silence is an uncomfortable one. For a while, the only audible sound is the chink of silverware on our plates. I make a few attempts at conversation, but he doesn't oblige until the very end.

"That was delicious," I say when we're both finished. "Laurel is amazing."

"She is," Kramer agrees. "Makes a mean casserole, too."

"What was the meat in that?" I ask him. "Ground turkey?"

"Venison," he says. "It was the deer I shot yesterday."

My gut tightens.

"He's tasty, isn't he?" Kramer smacks his lips together. "Put up a quite a fight, too."

I meet his eye line, but don't say a word.

I'm dying to know what he's thinking. *Is this his way of getting back at me? Is he still offended from earlier?* I have to find out.

"I believe that the smarter the animal, the better the taste."

My stomach does another backflip. "Jonathan," I start. "I

want to apologize for my question earlier. I didn't mean to offend you or—"

"Don't mention it," he says.

"Really, I only wanted to—"

Kramer slams his fist on the table. The sudden outburst makes me jump.

"Really, Fran," he says firmly. "Don't mention it."

* * *

I fall asleep quickly, but wake up what feels like moments later, struggling to breathe. Just like the night before. It's the rabbit dream again, haunting me like a song on repeat. Hunting yesterday made it resurface with a vengeance. I rub my eyes and remember what Dr. M said all those years ago. *Disassociate the recollection from the dream. Think of it as a television show.* The reframing technique is supposed to help prevent memory-induced nightmares. I try to do what he taught me, but it's impossible. The memory is too ingrained in my conscious and subconscious mind.

I step out of bed and find my pills. *The heavy-duty ones.* I'm only supposed to take them occasionally, but I don't know what else to do. I don't want to look like a walking zombie in front of Kramer tomorrow. This is a work assignment, and I need to sleep. So I pop the medicine into my mouth and drain my water glass.

The pills are fast acting. Within minutes, I feel a heavy pull dragging me into slumber. Unfortunately, the feeling doesn't stick. A persistently loud noise wins out—the same incessant creaking from previous nights. *Like a squeaky door opening and closing.* The sounds plague my head as I struggle to lie still. I turn over and moan in frustration. I know it's an old house, but this is excessive.

I force myself to keep my eyes glued shut until I nod off.

That resolve lasts for about two minutes. I've just about given up when I hear a different noise. *One I haven't heard before.* It's enough to scare me into alertness.

My eyes flit open to see something standing across the room. *Someone.* A slender shape pressed into the furthest corner, almost blending in seamlessly with the shadows. The figure travels like air: distant one second, and impossibly close the next. I can't even blink twice between the rapid movements. In mere seconds, it's managed to move all the way over to me. Teleported to my bedside. Then, suddenly, the figure is hovering over me.

My heart is squashed inside my chest. My lungs are devoid of air, and I can't draw in a single breath. *It's terrifying.* Even in the dim lighting, I know exactly who I'm looking at. I'm staring at myself.

This person—this woman—could be a carbon copy. She looks exactly like me, save for her hair. Where mine is wavy and blunt, hers is long and straight. *Is this really happening?* I blink in the darkness, almost expecting her to disappear.

As shocked as I am, I want to reach out and touch her. I extend my hand tentatively, fingertips inches away from grazing the woman's face. Then a loud noise startles us both. *A thud.* Before I can even react, she bolts. My eyes can barely track her movements. It's like watching an image vanish from a screen.

I look around for her—my mysterious double. But she's long gone. *Did I imagine her?* Surely, my mind conjured her up: hallucinated her into being. It must be my medication. *It has to be.* There is no possible way that she was real.

SIXTEEN

My senses are duller than a butter knife. Sounds are muffled. Vision is blurry. My limbs feel heavy, like someone attached little stones to my wrists and ankles. I'd check, but it's difficult to lift my head long enough to steal a decent look. I lie languidly against the warm mattress, sheets matted around my motionless body.

My neck is damp with beads of sweat as I struggle to reach across the nightstand. *What time is it?* My fingers brush the edge of my phone, but can't seem to fully grasp it. *Did I oversleep again?* Flashes of last night jolt me awake. *The medicine.* I took it because I couldn't drift off naturally. *The woman.*

Her face—my face—flickers through my head. *Did I dream that?* It must have been a nightmare. It was all just a mystifying, twisted, distressing nightmare. I feel my muscles relax at the realization. A wave of calm overcomes my body, easing me back into a light slumber.

I sleep for what feels like another hour. *Probably more like three.* But when I wake up, the tranquil sensation has entirely dissipated. I'm left with the same unsettling feeling I had before telling myself it was all a dream. *What if it wasn't?* What if the woman was indeed very real? The thought is enough to send chills down the length of my spine.

I grab my phone and look at the time. It's still morning. I exhale and check for texts or messages. *Nothing.* I resolve to call Edna as soon as possible, even if I have to hitch a ride into town. Kramer's property only extends so far, right? Thinking about his land—and the woods—makes me stiffen once again.

I'm instantly reminded of our hunting excursion. That's probably why I had such a hard time falling asleep—why I needed my medication in the first place. I glance across the bed and eye that small orange pharmacy bottle. My gaze slowly strays from it until I'm staring at the far corner of the room. *That's where she came from.*

It's been a while since I've taken one of those emergency pills. Definitely long enough to forget how awful they make me feel the next morning. I swallow hard and make a mental note to avoid them at any and all cost. Then I drag my body out of bed and trudge over to the dresser. It's a lengthy and laborious process. I need caffeine, and lots of it.

My eyes slowly scan the contents of my bag while I consider throwing on clean clothes and heading downstairs to get some coffee. The idea is tempting, but I decide to shower first. I gather up my toiletries and head towards the door. Something catches my eye before I leave the room. *A doll.*

It's sitting on a chair in the opposite corner. No more than one foot tall with a frilly gingham dress, porcelain face, and a pair of dark, hand-painted eyes. I move closer to examine it. Was the doll here before? *No.* I'm almost certain that it wasn't. I would have noticed. *But how did it get here?*

The doll stares back at me with a thin pinkish smile. The sight of it freaks me out. I've always hated dolls. I never wanted one when I was a child. They're like tiny, fake people. Everything about them is creepy. Especially old-fashioned dolls like this one.

I rack my brain for answers. How—and *when*—did someone put this here? I glance around, as if I'm going to find a clue or suddenly figure it out. This just doesn't make any sense. If the doll was here before, I'm ninety-nine percent sure that I would have noticed it. Well, maybe eighty-five percent sure. I waver for a few moments before leaving the room. Maybe a shower will do me some good.

The cold water actually works in my favor this morning, rendering me less of a zombie and more of a functioning human being. I let it drip down my dark hair and lashes as I lather up a loofah. I scrub my skin roughly, hoping to exfoliate away all remnants of lethargy and panic. Then I close my eyes and visualize them running down the drain. I even imagine the nightmare following suit, forever disappearing from my psyche.

How lovely it would be to wash away the events of last night, imagined or otherwise. But the dreadful thought lingers while I dry myself off. As I change into a fresh shirt and jeans, it feels more like a memory than a dream. By the time I start walking downstairs, it's at the forefront of my mind, threatening to dismantle my composure.

I glance around the lower level, looking for any signs of Kramer. *Maybe he's not awake yet.* The lamps are switched off, but early light fills the house with a bright yellow cast. I check inside the living room, library, and dining room. *Nothing.* He is probably irritated about our conversation last night.

Despite my sluggish haze, I feel like I'm on a hair trigger: suspicious of everyone and everything. I move slowly, half expecting someone—like my mysterious twin—to jump out. *She was real, wasn't she?* I find myself back in the entryway, staring at the sparse wall of pictures. My eyes linger on an old photograph of Kramer and Jane.

"Good morning," a voice chirps from behind me.

I flinch and turn around.

"Didn't mean to startle you," Laurel says warmly. "Are you all right?"

"Yeah!" I lie. "I'm fine. You didn't startle me."

I'm hoping that she believes my lie, though I doubt it. It takes a full minute for my heart to start beating normally again.

"Unfortunately, Mr. Kramer is feeling unwell this morning."

"Oh—really?"

"I'm afraid so. He asked me to make you breakfast and to let him rest for a few more hours."

I should just nod and accept what she's saying, but my curiosity gets the better of me. "Where is he right now?"

"He's resting," Laurel repeats.

"But where is he, exactly?"

She looks confused and a bit concerned.

"Where is his room located?" I take a breath and change my tone. "I'm just curious about the property, that's all."

Now Laurel looks suspicious of me.

"Sorry to ask," I continue. "But I'm trying to get a better understanding of the house's layout."

"Um..." she stammers, adjusting her wool turtleneck.

"It's for my article," I add sweetly.

"Oh, I see. Mr. Kramer sleeps on the first floor in a different wing."

I consider asking her more about it, but I'm worried that I've already come on too strong. Besides, this house is so large that it's reasonable to think Kramer has his own wing. Especially given his need for privacy.

"Can I make you something to eat or drink?" she offers. "We have juice, tea, coffee—"

"Coffee would be great," I say.

I sit at the dining table and sip from a large blue mug. It's strange to think that just last night, I was in this exact same spot, facing Kramer. We had a nice time together yesterday afternoon: the best conversation we've had all week. *Until it wasn't.* I actually felt relaxed before asking him that stupid question. I blame the mystery texter.

Still, I can't stop thinking about Kramer's odd reaction. *Or lack thereof.* It was yet another evasion—a complete avoidance of answering me. Then there was his reticence during dinner. I tried to fill the silence, but I'd take quiet any day over his eruption at the end of our meal. Kramer got so defensive when I tried to apologize. My suspicion heightens when I recall the loud sound his fist made as it slammed against the table.

I think about his strange comments, and then I remember the food. *Venison.* My stomach churns just thinking about it. Maybe that's why he is feeling ill. The image of Kramer shooting that deer is one I can't shake. Watching him hunt was the strangest juxtaposition: an old, frail man killing a young buck. Despite his fragile appearance, the artist is clearly more than capable of inflicting harm. *What else can he do?* I try to squash the thought as I finish my coffee.

The caffeine perks me up enough to ask Laurel if I can spend some time walking around the grounds. She hesitates at first, but eventually agrees.

"I can make a sandwich for your outing," she offers.

I thank her, but politely decline. Between the strong coffee and the events from last night, I don't have much of an appetite.

"Mr. Kramer should be up and about in a short while," Laurel tells me on my way out. "I'm sure he'll be looking forward to seeing you."

"Okay. I won't be gone for too long."

I walk down the driveway and look around. There are paths winding in all directions. Despite my efforts, I haven't yet gotten a decent lay of the land. Part of me wants to explore more of the area near Kramer's studio, but I decide against it. This is precious time, and I need to use it wisely.

I pause for a moment until an idea hits me. *That's it.* I'm going to leave the property. Kramer is resting, and Laurel has no idea where I'm headed. Besides, a nearby town can't be that far away. I'll hurry out, call Edna, and be back before either of them realizes where I went. Hopefully I'll even be able to figure out my location along the way.

I start on the paved road that branches off from the driveway. There's a hill in the distance, so I can't see what's on the other side. But this is the same route that my driver took when I first arrived. I'm sure of it. If I can follow this road long enough, it'll lead me off of the estate.

I haven't gotten very far when fear takes hold. *The mysterious woman.* She could be out here. *She could be watching me.* Though I initially suspected it was all a dream, I can't help but think she might be real. Paranoia amplifies as I increase my pace. The sun shines overhead, and a strong breeze rustles tree branches on either side. I turn back briefly to glance at Kramer's residence, which now looks like nothing more than a tiny dollhouse.

I try to focus on the road ahead. My feet carry me past a small pond with three mallards gliding along its surface. I watch as they dunk their heads, simultaneously searching for food. When I turn my attention back to the road, I realize that I'm not very far from the hill. I'm close: only about a hundred yards away.

I'm about to approach it when I notice my pocket vibrate. The feeling is foreign until I realize that a message probably came through. I grab my phone and stop walking. It's a voicemail from Liam.

"Hey, it's me. Haven't heard back from you yet. I just wanted to call and hear your voice. Being away from you... it's really hard. So much harder than I thought it would be. I miss you, Fran."

I move the phone away from my ear and take a deep breath. My thumb hovers over his number, daring me to call him. It probably won't even work, but I try anyway. I miss him too—more than I'd like to admit. Being out here puts everything into perspective. And although I'm not ready to get back together with Liam yet, I want to talk to him. I wait for the first ring, but it never comes.

I start on the hill, hoping that its peak might give me better reception. My breath is ragged as I race up to the top. But when I finally make it, my heart sinks. That's when reality hits. Far in the distance, I see a set of tall iron gates. They're locked shut, with some sort of golden crest in the middle.

I'm trapped.

SEVENTEEN

I stare at the gates as a cruel truth washes over me. There I was, thinking that I could leave the property. Thinking I could go into town, make phone calls, and figure out where the hell this is. It looks like I really *am* stuck here for the time being. At least until I finish this grating assignment. I definitely don't have the material that I believed I would, so I have to stick it out for the time being. My foreseeable future just got a whole lot drearier.

Technically, I have options I can exercise if I get desperate enough. I can demand to leave and tell Kramer that I need a permanent break from this cloistered setting. But doing so would inevitably ruin my chances of finishing this interview. I'm desperate, but not *that* desperate.

I take in the view from the top of this hill: trees in all directions. I can't even see past the gates. This estate must be nestled deep inside a forest, far from civilization. The thought is chilling. Looking around only leaves me more curious about where I am. Not knowing is really starting to eat away at me, and I'm not sure how much more of this I can take.

There's a jarring sound on my left side—a distant gunshot. The sudden noise scares me enough to hurry back to the house.

Kramer said that locals like to hunt in the forest, so that's probably all it was. But something still doesn't sit right with me. *Locals from where?* There must be neighboring houses or nearby properties. The idea gives me hope that this estate isn't as secluded as it seems.

*   *   *

Part of me is relieved to find out that Kramer is still resting. I'm not ready to face him yet. There's something suspicious about this entire situation, and I can't quite put my finger on its epicenter. I initially interpreted his extreme need for privacy as an artistic quirk or a personal preference, but certain things are making me reconsider. I'm starting to feel like Jonathan Kramer might actually be hiding something. There are no more messages from the mystery sender, but the last text still rattles me.

> For your eyes only. Jonathan Kramer says that
> his wife died from cancer, but I think he's lying.
> Don't believe me? Find out for yourself.

The more I read it, the sillier it sounds. *Who am I kidding?* I need to shift my focus and reframe the situation. I remind myself that paranoia can magnify other emotions. Dr. M told me that. It's time to face the facts. First, someone is messing with me. I am almost positive that it's another writer from work.

In terms of ill-intentioned colleagues, more than a few names come to mind. At the top of that list sits another young reporter named Randall Sacks. He's always looking to throw his peers under the bus. Everyone knows how badly he wants to be promoted. *Was it him who sent the message?*

Those stupid texts caused me to doubt Kramer's legitimacy, and now I view everything he does—and says—through a distorted lens. I shake off my frustration and continue filing through the facts.

Second, I had a nightmare about seeing myself last night, and I mistook it for being real. There's probably some complicated explanation for having a dream about oneself. Maybe I'm becoming more in tune with my emotions. *Sounds reasonable enough.* The reality is, I don't have a twin. There is no one else living in this house.

Third, the porcelain doll has been in my bedroom this entire time. I may not have noticed it before, but that doesn't mean it wasn't there. I probably overlooked it because I was so distracted by everything else. I feel myself relax as the logic washes over me. *Thanks, Dr. M.*

Laurel welcomes me back and fixes me a plate of crackers and cheese, which I quickly devour in the living room. I've just swallowed the last bite when an idea hits me. *Laurel.* I could ask her a few questions about Kramer. Not a full-blown interview, but enough to gather a different perspective on him.

I clear my plate and find Laurel standing inside the kitchen. She's frantically cleaning the countertop with a baby-blue dishtowel, rubbing the surface vigorously with soap and water. She looks so focused that I'm almost too hesitant to interrupt her. I even think about walking back out before she notices me.

"Yes?" Her tone is taut.

"Oh, nothing," I say quickly, noting the unusually red flush of color on her face.

"What is it?" she asks, setting down the towel.

"I don't want to bother you," I backpedal. "It's not really that important."

Laurel visibly softens. "That's all right."

I notice a stray tendril hanging out of her otherwise-perfect bun. The rogue strand of hair somehow makes her seem less prudish and more approachable.

"It's no bother," she adds.

"Well," I start as I set my plate in the sink, "I was wondering if I might be able to ask you a few questions."

"Questions? What kind of questions?"

"I'm just looking for additional insight on Mr. Kramer."

Laurel's eyebrows rise on cue.

"He mentioned that you've been working here for a long time," I continue.

"Yes." She nods in agreement. "I have."

"And he also told me that you two are pretty close. I think he described you as a *true-blue companion*."

Laurel parts her lips but doesn't say anything.

"I figured that you might be able to provide a different perspective for me," I explain. "I've asked Mr. Kramer about his sculptures and career path, but I want to know more about what he's like at home."

"I don't understand," she says stiffly.

"Just general questions about his everyday life. Nothing too serious."

Laurel stands up straighter, rolling back her broad shoulders. "No."

I am surprised by her staccato response. *Will she even consider my proposal?*

"I'm afraid that I'm not comfortable being interviewed."

"Oh, okay then." I try to hide the disappointment in my voice.

"I apologize," she adds dryly, though it doesn't exactly sound heartfelt.

"No worries," I hear myself recant. "It wasn't my original intention or anything, but I just figured I would ask. You know, with Mr. Kramer being unavailable and all..."

Laurel tucks the stray tendril securely behind her ear. "I'm sure that Mr. Kramer will regain his health soon."

"Yes, I really hope so."

"All we can do is hope for a speedy recovery."

I'm about to respond when she turns away to resume cleaning. I guess that's the end of that. I tread quietly out of the kitchen and return to the couch. Then I start typing up some more notes on my laptop—the bare bones of my eventual *SYNC* article. Unfortunately, I don't make much progress before getting distracted. I'm still thinking about Liam's message. I press the phone to my ear and listen to it once again.

I wish I could call him or at least send a text. I'm not even sure how I was able to send one before. Why do I get occasional notifications in random parts of the house, and why do those areas keep changing? The reception here is even more temperamental than I previously thought.

I trudge back upstairs to put my laptop away. I still have an imminent deadline, and Edna is probably furious that I haven't gotten back to her. *What can I say?* Getting Kramer to talk is not for the faint of heart. He's made it pretty clear that we're working to his timeframe. Besides, I can't exactly interview him while he's sleeping something off.

I pull open the door and walk into my bedroom. *The doll.* I almost drop my laptop before steadying myself. *The doll isn't here.* My eyes dart around as I look for it—high, low, and every place in between. But it's nowhere to be found. The doll is gone.

I jog down the staircase and find Laurel putting away dishes.

"Laurel," I say between quick breaths. "Did you see a doll earlier?"

She gives me a puzzled expression.

"In the bedroom," I clarify. "My room."

"A doll?"

"*Yes,*" I say quickly. "It was sitting on a chair in the corner."

Laurel shakes her head.

"It's a porcelain doll, about this big." I hold out my hands and look at her expectantly.

"I'm afraid not." She opens up a cupboard and sets two mugs inside.

"Are you sure?" I ask, desperate for confirmation. I need some sort of proof that I'm not crazy—that I didn't just imagine the doll earlier.

"Positive," Laurel says. "Is it missing?"

"Yes." I decide to spare her the entire story. "I saw it this morning, and now it's gone."

"Sorry to hear that, but I wouldn't be much help anyway." She frowns at me. "I haven't even gone into your room."

As I take in her words, it dawns on me that they do not sound sincere. In fact, they aren't even true. *Not in the slightest.* Didn't Laurel put the comforter and fleece blankets on my bed? I want to call her out, but something stops me.

"Maybe you should get a bit of rest," she says.

I nod as she regards me with apparent concern. Even Laurel's frown looks pasted on, just like the doll's chilling smile.

EIGHTEEN

The missing doll renders me fully panicked. All of my reframing work goes out the window once I realize that someone moved it. My growing suspicions return with a vengeance as I search for answers. The next several hours drag on like molasses. By the time night falls, Kramer is still resting in his room.

"I just checked in with him," Laurel tells me as I enter the kitchen. "He's not feeling well enough to get out of bed."

"That's too bad," I say, trying to gauge her demeanor. After our tense exchange earlier, I'm trying my absolute best not to get on her bad side.

"Yes, it really is." She looks down at her feet. "He's definitely fallen ill."

"I'm so sorry that he's sick. Do you have any idea what it is?"

She shakes her head. "Probably just a bad cold."

"Okay. Well, I hope that he feels better soon."

Laurel smiles faintly. "Why don't I make you some dinner? It's been a long day."

The thought of leftover casserole makes my gut tighten.

"How about a bowl of stew? I made some last week, and I still have a batch in the freezer."

After politely clarifying that I'm not eating venison in any way, shape, or form, I dig into a simmering bowl of vegetable stew. The hot liquid slides down my throat and fills me up. It's delicious, and the warmth is enough to make me sleepy. I thank Laurel again and tell her that I'm going to bed.

"Sleep well," she calls after me.

I head upstairs and pause when I reach the landing. My door is visible, but the rest of the hallway is too dark to see. When I first arrived, it seemed like the other rooms were either locked or empty. But if Kramer sleeps on the first floor, there's no reason for them to stay closed all the time. *Unless they're hiding something.* Part of me wants to investigate, but it's too risky. What if someone caught me sneaking around?

I finally come to my senses and decide against it. People keep their doors closed all the time, don't they? *Especially if a stranger is staying in the house.* A long shower relaxes me enough to forget—albeit momentarily—about the unappealing situation I'm in. For a short while, it's just hot water, skin, and soap bubbles. I dry off and swipe across the fogged-up mirror. One glance at my own reflection is enough to undo my fleeting sense of calm. It reminds me of *her.*

I crack open the bathroom door and watch as steam disappears into the dark hallway. Unfortunately, the urge to search it is still very much inside of me. Forget Kramer, I'm now completely fixated on the woman I know nothing about. *Does she sleep in one of these rooms?*

There I am, with sopping wet hair and a dirty bundle of clothes. I leave the bathroom light on and the door partially open, illuminating a thin sliver of the hall. Most of it is still obscured, though. Cold water drips down my back as I approach the edge of the darkness.

My feet tread lightly, taking small, measured steps. Then a

creaking sound stops me in my tracks. I can't tell if I'm causing the noise, or if it's the same one I've heard before. I try to tiptoe even more gently, like a ballerina dancing on pointe. I haven't made it very far when I hear someone behind me.

"Fran?"

I turn around to see Laurel, standing only a few feet away. She's clearly much stealthier than I am. Her face is lit from the side, emphasizing a collection of lines and wrinkles I haven't noticed until now. For a moment, she looks like she could be Kramer's age.

"What are you doing?" Her tone is impossible to read.

"Oh—nothing," I lie.

"Can I get you something?"

"No," I say quickly. "I'm fine. I just took a shower." I gesture to my wet hair. "I guess I just went the wrong way coming out of the bathroom."

Laurel doesn't respond.

"Anyway," I add, trying to break the silence. "Goodnight."

Her expression doesn't change as I walk past her and approach my room. I linger for a few seconds, hoping to see where she's headed. But Laurel turns around before I can figure it out. She stands still, staring at me until I shut my door.

The exchange leaves me with an unshakable feeling. *Where was she going?* Kramer told me that she sleeps in the guest-house. Maybe she was checking on the main wing one last time before bed? That's probably all it was. Still, Laurel caught me snooping. And I don't think either of us bought my lame excuse.

I decide to lock my door tonight. I don't want any strange visitors creeping in. I fall asleep unexpectedly fast, especially considering how anxious I am. I sense the heavy pull of slumber and feel my body give in. Then I dream of *her*. At least, I think it's a dream.

It's like reliving the previous night—watching that shadowy figure in the far corner of my room. In my dream, she moves just as fluidly as before. Then she comes closer and sits down on my bed. This time, I'm not alarmed or afraid. I reach out for her and touch her face. *My face.* Her face.

In the morning, I wake up feeling refreshed. I'd even venture to say *serene.* I get out of bed slowly, stretching as I go. Overcast light creeps in from the bedroom window. It's another cold, moody day. I walk over to the dresser and fish through my bag. I'm running out of clean clothes.

It isn't until I unplug my phone that my tranquil energy evaporates. Sitting on top of the nightstand is a tiny scrap of paper: a note. Three inky words are written in the neatest cursive I have ever seen.

Check the library for answers

I stand frozen for what feels like hours. *Who left this note?* Although the handwriting is different than the style Kramer used on his welcome message, I can't help but compare the letters. I obsess over the possibilities until I finally accept that there is only one reasonable answer. *Her.* I locked my door last night, but she still managed to get inside. Maybe she didn't even come through the door. The realization leaves me feeling equally curious and terrified. It wasn't just a dream.

I check my phone and can't believe how late it is. It's already past noon. I haven't even gone downstairs yet. Kramer is probably waiting for me, wondering what the hold-up is. I should go meet him. But before I do, I can't help but look around the room. I check everywhere for some sort of hidden passageway or secret door. *Nothing.*

I change into jeans and a cardigan before heading to the kitchen. I half-expect Kramer to make a quip about how late I slept in, but he's nowhere in sight. I walk around the lower level looking for any signs of life. *No Kramer, no Laurel.* Maybe they're outside or something.

I glance around the kitchen and feel my stomach grumble. I wonder if it's okay to make myself something to eat. Then again, someone will probably be back soon. I'm about to brew a pot of coffee when I hear the front door swing open. I listen for voices, but only hear a pair of footsteps. It must be Laurel.

"Hello," I call from the kitchen.

"Oh!" she shouts. "You're finally awake."

"Yeah, I definitely slept in a little later than I meant to."

Laurel rushes into the kitchen. "I'll get that for you!" she exclaims as she moves towards me.

"I really don't mind," I start to say.

But she takes the mug from my hands and hurries me out of the room. I take a seat at the dining table and wait for her to re-emerge. After our odd run-in last night, I wonder if she's suspicious of me.

"Here you go," Laurel says as she sets the coffee down minutes later. Her gray wool turtleneck looks baggier today, hanging from her thin frame like an oversized pillowcase.

"Thank you." I offer her a manufactured smile. "I really could have made it myself, you know."

"Oh, it's all right," she says with a wave of her hand. "You don't need to concern yourself with that."

I scan her expression for signs of wariness, but it's impossible to tell what she's thinking. Apparently, Laurel is just as inscrutable as Kramer.

"I was working out in the front yard," she tells me. "Cleaning the windows from both sides. Mr. Kramer likes them *spotless*."

"Is he feeling any better?"

"I'm afraid not," Laurel says sadly. "Still under the weather."

"Oh." I can't conceal my disappointment.

"He sends his apologies," she adds. "Mr. Kramer says that he'll be back on his feet in no time."

"Okay. Can I help you at all?"

She shakes her head. "Just relax and take the day for yourself."

"Are you sure?"

"Yes!" she says a little too loudly. "I'm going to keep cleaning the house. Just let me know if you need anything."

And with that, she walks back into the kitchen. This is perfect. With Laurel being busy, it'll give me a chance to check the library. I drain the rest of my coffee and clear my plate. Then I head down the hallway. But no sooner do I get to the library, than I find out that it's already occupied.

"Hello, again," Laurel says. She's dusting one of the wooden bookshelves with a fresh rag.

"Oh—hi. I thought you were cleaning the windows outside?"

"I'm all finished," she replies with a quick shrug. "Can I get you something?"

"No, that's okay. I was just going to do some reading." I gesture to Kramer's collection of first-edition novels.

"Of course," she says lightly. "Don't mind me."

There's no way I can perform a thorough search with Laurel in here. I consider waiting, but she shows no signs of being finished anytime soon. I'll have to switch plans. Maybe I can wake up early tomorrow morning before everyone else rises. That'll give me a chance to look through the library undisturbed. And more importantly, without getting caught.

I set up my laptop in the dining room and busy myself with more transcribing. I work intentionally slowly to pass the time, but I'm already running out of recorded segments to transcribe. I didn't bring any reading material with me besides a hard copy of Kramer's verbose contract. SYNC's lawyers examined the document on my behalf, so I only scanned it briefly before signing. Maybe I'll look through it and see if there's anything that they missed. Not very likely, though.

I walk upstairs to get the contract out of my bag. It's even thicker than I remember—all one hundred pages of it. Only a *slight* exaggeration. I stop after I come out of my room, stealing a quick glance down the hall. I lean over the banister to make sure Laurel is still cleaning. Before I head back down, I decide to take a little stroll around the upper level.

The hallway is far less ominous during the day. Light floods the length of it, making all of the doors visible. Every one of them is closed, save for the bathroom that I use. I peer over the banister one more time. Then I muster any remaining courage I have and approach the first closed door. *It's locked.*

I move on to the next door, turning the knob slowly in case Kramer happens to be inside. *God, what if he actually is?* I could potentially save face by saying I wanted to check on him, but even my hypothetical reasoning seems inappropriate. I stop and try to figure out whether or not this is really worth it.

I am technically here in a professional capacity, which means I really shouldn't be spying. *I shouldn't be snooping regardless.* But I am also a journalist. It's obvious that the doors are intentionally kept closed and locked. So what's behind them? *What are they hiding?* Any way you slice it, the situation seems sketchy.

My curiosity wins out, though the victory is fleeting. I try one more handle before going back downstairs. It starts to feel like I'm pushing my luck in a way that could be dangerous. Laurel has a way of sneaking up on me, and I don't want another encounter like last night.

The rest of the day passes quickly as I comb through the contract. Aside from the odd transportation requirement, everything I read seems boilerplate. To be fair, I have extremely limited legal knowledge. I probably should have hired my own attorney to read this over before signing it. *Classic hindsight.* I trusted SYNC's lawyers, although I'm just realizing that their priority is to protect the publication, not to necessarily look out for me.

I flip through more pages and toss the packet aside. This is becoming pointless. At the end of the day, there's no way to know exactly what's going to happen. There's no clause about Kramer being under the weather or about me growing more impatient with each passing day. If I want to finish this interview properly, I'll just have to wait until he's feeling better.

Laurel heats me up some leftover stew for dinner. After I eat, I'm left deliberating my limited options. I should leave. *Shouldn't I?* I consider this for a long time, turning over the idea in my head. The logical option is to get the hell out of this place. But despite everything telling me to go, there's an irresistible pull to stay. I'm not sure what's keeping me here more: this interview, or my conviction that there is a secret woman living inside of this house.

NINETEEN

I lie unnervingly awake, mentally filing through the events of this week. *Strange* doesn't even begin to cover it. When I first agreed to this, it seemed like an incredible opportunity—a dream interview. In my mind, there wasn't even a decision to make. It's hard to explain how differently I feel about it right now. If there's a spectrum of certainty, I've completely migrated to the lacking side.

The trajectory of my career seems minuscule compared to the possibility of me having some sort of twin. Or whoever that inexplicable woman really is. Is she a clone? Is she my long-lost sister? *Did I imagine her?* It wouldn't be the first time my medication has caused hallucinations.

Even if I did conjure her up, the note is still unaccounted for. *Check the library.* Someone left a scrap of paper on my bedside table last night. There's no question about it. Could it have been Laurel? The only way to know for sure is to ask her. Still, she had several opportunities to deliver the message to my face. She could have said something yesterday. Besides, Laurel's caginess just doesn't add up.

All things considered, I have to follow the message. *Regard-*

less of who left it. My priority right now is to figure out if there's really something going on here, whatever that might mean. There's a chance I'm reading too much into things, but my gut tells me I'm not reading into them enough.

I doubt I'll get a wink of sleep, but I have no choice. There'll be no medicine for me tonight. *This takes precedence.* I need to go downstairs before Kramer wakes up. I have to search the library.

After forcing myself to stay in bed for what feels like hours, I glance at my phone and check the time. It's only 3 a.m. I feel anxious and impatient as the next hour drags along. Even *restless* is an understatement. When I can't handle it anymore, I change clothes and decide to venture downstairs.

My door creaks slightly as I inch out of the bedroom. The pitch-black hallway looks nothing short of ominous. I still haven't seen the rest of the rooms. *What if Kramer is in one of them?* I turn the brightness up on my phone and use it to guide my path. Step by cautious step, I descend the staircase as silently as possible.

When I finally arrive at the library door, I'm surprised to find it closed. It's been open the entire time I've been here. Laurel must have shut it after she cleaned earlier. I glance around before reaching for the knob. Half-expecting it to be locked, I rotate it clockwise and push forward. It opens.

My heart rate picks up as I enter the room. I feel watched— tracked in some way. The still air makes me tenser than I've been in a while. *Like something could change on a dime.* I could be caught—penalized for snooping in Kramer's office. But most of all, I feel guilty. I still have no evidence that anything sinister is going on here. There's a chance I hallucinated the entire thing. There's a chance I'm just going crazy.

But I went through all of this earlier, and it still doesn't explain the note. *Check the library.* I'm not even sure what I'm looking for. Is she going to meet me here? Is there something I'm supposed to find? I use my flashlight to illuminate different areas of the room. I'll have to work in sections.

I start with Kramer's desk. A spiral notebook sits atop an outdated stack of *National Geographic* magazines. I crack open the notebook, only to find a series of blank lined pages. There's not much else on the desk's surface. I only see a ballpoint pen and an empty mug with coffee rings inside the rim.

Then I notice the drawers. There are five of them altogether: three on one side and two on the other. I open the first, but am disappointed to find a sparse array of rubber bands and paperclips. The second one houses only a thick ream of printer paper, though I don't see a printer anywhere in this room. The third drawer is vacant, save for a used staple in the corner. The fourth and fifth drawers are locked. *Perfect.* I start searching for a key when I feel my phone vibrate. It's a message from Edna.

> Francine—why haven't I heard from you? Call me!

I immediately try to call her, hoping that my cellular signal might be strong enough in this spot. The phone rings once, twice... then it stops. I try again, but the same thing happens. *Shit.* I sigh and type back a quick response.

> Hi Edna! Extremely spotty service here. I've been trying to find better reception, but no luck. Will keep trying. Hoping to get out of here in a few days!

I hold my phone light back up and turn to the bookcases. Kramer's astounding collection of classic novels and first editions stares back at me. I start running my finger along the well-preserved spines, hoping for an epiphany. Maybe she left a note inside one of them. Their titles could be hints or little messages: clues to a bigger picture. I feel like some sort of makeshift Nancy Drew. *A sad-sack one at that.*

I pull the books gently out from the shelf, one by one. Then I quickly—but carefully—flip through their pages. Unfortunately, my quest is unsuccessful. I find nothing but dust and a bit of mildew. I'm about to open *East of Eden* when something startles me. The light turns on.

"Fran?" Kramer's voice instantly halts my search.

I whip around to see him lingering in the doorway. *How long has he been there?* The old-fashioned wheelchair creaks as he slowly enters the room.

"Are you all right?"

I snap the book shut and shove it back in the bookcase. "Fine," I lie.

Kramer's gaze remains fixed on me.

"Just looking through more of your first editions. Hope that's okay?"

"You're up early."

"Yes—couldn't sleep."

"I'm sorry to hear that," he says. I think I detect uncertainty in his voice, but I can't be sure.

"Are you feeling any better?" I ask in a quick attempt to change the subject. "Laurel said you've been ill..."

"I'm fine," he mutters and waves me off.

"That's great." I feel my heart racing as he moves forward.

Kramer stares at my face for a moment. "You seem unwell, Fran," he says.

I shake my head and take a step back. "Not at all. I'm perfectly fine." I cringe at the slightly higher-pitched sound my voice makes when I lie. *Maybe he's picking up on it too.*

"Hmm." He moves even closer, peering up at me from his chair.

I feel like I'm being examined. "I'm just restless, that's all. I probably had too much caffeine today."

"You don't look good," he says decisively.

I take another step back and feel the shelf pressing into my leg.

"You seem anxious."

The pounding in my chest grows louder. *Can he hear it?*

"Are you sure that you're okay?"

"I'm fine," I repeat, trying to steady my voice.

He still seems unconvinced. Or maybe he just knows I was up to something.

"You're pale, Fran. Maybe you should eat something."

"I'm all right. I actually had a late dinner."

"I can have Laurel whip something up," he says. "It's early, but I'll call her—"

"That's okay," I decline. "I'm *really* not hungry."

"You should eat," he urges.

"I said I'm not hungry!" The words come out louder and more direct than I intend them to.

The room is silent until Kramer finally speaks again.

"I didn't mean to upset you," he says.

"No, it's okay," I say quietly. "I'm actually feeling pretty tired again. I think I'll go back upstairs and try to lie down."

"You don't have to leave," he says. "I'll go."

"No—please," I stop him. "I'm going to try to rest. I probably just need some shuteye."

"Okay." He nods. "Sleep well."

As I walk out of the library, a disconcerting feeling overcomes me. *I've been caught.* I know it, and Kramer knows it too. He clearly sensed how nervous I was. It was obvious, wasn't it? I had no choice but to leave the room. Still, I can't stop thinking about that note and my inconclusive search.

* * *

I may have confined myself to this bedroom, but my thoughts run wild for the next several hours. Completely rampant. I dwell on hypotheticals and impossible questions... what ifs and worst-case scenarios. Just before my brain starts to short-circuit, I shift my focus to more productive thinking.

I need to keep following the note. *Check the library.* How can three little words hold so much ambiguity? On one hand, the effort seems futile. But on the other, it's the only lead I have. Then I realize how to get into the desk drawers. *The key ring.* Kramer's clunky set that he takes wherever he goes.

How on Earth am I supposed to get hold of them? Maybe I can distract him while we're eating. Then again, Kramer keeps those keys on him at all times. If they're not in his pocket, they're in the zipper pouch attached to his wheelchair. *I've never even seen him get out of that thing.*

Every idea I come up with has a gaping hole in it. *There's nothing I can do.* Even trying to pick the locks won't work. I could mess something up and damage the drawers. If anything went wrong, it would be way too obvious. I give up. *For now, at least.* I just wish I could ask someone for help—anyone at all.

I scan through my phone and reread old messages. In a sense, I feel like I've lost communication with the outside world. I essentially have. This estate is cloaked in a veil of secrecy, just like its owner. But there are answers hovering just beyond my reach. I'm sure of that.

I decide to dial Edna again just for the hell of it. At this point, it couldn't hurt to try one more time. Imagine my surprise when the phone actually starts ringing.

"Francine?" she answers quickly.

"Edna!" I shout into the phone. "It's me!"

"Finally," she huffs.

Relief floods my entire body. *It worked.*

"Where in God's name have you been?"

"I've been trying to reach you constantly, but the service here is pretty much nonexistent."

"I... from you... long..." Her voice starts to break up.

"Edna!" I shout again.

"Francine?"

"Edna! I'm here—"

"Francine, I can't hear you."

Wait. Hold on!" I stand on the bed and raise my arm up, desperately searching for a stronger signal.

"I'm not sure if you're getting this," she says. "It's difficult to hear—"

"Yes!" I yell before consciously lowering my voice. "I can hear you. Can you hear me?"

"Now I can," she answers.

Perfect. I won't move from this spot.

"How is the interview progressing?"

"Honestly, it's going slower than I hoped it would."

"You should be finished by now," she shoots back.

"I'm trying," I counter. "But Jonathan Kramer is... well, he's extremely difficult to work with."

"I see." Her tone is dripping with irritation.

"I'm doing my best, Edna. *I really am.* But the man is tricky."

She lets out a heavy sigh. "I still don't understand why he requested you in the first place."

"What?"

"Yeah, Kramer wanted *you.* He would only agree to..." Her voice disappears.

"What do you mean?" I ask, still frozen in place. "I thought you chose me."

I don't hear anything on the other end.

"What do you mean, Edna?"

"He... you specifically... requirement... non-negotiable." *More silence.*

"What? You said that *you* picked *me.* You were giving me a chance, remember? A shot at my first big break."

"Francine?"

"Yes!" I can hear her clear as day now, but she obviously can't hear me at all.

"Francine, I'm sorry... shouldn't... agreed to..."

"Edna—you're breaking up again."

No sounds. *Nothing.*

"Hello? Edna? I can't hear you!"

The line goes dead.

I stand on the bed for a while longer as her words sink in. Kramer wanted me specifically. Edna made it sound like he would only agree to the interview if I was involved. *But why?* It doesn't make any sense. I'm a newbie reporter who writes fluff pieces for a living. *Why would he want me?*

I finally sink back down and lean my head against the pillow. My heavy lids close almost involuntarily. *Like little fairies are pulling them shut.* I'm suddenly feeling very exhausted, just like I do after a long workout. I let myself rest for a few more minutes before vowing to stay awake.

It isn't until I open my eyes again that I notice something. Something chilling. A sliver of dim light shines underneath the closed door, probably emanating from the bathroom. But it isn't the light that scares me. It's the shadows: two feet stationed right outside the door. *They don't move.* Someone is spying on me.

Who is it? Kramer doesn't come upstairs, so it has to be Laurel. *Was she listening to my phone call?* Maybe she was just eavesdropping. I stay completely still, waiting for her to walk away. But she doesn't move. The shadows remain fixed under my door.

Another thought crosses my mind. *Could it be her—the unidentified woman?* Is this her way of reassuring me that she's real? Maybe it's a confirmation that I'm not imagining things. Proof of her very existence. Maybe she's here to deliver another note. The possibility that it might be her is somehow more palatable than the idea of Laurel standing right outside. Then again, neither option is easy to swallow.

There's no way to know for sure. Not unless I'm willing to leave this bed and venture across the room. My trepidation, which is currently a thousand times more powerful than my sense of curiosity, wins out this time. I'm much too terrified to move.

The longer and more intently I stare at the door, the harder it is to sit still. But I refuse to shift an inch or make even the slightest sound. Whoever it is knows I'm in here, but I won't give them anything else to listen to, or any other reason to stay. It's too risky. Right when I don't think I can take it any longer, the shadows move. They disappear quietly down the hall.

Just as quickly as they came.

TWENTY

I do my best to deep breathe and steady my rising heart rate. *In for four seconds, hold for seven, exhale for eight.* I repeat the exercise a few more times until I feel my body starting to calm down. Dr. M taught me that technique to help release some of my pent-up anxiety.

I think of my old psychologist and his practice. I wonder exactly how he would analyze Kramer, given the opportunity. *What would his prescription be?* The thought brings a wry smile to my face. It's been years since I've seen Dr. M, but he left a lasting impact on me—a profound one. He never judged me for my condition or made me feel like I was irrational. For that, I am forever grateful.

I've had more than a few episodes in my life. There are some that blend together like strands of yarn in a scarf, impossible to distinguish unless I unravel everything. *I can't.* Then there are other episodes: ones that stick out like flashbulb memories. Ones that I wish I could forget.

The rabbit incident is high on my list, but the night with Liam is higher. Both of them are seared into my being, eternally a part of who I am. There's another episode that I don't think of very often—one that I've tried to push deep down. Still, it continues to haunt me. I wish I could erase that memory more than all of the others combined.

I was in middle school at the time. It was a standard seventh-grade landscape: cliché social groups, bullies, and cliques. I usually kept to myself, save for the occasional lunchtime art club meeting. I never really got along well with the other students. Most of them didn't care, though. They left me alone just like I did to them.

There was one person, however, who never left me alone. Her name was Molly Sanders. *Typical mean girl.* Perfect blonde curls, big doe eyes, and pillowy lips swiped with sparkly gloss. She used to tease me about virtually everything, from my frizzy hair to my knobby knees. She even made fun of me for bringing a unicorn lunch-pail to school. Her relentless taunts bothered the hell out of me, but I never let it show. Except for one time.

Molly caught word of my mom being a single parent. The thing is, I never really thought it was that big of a deal. I asked about him every now and then, and Mom's answer was always the same. *He died before you were born.* Maybe her response sent a shock of fear through me. Or maybe I just trusted her so much that I didn't feel the need to pry. Either way, I stopped bringing him up.

But then Molly started spreading rumors about my mom— calling her horrible names and telling ugly lies. Each one hit me like a cruel rock, heavier than the last. I begged her to stop, but she persisted. The insults built up until I couldn't take it anymore. The last thing I remember is running towards Molly.

I woke up in the nurse's room shortly thereafter, upset and completely disoriented. She told me that I passed out on the play yard. Mom met me and escorted me to the principal's office for a meeting. She held my hand, but didn't speak a single word as we walked down the hallway.

Molly Sanders and her mother were already sitting inside when we arrived. My jaw started to drop the second I saw her face. It was bruised and bloody, with a long cut traversing the length of her cheek. Mrs. Sanders held an ice bag against her daughter's forehead and shot me a dirty look.

I told them all that I didn't remember anything. It was the truth. Unfortunately, Molly recalled *everything*. The principal informed us that several students witnessed the incident and corroborated her story. I was suspended for a week and had to apologize to Molly.

I still remember hearing the pain in my mom's voice... seeing the shame in her eyes. She never made me feel bad or said anything hurtful, but I could tell that something had changed between us. I swear that she never looked at me the same way again.

It was almost like my mom was scared of me—terrified of what I was capable of. I wanted desperately to ease her pain. I wanted to make her proud. I wanted to get better. I started seeing Dr. M every single week after that incident. I didn't stop until my mom died several years later. Looking back, I really could have used therapy to deal with my grief. But after that tragedy, the last thing I wanted to do was discuss my mother's passing.

* * *

Somewhere between desolation and fear, I'm able to drift off to sleep for a while. I guess it's just testament to the fact that I'm drained—mentally, physically, and emotionally. Two quick knocks on the door startle me awake a few hours later.

"Fran?"

I sit up straight. *It's Laurel's voice.*

"Are you up?"

I think about hiding under the covers and pretending to be asleep, but decide against it.

"Hello?" she asks a little louder.

I hop out of bed and open the door. Laurel looks surprised to see me standing in front of her.

"Hi," I say quickly. I can't help but wonder if it was her standing outside the door earlier. *Was she the shadow?* I study her face for signs of recognition, but can't detect anything one way or another.

"I just wanted to check on you," she says. "How are you feeling today?"

What a loaded question. "Um…" I trail off. Then I have an idea. "I'm actually not feeling very well."

Laurel knits her brow together. "Really?"

"Yeah," I lie, trying to make my voice sound nasally. "I think I might have caught something yesterday."

"Oh, no." She wears a look of concern. "I hope it's not the same thing that Mr. Kramer had."

Had. I guess he really is feeling better.

"Hopefully it'll pass quickly," she adds.

"I'm sure it will." I wonder if Laurel knows about our little library encounter earlier this morning. *Did Kramer send her up here to see what I was doing?*

Just then, a vibration sounds. It's definitely coming from Laurel's coat. *Does she have a phone?* More importantly, does she have service?

"Well then," she says suddenly, "I'll bring you up some chicken soup and saltine crackers."

"That would be great." My eyes linger on her jacket pockets, trying to figure out exactly where the vibration came from. "Thanks, Laurel."

She definitely sees me looking, but neither of us says anything about the sound. When she brings up my meal tray, I thank her again and ask if she'll apologize to Kramer for me. He's the last person I want to see right now. Besides, staying locked in this bedroom sounds much safer than traversing the rest of the house.

My plan is to stay put for the time being and hopefully call Edna again. I'll be able to talk to her for as long as my spotty signal cooperates. I need to know more about what she told me near the end of the conversation—the part about Kramer requesting me specifically.

Unfortunately, my plan is short-lived. Laurel's hearty soup makes me tired all over again, and I nod off earlier than I even thought possible.

For most of the night, I straddle the intangible space between asleep and awake. It's a feeling of both ease and discomfort. *A dichotomy of unconscious and conscious.* The state makes it nearly impossible to discern a dream from an actual event. Still, I try.

The woman visits me again tonight. Now I know that she isn't just a dream. *She can't be.* Her appearance is quick—just a transitory dance from wall to wall. She pauses in front of me again, staring deep into my soul like a psychic would. I try to touch her, but she leaves before I can reach out far enough.

When I wake up, I'm left with only an ethereal image of the woman. A brief vision of her moving through the shadows of my room. *So fluid that she barely created any of her own.* My fleeting excitement is replaced with disappointment when I realize that I still have no confirmation of her existence. Well, at least not outside the confines of my mind.

I peel off the covers and venture across the room. That's when I see it: the answer to my question. *Sitting in the exact same place where the note had been.* Inside my bag is a shiny golden key. Without even examining it, I have a strong feeling what it unlocks.

TWENTY-ONE

As much as I want to avoid Kramer again, I decide to brave the beast. *I have to face him at some point*. It might as well be now. The time I've spent here has already exceeded what I so naively anticipated before the trip. After a sobering shower, I gather all the nerve I have in me and venture downstairs. I find Laurel washing dishes in the kitchen.

"Hi," I say as cheerfully as I can. "How are you?"

"Just fine," she responds, taking the dirty soup bowl out of my hands. "Are you feeling any better?"

"A little, but still not great," I lie. That response seems more believable than a solid yes. Besides, it might come in handy later if I need another excuse.

"Sorry to hear that," Laurel says with an unconvinced look on her face.

Why doesn't she believe me?

"How about some orange juice? Vitamin C can work wonders, you know."

"That sounds great," I say with an appreciative smile. "Thank you."

"Go ahead and take a seat," she urges. "I'll make you some toast."

"Do you know if Mr. Kramer is—"

"He's working in the studio today," she says quickly. "Doesn't want to be disturbed."

"Oh. Really?"

"Sorry, Fran." Laurel senses the disappointment in my voice. "But he told me this morning that he's suddenly feeling very inspired."

Half of me is irritated, but the other part is just plain impatient. So many things are on my mind. Now that I am armed with this key, all I want to do is check the library.

"Hopefully Mr. Kramer won't be long," she adds. "I'm sure he will be back soon."

After breakfast, I head straight to the library. But before I can try the key, I become aware of Laurel's presence. She walks by and glances at me before dissolving into the hall. When this happens a few more times, I realize that I won't be able to investigate until I am alone.

So in an effort to avoid being caught, I browse books. I start with a few chapters of *The Sun Also Rises*, and end up reading for most of the day. Sitting in close proximity to the desk tempts me unlike anything else, but I resist the urge to try out my new key. Instead, I bury my thoughts between the addictive words of Hemingway, Kafka, and Thoreau.

Nightfall arrives quicker than I expect. Kramer finally returns around 8 p.m. with a revved-up appetite. He and I eat an early dinner in silence, save for the occasional surface-level comment about the weather. I try to ask him about his day in the studio, but he's unforthcoming. Something is definitely off with him tonight—probably whatever cold or sickness presented itself a couple days ago. He was fine during our surprise meeting in the library, but that could have been a fluke. Or maybe he's just drained from working all day. Still, Kramer seems particularly under par, with sunken eyes, pale skin, and a lethargic demeanor to show for it.

Once we finish eating, I excuse myself and say that I want to turn in early. I even tell him that I'm feeling a bit sick. Kramer seems to buy my explanation, but as always, it's difficult to tell. I go upstairs and lock myself inside the bedroom. Then, I wait.

I busy myself for a few hours until I am sure that everyone has gone to bed. *Even Laurel.* Then I make my way quietly downstairs, sans creaking. The unpredictability of the settling cracks—or whatever those noises are—still freaks me out. It just doesn't really make sense.

I reach the library and walk over to Kramer's desk. Then I pull out the shiny golden key gifted to me this morning. *How did the woman get it without him knowing?* I shake off the thought and start unlocking drawers. There is no time to waste.

I try the first two drawers with no success. They open just fine, but there is nothing inside. *Completely empty.* Then I stick the key into the third lock and turn. The drawer doesn't slide open so much as it screeches furiously. The volume of the sudden sound startles me. I turn around to make sure no one is here.

Inside is a small black object. It takes me a moment to realize that it's a cell phone. *An outdated model.* Is it Kramer's? He doesn't even have a landline. Besides, I have learned first-hand that reception here is basically nonexistent. Maybe that is why his phone is tucked away in a locked drawer.

I reach for it tentatively, looking over my shoulder once or twice before making contact. I can barely keep my shaky fingers calm enough to pick the phone up. *What would happen if Kramer came in right now?* I can't even fathom the answer. Instead, I flip open the cover and power it on.

The tiny screen illuminates to reveal a simple background. *Probably just a stock photo.* The display shows the time and date, with a little envelope icon in the bottom corner. I click on it without thinking. My eyes widen as I stare at a series of recent text messages. One of them in particular stops me in my tracks.

> She's going outside. Be careful.

The message was sent two days ago at 10:52 in the morning. *The same time I went walking around the property.* It's also when Kramer was supposedly resting. Laurel told me that he was still feeling ill and unable to get out of bed. Wishing that I had more information, I wonder desperately who the sender might be.

I stare at the phone in disbelief. *Be careful.* What does the sender mean? Why were they texting about me in the first place? I scroll through more messages from the past several days. All of them are between Kramer and the unknown sender. *There are so many.* They've been doing this the entire time.

I read a few more before realizing that I need to hurry. I don't have much time. Kramer will probably be downstairs soon, and I refuse to give him another reason to be guarded around me. *Him* not trusting *me* is ironic, to say the least. I power the phone off and stick it back in the drawer. Then I lock everything and place the key inside my pocket. *Does he even realize it's missing?*

I think about sitting in one of the cushy armchairs and reading another book, but quickly change my mind. It makes more sense to go back upstairs and pretend like I'm still sleeping. It *is* only 3 a.m. That way, he won't even know I was ever here.

I walk through a long patch of darkness and ascend the stairs to my temporary bedroom. I have the unnerving feeling that I am constantly being watched. Monitored, somehow. Now I know that it is more than just a suspicion. It's the truth. I just confirmed it when I read those text messages. Someone is tracking my every move. They are spying on me.

When I start to open the door, I feel a painful tightness in my lungs. It continues as I step inside and intensifies once I lock up behind me. *It's hard to breathe.* They are watching me. *I'm trapped.* An image of the property's iron gates is plastered at the forefront of my mind—a warning sign that will not disappear. The realization that I might not be safe here is enough to send me reeling into a full-on panic.

Dr. M once told me that extreme emotions are like poison. *Certainly not conducive to the healing process.* I remember him giving me some advice that actually seemed sound at the time. *Steer clear of intense situations when possible.* He said to protect myself by putting up barriers between unnecessary stress and anxiety. Just as it was challenging then, the skill is still very difficult to master.

That was years ago. Long before I joined the overrated ranks of working adults, and well before I accepted this assignment. I wonder what he would think of my current predicament. Dr. M always disapproved of anything—activity or otherwise—that could trigger an episode.

If only he could see me now.

TWENTY-TWO

There is not a doubt in my mind that Jonathan Kramer is guilty of something. There have been signs—*so many signs*—over the past several days that I have chosen to ignore. The first clue was that excessive contract he forced me to sign. His obsession with privacy defies normal human behavior. I should have realized that it was a major, deal-breaking red flag.

The second clue was my short, choppy phone call with Edna. She revealed that Kramer requested *me* specifically for this interview. I am still annoyed that she even pretended like she was giving me a shot: a chance for my very own big break. I guess I should have known better. It doesn't matter anymore, though. What matters is figuring out why Kramer wanted *me* to write this story. Why did he choose me?

That brings me to the third—and most damning—clue. *The messages.* I can't shake what I just found in his locked desk drawer. Why does Kramer have a secret cell phone? And more importantly, why is he texting someone about me?

I pace restlessly around the room and scour my brain for answers. There is a chance that I'm just being paranoid, but the evidence stacks up. There is also the fact that I have seen someone who looks exactly like me lurking around my bedroom. *Where did she come from?* Does Kramer even know about her? The sun rises before I am able to come up with any viable theories.

I grab my phone and make one last-ditch effort. *No new messages.* Nothing has changed reception-wise, but it can't hurt to try. I dial Liam first, then Edna. Neither call goes through. I open my Internet browser and map application, just on the off chance that my location might pop up. *Nothing.*

Even those mystery texts don't seem like a scam anymore. Maybe they are actually onto something. That still doesn't explain who the sender is, though, and how they got my number in the first place. There is a story here, but it's not the one I thought I was going to write. This is not the interview I signed up for. I look around the room and swallow hard. A disturbing secret lives within these walls, and I am going to drag it into the light.

* * *

Kramer is in much better spirits this morning than he was yesterday. "Shall we continue the interview?" he asks.

I am surprised that he wants to talk, but of course I agree. "Let me just get my recorder," I say on my way back upstairs.

"Take your time, Fran," he calls after me.

When I return, there are two hot mugs of coffee on the table. *Laurel.*

"Thought you might like some caffeine," Kramer says excitedly.

His face is more animated than it's been this entire time— almost caricature-like. It's impossible to look at him the same way I did before. *The man is hiding something.*

"Whenever you're ready," he urges.

I flip on my recorder and refresh my memory. *Where to*

resume? Our last session went well, but we mainly spoke about the early part of his career. "So," I start. "How do you conceptualize your pieces?"

"Well, they're all different. Some of the ideas come to me in dreams. Others take a little more... patience."

"How about your most recent sculptures?" I suggest. "How did you envision them?"

"I haven't finished anything in so many years," Kramer says sadly. "But let's see." He taps a finger to his lips. "I believe that the last real piece was *Fear*, so that must have—"

"Fear?" I ask suddenly. "Is that the name of it?"

Kramer looks away. As far as I know, he's never named any of his sculptures. It's one of the many elements that sets him apart from other artists.

"Oh, no," he finally says. "That's just a silly way I keep track of them in my head." He waves a hand through the air and takes a sip of coffee.

He clearly wants to move on, but I can't help myself. "Do you have names like that for the other pieces?"

He shakes his head.

"With *Fear*, I'm wondering if you—"

"Let's just move on," Kramer says.

Fine.

"If that's all right with you?" he adds, but it's clearly not up for debate.

"Okay. How long does it take you to produce a piece, start to finish?"

"Difficult to say," he begins. "Probably at least three to five weeks for most of my work. Of course, each one has quite a unique process."

I wait for Kramer to continue, but apparently he's prompting me now. I reluctantly take the bait. "And what is that process like?"

"Well," he says with an impish smile, "I'm glad you asked. I work with so many different materials when I create a new sculpture... resin, cement, glass, you name it."

Kramer keeps speaking, but I tune him out. I can't help it. I try to focus on the questions at hand—the ones about his career —but my growing suspicion is too distracting. I want to delve deeper.

"What else would you like to know, Fran?"

"Do you like having the studio so close to your house?"

"Very much," he says without missing a beat. "It's very convenient since I don't have a car."

He doesn't even own a car? How does he get around? Does he have a driver?

"Laurel does," he adds, as if reading my mind. "But I don't leave the estate much."

"I know that you won't reveal the exact location of your property," I venture. "But what was it that drew you to this place?"

"Jane," he says quickly. "She fell in love with it as soon as Laurel showed it to us."

My stomach tightens. Laurel told me that she never knew Jane. "I didn't realize that they ever met each other..."

Kramer flinches. "They—they didn't. I meant it in a different sense."

I'm sure that my face is cast in incredulity.

"I—I misspoke. It's my memory, you see... not as sharp as it once was." He lets out a forced laugh.

"How did you hear about the house?" I press.

"Oh, I don't remember," he says, averting eye contact once again. "It was a long time ago."

"Do you remember—"

"You know what?" he cuts me off. "I'm not feeling very well, Fran. I think we're finished for today."

TWENTY-THREE

I wake up between jarring dreams to see someone standing in the corner of my room. *It's her*. I lie motionless as she moves across the floor, gliding just as fluidly as she did the previous nights. I'm sure that this isn't a fantasy or hallucination.

I am wide awake. *She's real*. She is here.

I watch her move through the shadows until she is standing over my bed. She is more visible now: pale flesh, dark eyes, and sleek hair falling over her shoulders. I sit up slowly, careful not to make any sudden movements. I don't want to scare her.

"Who are you?" I ask quietly.

She stares back, eyes burning into my own.

"*Please*," I beg. "I need to know."

She lifts a slender hand to her throat, then taps her lips.

"I—I don't understand."

She keeps a finger on her mouth and shakes her head.

"Oh," I whisper. *Maybe she's mute*. "You can't speak?"

She takes a step towards me.

I notice the closing gap between us. We're mere inches apart, face to face. *It's like looking into a mirror*. She seems as fascinated by me as I am by her. The resemblance is uncanny.

"Are you..." I pause. There are so many questions I want to ask her. *Where do I even begin?*

She reaches out and takes my hand. Her palms are soft, but cold as ice. I take a deep breath before speaking.

"Are we sisters?" I finally ask. "Twins?" Part of me already knows the answer.

She nods and squeezes my hand.

The emotions whirling inside me are overwhelming. I can barely think. *It doesn't make sense.* I don't understand how this is possible.

Just then, she pulls a tiny piece of paper out of her pocket. It's wrapped up like a scroll.

"For me?"

She nods and hands it to me.

I unwrap the paper and read the cursive words out loud. "Inside the sculpture."

She blinks in the darkness.

"Kramer's sculpture?"

She nods again.

"I don't understand. What's inside?"

She just points to the inked words.

"Which sculpture?"

She gestures downstairs.

I glance around the room and have an idea. "Hold on," I say calmly. "I'm just going to grab my notebook and a pen." At least we'll be able to communicate more effectively.

She moves aside so I can get out of bed. When I stand, I realize that we're exactly the same height and build. It's somehow more startling than our faces being identical.

"Okay, I'm going to walk over to the dresser and find my supplies. They should be right inside my bag." I'm not sure why I feel the need to narrate my every move, but it seems safer than assuming she'll know what I'm doing. I unzip my bag and look for my trusty black spiral notebook. Then I grab a pen and turn around.

She's gone.

"Are you there?" I whisper.

She's definitely gone. I'm not sure exactly how she left in the three seconds I was looking through my bag. *Fast* is an understatement. *Why did she go? Where did she go?* She obviously didn't escape through the bedroom door, because I would have seen her.

I look around and wonder how she got out. Maybe there is some sort of secret passage or hidden door in this room. I flip on a low light and start searching: under the bed, inside the wardrobe, and behind the curtains. I don't stop until I am certain I have scoured every inch of this space. If nothing else, my twin is incredibly stealthy.

My twin. The words dance around my head until I truly acknowledge them. I have a twin—a sister. It seems far-fetched, too strange to be real. She lives here... sort of. I still don't understand what is going on in this house. Nothing really makes sense. I feel like I have been yanked out of normalcy and dropped into some sort of horror movie. Then again, normalcy is relative.

I try to calm down, but it is impossible. I can't even stay still. My journalistic instinct tells me to keep chasing clues. I should go downstairs and find the sculpture that she refers to in the message. But the better part of me realizes that Kramer—and Laurel—could be dangerous. They may not be physical threats, but who knows what they are capable of? This assignment has driven home the point that things are not exactly what they seem. *They're far from it.*

I crack open my laptop and begin to write. My fingers fly across the keyboard in a mad dash. The rapid pace is all-consuming, pulling me out of my own head. Details slip onto the page in front of me... interesting facts come out of the woodwork. But it isn't until I stop to review what I have written that I realize what I need to do.

I think for a while until my gut wins out. I'm going downstairs. A quick glance at the time tells me that it's only 4 a.m. *Perfect.* It's early enough that Kramer should still be asleep. With nothing more than my half-charged cell phone to keep me company, I open my door and step into the hall.

I peer over the banister and take in the stillness of the house. Everything is obscured, save for a small patch illuminated by my phone. I turn up my screen brightness instead of using the light, just in case someone happens to be up. Then I tiptoe downstairs as quietly as my ragged breath allows.

The floor creaks shrilly beneath my feet, making me freeze in place. I think about turning around, but I'm committed now. *I can't go back.* I attempt even lighter steps for the remainder of the staircase and breathe solely through my nose. Going slowly seems to be the trick, so I take my time with the rest of the descent.

When I finally reach the bottom, I realize how difficult this is going to be. *Which sculpture does she mean?* Kramer's art is displayed all over the lower level, so this could take forever. Even after I find the piece in question, how will I look inside? *Does she want me to break it open?*

I decide to start at the front of the house. I'm here already, so I might as well. I take a deep breath and head towards the entryway. Just as I round the corner, a flash of light steals my attention. It's quick—almost imperceptible. Someone else might think their eyes are playing tricks on them, but not me. *I know what I saw.* I think it came from the library.

I wait for a moment before proceeding down the hall. My route is dark and tension-filled. *Is Kramer inside?* I take several slow, delicate steps until I approach the living room. Then I hear a sharp sound. I press my body into a dark corner, hoping not to be seen.

There's a low humming emanating from a different part of the house. I quickly identify the noise as the motor on Kramer's chair. It grows louder and louder until I'm sure he's about to find me. *Don't make a sound.* I push my back harder against the wall and hold my breath.

I see the blinking light on his chair and stiffen. He's across the room, headed for the library. My eyes have mostly adjusted to the dark, but it's still difficult to make everything out clearly. Thank God for that green light.

Kramer enters the library and parks his chair. I watch the light disappear and listen to the motor switch off completely. *What's he doing?* The better part of me wants to retreat to my room. Every fiber of my being knows that this is a bad decision. But I can't pull myself away from the urge—the need—to follow him.

I steady myself and start making my way across the room, slowly but surely. I stay as close to the wall as I possibly can, hoping that my movements will be less obvious that way. Channeling my twin's fluidity isn't nearly as effortless as she makes it look. I feel awkward and clumsy as I take the last few remaining steps to the library entrance.

I position myself on the left side of the door. *There's no way I'm going inside that room.* Hopefully this spot will give me a decent vantage point without being detected. I don't hear anything for a long time, and the silence renders me even edgier. Kramer must be sitting still. Does he realize I'm here?

After a few more minutes, I hear a shuffling noise that reminds me of book pages turning. It intensifies before stopping altogether. Then there's a small thud, followed by something that sounds like a heavy door opening. I hear Kramer's chair turn back on, with the motor humming softly just like it did before.

At this point, I cautiously inch closer to the doorway. Ever so slowly. Then I crane my neck and peer through the crack between the hinges. The chair's green light blinks intermittently from the far side of the room. It's bright enough to make Kramer visible, albeit momentarily. He faces the bookcases and waits.

Then I realize that there's something else: a hollow between the stacks. It looks like some sort of secret entrance. I squint and try to figure it out, but my eyes betray me. Kramer moves towards the void until his chair motor is nothing but a whisper. The green light grows fainter until it disappears completely. *He's gone.*

I work up the nerve to go after him. If not, then why am I even doing this? My feet carry me into the dark library and towards the even darker hollow—the mysterious entrance where Kramer vanished. Sure enough, there's a doorway between two of the bookcases.

I hesitantly hold my phone up so I can see more clearly. Beyond the entrance is a long chamber leading to another set of doors, sleek and silver. It takes me a second to realize what I'm staring at. The second set of doors doesn't lead to another room. It houses an elevator shaft.

I muster my last few drops of bravery and move towards the opening. But before I can step inside, the bookcases slide swiftly back together. The hollow is gone just as quickly as it appeared. I inhale sharply and step backwards. *What the hell?* I'm left with a sour taste in my mouth as I process what just happened. I need to figure out why Kramer has a secret passageway in his library. *I need to know where the elevator leads.* I need to know what lies beneath this house.

TWENTY-FOUR

Half of me is still in disbelief. *Is any of this real?* I think about my twin and Kramer's secret phone, along with his mysterious elevator that leads to who-knows-where. If someone had warned me about this place—told me what I would find here—I would have called them crazy. Just thinking about it makes me question my own sanity.

I sit in bed and shut my eyes tightly. Then I draw in a deep breath and hold it for a few seconds before exhaling. Dr. M tried to teach me visualization years ago. It used to help, but so many years have passed since I have done it. Too many years. Still, I sit here for several moments and try to picture myself at the beach. *Sand wedged between my toes, ocean water splashing my legs.* I imagine it washing away my doubts—drowning my fears.

I open my eyes with a potent sense of clarity. I am going to confront Kramer. If he doesn't tell me the truth, then I am leaving. He will have to let me go. Enough people know that I'm here. Liam does. The entire *SYNC* staff does. Then again, where is *here*?

When I feel myself starting to spiral again, I shake my head and stand up. It's done. My decision is made. I am going to get to the bottom of this one way or another. If Kramer resists, I will pull the truth out of him. If he refuses, I will leave.

The remaining hours drone on until my patience eventually runs out. I decide to change clothes and go back down. At least I will be ready before Kramer gets back. Early morning light paints the house in a deep blue-gray while I descend the staircase. For the first time, I am not worried about making a sound. The steps creak in a shrill chorus as I go.

I am surprised to find Kramer sitting at the dining table. There is a cream-colored folder in front of him, along with a steaming mug.

"Good morning, Fran."

"We need to talk," I say firmly.

Kramer looks up from his coffee.

"*Now.*" Even with my newfound resolve, I'm surprised at how bold I'm being.

"All right," he says gravely.

I take the seat opposite him.

"I actually want to talk to you as well."

"What is it?" *I'll let him go first.*

"Well, Fran," he starts, "I haven't been entirely honest with you."

I swallow hard, because I certainly wasn't expecting this.

"In fact, I've been very deceitful."

The acid in my stomach rises as I wait for him to continue.

"You see, I had other motives when I contacted you a few weeks ago."

I pause for a beat to catch my breath. "What were they?"

Kramer looks at me with a remorseful expression. "What I'm about to tell you will come as a shock..." He trails off.

The anticipation is agonizing. *Is it something that I already know?*

"Fran," he says, voice faint. "I'm your father."

My entire body tenses as his words sink in. *My father.* I struggle to process, unable to make sense of this bizarre information. It's paralyzing. Neither of us speaks for a few minutes.

Then I finally break the silence. "You can't be."

He sighs and looks at the table between us.

Obviously, I never knew my dad. But Kramer can't be my father. Like Mom said, he died before I was born.

"Fran." Kramer looks me straight in the eyes and speaks softly. "I *am* your father. I can prove it."

I wait as he picks up the folder in front of him.

"This has some of your baby photos inside," he tells me.

I reach across the table and take it from his shaky hands.

"Your given name is Rochelle Francine Kramer," he adds. "That's why some of the pictures say *Rochelle* on the back."

He watches me intently as I open the envelope. A series of photos slides out in a messy stack. My eyes scan them one by one, searching for some sort of connection. A newborn bundled in a pale pink blanket. An infant sleeping next to a tiny stuffed elephant. A baby crawling across a stark white carpet. This little girl might as well be a stranger.

"There's no proof that this is me," I say. "It could be anyone."

"Keep looking," Kramer urges with a twinkle in his eye.

I briefly wonder if this is some kind of sick joke. *But what if he's really convinced himself that I'm his daughter?* What if he's insane?

I continue examining the pictures until one stands out. It's faded over time—worn at the edges—but I've seen it before. *A toddler in a purple tutu and ballet slippers.* It's the same photo my mom used to keep on her nightstand.

"Fran?" he asks hopefully.

My mouth goes dry. *This doesn't make sense.* How did he get this photo?

"Do you recognize something?"

"How did you get this?" I demand. "*How?*"

"I took the picture."

I search Kramer's face for signs, answers—anything—but he just smiles sadly.

"God," he says. "That was just about thirty years ago."

"You and my mother... why? How?"

He parts his lips, but doesn't speak for a while. "Well," he says hesitantly. "That's the other piece of this puzzle."

I wait for an explanation, but he doesn't give me one. *It's infuriating.*

"Maybe it's better if you just keep looking through the photos," he suggests.

I shuffle through them, expecting to find one of my twin. *A picture of us together.*

"Probably towards the end," Kramer says.

I continue sorting, but there are only pictures of that same little girl, always alone. I compare her face to the one in my mom's photo and can't deny it anymore. She's definitely me. The confirmation is absolutely unnerving. *Kramer is my father.*

"But I—I don't understand," I stammer. "How did you meet my—"

"Please, Fran. Please just keep looking."

I sigh and return my attention to the stack. Then I see what he's talking about. It's a photograph of me laughing on a swing set, with a woman pushing me. *It's Jane.* I recognize her from the frames on the wall.

"Yes," Kramer whispers. "That's the one."

My eyes are still plastered to the black and white image. The sight of it hits me like a landmine.

"Do you understand?" he asks gently.

No. I can't speak. *There's no way.*

"You were adopted, Fran."

"No..." My voice is barely audible. I feel my heart rate start to quicken.

"Mary Hendrix—the woman you know as your mother—wanted a child more than anything in the world," he says. "We chose her because—"

"*No*," I say more forcefully. "I wasn't adopted." My heart is racing now, pounding against my chest like a beating drum.

"Yes," he says resolutely. "You were. Jane was your birth mother."

His words hit me like bullets.

"No," is all I can say as I look through more photos. There she is again. *Jane*. She's holding my hand as we walk through the forest. *This forest*. The one we just went hunting in.

"I'm sorry, Fran," Kramer says. "I wanted..."

But his voice fades to a background noise.

All I can think about is how this could even be possible. My mom lied to me. Kramer lied to me. Everyone lied. I can't quite make sense of it. And after a while, I can't even think. *No thoughts, only sensations*. All I feel is anger—white-hot rage. The emotion overcomes me like a tidal wave, hitting me hard and pulling me under. My heart beats violently inside my ears until I lose track of place and time and meaning.

Then everything goes black.

TWENTY-FIVE

When I come to, the first thing I feel is a dull ache. It stems from my right palm and covers the length of my wrist. I'm sitting on the floor, slumped against a leg of the dining table. The pointy edge juts into my back before I sit up straighter. *What happened?*

I massage my shoulder and look around the room. There are plates shattered on the hardwood, chairs broken, and photos torn in half. I quickly realize what just took place. It reminds me of waking up in my living room several months ago. *I had another episode.*

I hear the low hum of Kramer's chair before he enters the room.

I feel tired, almost out of breath.

He approaches me, wheels only a foot away. "Fran," he breathes.

I look up from the floor, neck straining to see him.

"You're just like her." His voice is a muffled whisper.

I expect him to look horrified, but his expression is quite the opposite. He looks fascinated—fully entranced.

"Remarkable..." he muses.

I try to stand, but my legs betray me.

"It's okay," Kramer says. "No need to get up just yet."

"Wh—what happened?" I ask. *Did he see the whole thing?*

"Shh," he whispers. "You need to rest." The words sound bizarre coming out of his mouth.

I try to stand again, but my knees give out. I'm physically exhausted.

Kramer reaches into his pocket and produces a tiny vial of liquid. "Drink this," he says while quickly pouring it into my mouth.

I try to spit it out, but some of the syrup slides down my throat before I can.

"There you go. It's okay," Kramer soothes as I struggle against the floor.

The syrup is potent and fast acting. I feel my senses growing hazier by the second.

"Sleep now," Kramer tells me.

I watch him lean down and place his hand on my arm. It's cold, just like my twin's. *Where is she? What did he do to her?*

Just then, I hear footsteps.

"Oh, my." It's Laurel's unmistakable voice. "She caused quite the commotion, didn't she?"

"Let's clean this up," Kramer says, removing his hand from my arm.

Everything looks blurry before my eyelids fall shut. I can still hear them speaking, but their voices morph into confusing sounds. *I can't make out the words.* I feel a familiar pull start to overpower me. The more I try to fight it, the stronger it gets. Then it wins out completely.

* * *

I stir slowly, resisting the sleepy feeling emanating from my core. The couch is soft beneath the warmth of my body. It's more comfortable than my bed upstairs, but not as cozy as the one I have back home. I peel my eyes open and take in the stillness of the living room. *What time is it?* It's starting to get dark outside, and I don't remember how I got here.

My mental fog starts to wear off as I sit up. The events of this morning come crashing down on me one by one: Kramer's confession, the photo reveal, and my episode. I bring my hands to my head and massage my temples. Then I remember what else Kramer did. *The liquid.* He gave me some sort of heavy sedative.

I inhale sharply at the realization. I'm not safe here. I should leave before he does anything else. *But where will I go?* I brush off my jeans and stand up. Then I hear a sound behind the couch and whip around to identify it. *Kramer.* He's hovering in the library doorway.

"How are you feeling, Fran?"

"You," I say under my breath.

He starts coming towards me, wheelchair humming as it moves.

I have half a mind to lunge at him right now, but what good would that do? He's an old man in a wheelchair, not a physical threat.

"Please don't be mad." He comes around the couch and parks his chair in front of me. "Laurel helped me put you onto the sofa. We thought you'd be more comfortable—"

"You drugged me," I cut him off.

"Fran, you have to understand that I was just trying to help."

"Help with *what?*"

"With your..." He gestures to me. "Look, I have experience with this. I just thought you might need to rest, that's all."

I glare at him while he continues talking.

"Let's just start over, okay?" he pleads.

"No," I say steadily. "You're going to answer all of my questions."

Kramer nods and inches his chair back slightly.

"Right now," I add.

"All right," he agrees. "Won't you please sit down?"

I take a breath and steel myself. Then I sink back into the couch and meet Kramer's gaze. His entire face—lined with creases and wrinkles—looks different to me now. Maybe it's just the realization that he's my father.

"What would you like to know?" he asks softly.

"I want to know exactly what happened. Why did you give me up?"

"We never planned on having children," he starts. "But when Jane found out she was pregnant, we were overjoyed."

I flash him an incredulous look.

"We fully planned on raising you ourselves," he continues. "But Jane got sick shortly after you were born. *Cancer.*" His voice is strained. "I was grieving so hard, and I knew that I wouldn't be able to give you the life you deserved."

"She died when I was a baby?" I ask quietly.

He nods solemnly. "I'm afraid so."

We sit in silence for a moment until I realize that his story doesn't add up.

"You're not telling me the truth," I say. "Not the *entire* truth."

He wears a quizzical expression.

"What about my sister?"

Kramer furrows his brow.

"I know about her," I continue. "I know about my twin." The word is foreign on my tongue. *Twin.* I still find her existence difficult to believe. Wouldn't I have suspected something?

"That's impossible," he says firmly. "You don't—"

"No it's not," I shoot back. "She's been leaving me notes."

He looks bewildered.

"That's right. The other day, she told me to look in the library."

Kramer parts his lips, but I continue before he has a chance to speak.

"I found your little cell phone. The one you've been using to text about me."

"I... I don't know what you're talking about."

"Oh, c'mon," I say loudly. "I found it. I read the messages with my own eyes."

"Fran—"

"Then she left me another note," I tell him. "This one is a little more confusing. *Inside the sculpture.*"

The blood drains completely from his face. "What are you talking about?"

He's playing dumb, and I'm getting more irritated by the second. My eyes search the room and land on the vibrant piece in the middle of the coffee table. Layers of red and purple blown glass form a magnificent, nebulous shape.

"Maybe I should follow her clue," I breathe. "There's a sculpture right here." I gesture to the coffee table between us.

"Fran, *please.*" Kramer sounds worried. "Please just listen to me."

But I'm already reaching across the table.

"No!" he objects as I take the piece between my hands.

"I have to," I say while eyeing the work of art. It's so beautiful, but I *have* to know what's inside. I exhale and lift the sculpture high above my shoulders.

"No!" Kramer shouts right before I send it crashing onto the ground.

Broken pieces fly everywhere, scattering around my feet and collecting in an amorphous pile of debris.

"Oh, Fran." Kramer's words are a pained whisper. "What have you done?"

He keeps speaking, but his voice fades out as I examine the wreckage. Then I see it.

Amidst the fragments and shards of glass is something else. *What was inside the sculpture all along.* It's fully intact, lying smack against the aged hardwood floor.

It takes more than a minute to work out exactly what I am staring at. If it weren't for my honors biology course, I wouldn't recognize it at all. But sure enough, I am able to identify the slimy scarlet organ lying on the ground. It's a human heart.

TWENTY-SIX

I want to bolt, but I am frozen in shock. Every cell in my body tells me to run—to get out while I can. But my legs won't move. I stare at the heart, willing myself to spring into action.

"What the hell?" I try to say, but end up mouthing the words silently instead.

"Fran," Kramer says anxiously. "Let me explain."

Explain? How can he possibly explain this?

"I—I can clarify," he says, voice quivering.

I break my stare and step backwards. "I'm leaving," I say decisively.

"Wait," he protests. "Just hold on for one sec—"

"Take me home!" I shout. "I want to leave *right* now."

Kramer eyes me vigilantly.

"*Now.*" I glare back at him, lips pursed into a hard, thin line.

He nods gravely and tells me to collect my things. "I'll arrange for a car," he says.

I leave Kramer and the heart behind as I run upstairs to pack. If he posed more of a physical threat, I'd be looking over my shoulder. But he's a frail septuagenarian. *What could he really do?* I definitely have the advantage here.

Then I think of Kramer's guns and the broken sculpture. *The organ.* An image of the heart is permanently seared into my mind—my conscious. He killed someone. *He's a murderer.* I need to get out of here as quickly as possible.

My shaky hand reaches for the knob as I approach my bedroom door. I pull it open swiftly and jump. *The doll.* Those hair-raising eyes and that pale, porcelain face. It's sitting on the duvet cover, propped up against a decorative throw pillow.

I walk over to my bed and eye the toy. It stares back at me, mouth painted into a skinny smile. *Is this Kramer's sick way of messing with me?* I immediately grab the doll and run back downstairs.

"What the hell is this?" I call down from the landing.

Kramer looks up from the entryway and squints.

I hold the doll by the leg and dangle it in front of me.

"My God," he breathes, beady eyes expanding.

"Is this your way of messing with me?" I ask, swinging the doll back and forth.

A horrified expression takes hold of Kramer's face: mouth agape and lines etched into his brow.

I release a heavy sigh. "This stupid doll is—"

"Where did you get that?" he demands with an unmistakable edge.

The severity of Kramer's tone catches my attention. *It wasn't him?*

"Fran," he says fatally. "You have to listen to me."

"Listen to *you?*" I don't even bother trying to conceal the repulsion in my voice.

"We don't have much time."

I set down the doll. "What on Earth are you talking about?"

"You told me that you've seen your sister..." His pale complexion whitens even further.

"I have."

"When?" he asks charily.

"At night." I move down a few stairs. "She came into my room."

"You're not safe, Fran." His voice is hushed.

What does he mean?

"She's dangerous. She's... pure *evil*."

"How can you say that about your own daughter?"

"You need to believe me—"

"Why should I believe you?" I raise my voice. "You've been lying to me this entire time!"

"Please!" Kramer begs. "Please just listen to me."

I take another step towards him. "There was a human heart inside your centerpiece, and you have some sort of secret elevator in the library that leads to—"

"You know about that?" he asks incredulously.

"Yes. I do."

"That's where Ramona lives," he says quickly.

"Ramona?"

"That's her name—your sister. Your twin."

Hearing Kramer confirm her existence is shocking, but hearing him say her name is beyond strange. I still find the entire situation surreal. It's like reading about someone else's life.

"She's down there right now."

"Down there? Wait, so she lives what... *underground*?"

"Yes. That's where I keep her."

"You keep her there?" I look from Kramer to the heart, and then back again. Can he see the judgment in my gaze? Does my face betray the utter dread I feel? *Does he even care?*

"Fran, she's—"

"You're sick," I say through gritted teeth.

His face falls.

"I—I can't believe this," I stammer, placing a palm on my forehead. I can't trust him to let me leave safely. I glance around the room and try to come up with a better plan. *What should I do next? How do I get out of here?* I feel like my entire life is turning upside down before my eyes.

"You were never supposed to find out about her," he whispers.

Ramona. *I need to save her.* I need to save us both.

"She was never supposed to remember you."

I descend the remaining steps until I'm standing no more than a few inches from Kramer. "Take me to her," I say.

"There's no way—"

I reach down and put my hand around his throat—an instinctual reaction. "Take me to her," I repeat.

Kramer stares back at me, eyes deep and conflicted. Then he nods. "Okay."

I take my hand away and follow him into the library. He's a few feet in front of me, but I'm watching his every move. I see a letter opener on the desk and grab it before he turns around. It can't hurt to have a pseudo-weapon with me. Kramer may be in a wheelchair, but I've already seen what he's capable of. I stash it in my jacket pocket and keep my eyes fixed on him.

"Fran," he says as he stops in front of the bookcases. "Are you sure you want to do this?"

"Positive."

He nods gravely and reaches behind the third shelf. Then he pulls some sort of lever or switch—impossible to see from my vantage point—that activates the system. Within seconds, the bookcases begin to slide apart. *A mild thud, then a heavy, muffled noise.* It's the same sound I heard last night.

They open to reveal a long, dark hallway. Kramer flips on a small wall lamp that partially illuminates the entrance. The light flickers as I take it all in. *The void.* It looks like a sleek tunnel, with smooth metal walls and silver elevator doors at the end.

He looks back at me before moving forward. I follow him inside, jumping slightly when the bookcases begin to close behind us. There's no changing my mind now. The space gets darker as the gap of light narrows. I start to follow Kramer down the hall until I have trouble seeing him. A few seconds later, it's completely pitch black in here. I immediately reach for my phone, but can't find it anywhere. My fingers fumble around my coat and inside my jean pockets. *Nothing.*

"Where is my—"

Just then, a panel of harsh overhead lights turns on. It blinds me momentarily—stark white bulbs shooting into my open eyes.

"Sorry," Kramer says. "I should have told you about the automatic lighting."

"Why does it take so long to turn on?" I ask, hand still covering my face.

"I usually come down here at night, and I didn't want you to find out about this. I figured the light might wake you up."

At least he's being honest. I'm about to ask for my phone when the elevator doors at the end of the hallway shoot open.

Kramer moves his chair backwards rapidly until the wheels hit me.

"Watch it—" I start to say.

He turns his chair around to face me before speeding up. Then he does it again. But this time, he knocks me over.

I fall knees first onto the ground, which feels like cold cement. What is he doing? I hear the chair motor intensify briefly, then shrink back down to a low hum. He's too fast. I crane my neck to see him heading towards the elevator.

"Kramer!" I shout as I peel myself off the floor. My legs are definitely bruised.

But he's already inside, pressing a button repeatedly until the elevator doors start to close. *Shit.* Our eyes lock for brief a moment as I start running towards him. *It's too late.*

"I'm sorry, Rochelle." *My birth name.* Those are the only words to escape his lips before the doors slam shut.

TWENTY-SEVEN

I reach the elevator and search for a button—anything to call it back. But there's nothing on the wall. No panel or switch or button to press. *Nothing.* I wait for several minutes, hoping for the elevator to return, but it never does. Kramer probably made sure of that when he designed the damn thing. For now, I'm stuck in this sealed-off hall.

I shift my focus to the large doorway we came through together: the one that leads to the library. I'll just go back into the main house and wait for Kramer to return. *He has to eventually.* I walk over and look for some sort of trigger to open the passage. All of the walls are blank—nothing but smooth metal in all directions. *How do I get out of here?*

I try to pry the door open with my hands, but it doesn't budge. All I'm doing is tiring myself out. I'm out of breath, and my knees still ache from falling on the ground. Or more accurately: from Kramer shoving me down. I'm about to walk back over to the elevator bank when the lights flicker.

Then they turn off. I'm stuck in complete darkness. My breathing is shallow as I wait for the lights to switch back on. I wave my arms around in case they're automatic, but no luck there.

"Hey!" I shout. "Let me out!"

I'm not even sure who I'm talking to. *Kramer can't hear me.* He's long gone. Maybe he's going to leave me for dead. *Or worse.* Maybe he's going to kill me himself. He's going to murder me just like he did to the owner of that heart.

I think of the magnificent blown-glass sculptures—Kramer's entire body of work. *What else is he hiding? Has he killed more people?* Does every piece have an organ inside? How has he got away with it? The questions keep coming, but the answers are nowhere in sight.

He's been lying to me ever since I arrived. Before that, even. Maybe it was all a lie... the whole thing. Maybe there's no Ramona. Maybe Jane was never real. *Maybe Jonathan Kramer isn't my father.*

As desperate as I am for that to be true, I know better. He showed me irrefutable proof. I can barely choke down the fact that I was adopted, much less the idea that my biological dad is so twisted. Has he been manipulating me this entire time?

Reality hits hard that I'm really trapped in here—stuck inside this pitch-black void. Sharp pain shoots through my lungs as I try to inhale deeply. My breathing grows ragged. I feel the darkness closing in on me, swallowing me whole. There's no escape.

I open my mouth and let out a high-pitched scream. Then another, and another one after that. "Help! Help me!" I pound on the door until my fists are bloody. "Let me out!" I yell until my throat runs dry, rough as sandpaper. But my cries are useless. They disappear into obscurity and evaporate without a trace.

After a while, I press my back against the wall and slump onto the floor. I can't scream anymore. *There's no point.* I decide that Kramer will be back soon enough. He has to come back, doesn't he? But I'm eventually proven wrong. What feels like two hours—or longer—passes without any sign of life. *Where is he?*

Just when I've started to lose my last shreds of hope, there's a sign. *A sound.* I hear something on the other side of the bookcases. I can't make out what or who it is, but that doesn't matter. I have just enough strength to stand up and start banging on the door again. "Help me!" I shout. "*Please!*"

I don't hear anything for a few minutes. *No response.* I wonder if the person left the room, or simply didn't hear me at all. Maybe there was no one there in the first place. Then the door starts to slide open. *Thank God.* Relief floods my body as I wait for the first shred of light to come through.

The passage is almost fully open. Light floods my face and I feel my muscles finally starting to release. I begin to step back into the library when something stops me. *A shovel.* The entire thing happens so quickly. I can't even see my attacker's face before I feel myself plummeting back into the darkness.

TWENTY-EIGHT

Pain. That's the first thing I feel when I wake up. My neck is stiff and my head is throbbing. What happened? My eyes flit open to see a blurry splash of light. Everything is cast in a murky gray. There's a lumpy mattress underneath me, and a cup of water at my side.

I wince as I sit up. The heaviness in my skull gets worse with every movement. *Where am I?* I lift a hand to my face and instantly remember getting hit. *The shovel.* There's a lump on the top of my head, tender to the touch. I massage it with my fingertips and look around.

The room is dim and bare. Aside from this bed, there's nothing else here. No furniture to sit on or windows to look through. My vision is still blurry, but I think that this is some sort of cell. *Like a prison cell.* There's cinderblock on either side, with cold cement floors beneath my feet. The air is frigid, with a sterile lemon scent wafting through.

The more I try to focus, the harder it becomes. Everything appears to be vibrating or pulsating. I see iron bars, but it's difficult to make them out. They look wavy, like they're shifting back and forth. I squeeze my eyes shut and open them again. Then I hear Kramer's raspy voice.

"Hello, Fran." He's sitting several feet away from me, just outside the cell.

I glare at him through heavy lashes and wonder why he's calling me *Fran* again.

"I'm so sorry it's come to this," he says remorsefully.

I massage my temples while he speaks.

"This isn't how it was supposed to go." His mouth presses into a thin, hard line.

What does he mean? Recent events continue to flood my memory.

"Where am I?" I ask between heavy breaths. "Where's Ramona?"

He purses his dry lips again. "You're in an underground room, same as Ramona."

"Room?" I sneer. "This is a *cage*."

"It's actually more—"

I scoff. "So you keep your daughters locked in cages?"

"Please don't think of it like that," he says. "This is temporary. I just need to keep you separate."

"You *bastard*." I raise my voice. "You're insane." My words echo through the space, ringing around me in a dizzying coil.

Kramer moves his chair forward until he's sitting a mere two feet from the bars: just far enough away so that I can't reach him. His silhouette is still fuzzy.

"This is ibuprofen," he says. "I know you don't trust me, but it'll help with your pain."

He's right. *I don't trust him.*

"This will bring the inflammation down," he adds.

"How do I know that it's really ibuprofen?"

"I thought you might ask that," he says. "This is an unopened bottle."

I look at him skeptically.

"I'm going to slide it through," he tells me, gesturing to a space between the bars. "You can see for yourself."

I don't want to take anything Kramer gives me—medication or otherwise—but the throbbing is intensifying by the minute. If I don't take this, my pain is only going to escalate. It's already approaching unbearable.

"There's some water next to the bed."

I stand up slowly and examine the bottle before breaking its seal. Then I take a long swig and swallow down two orange pills.

"What the hell did you do with my phone?" I ask him.

"I don't have your phone, Fran," he says, matter-of-factly.

"Yes, you do," I insist. *He took it.* My only tether to the outside world. My main connection to work and home—my real life.

"Stop lying! You must have taken it when I blacked out."

"Is that what you call it?" He sounds amused.

I'm not going to answer any of his questions. And I'm sure as hell not going to discuss my episodes with him.

"Watching you in the dining room reminded me so much of her..." He trails off.

Ramona. I need to find her. Does she even know I'm down here?

"It's uncanny—"

"Where is my sister?" I ask sharply.

"I told you. She's down here too."

"Where exactly?"

"Down the hall," he says.

"Ramona!" I start screaming. "Ramona!" But even if she hears me, there's no way she'll be able to respond. *She can't speak.*

"I hate to break it to you, Fran," Kramer stops me, "but she's in a different type of room than you are. Hers is a little more secure."

I flash him a look and gesture to the cell bars.

"I know." He shrugs. "But once you told me that Ramona had been visiting you at night, I realized that she'd found a way out of her former... residence."

I stare down at my feet and don't respond.

"She's actually quite happy down here, you know," he continues. "Well, maybe *happy* is too strong a word. *Amenable* is a bit more accurate. Yes, I believe that Ramona has come to accept these circumstances and—"

"She doesn't exactly have a choice," I cut in.

He looks at me quizzically.

"Does she?"

"Well, not exactly. But this is the best arrangement I could come up with," he says.

It's hard to digest how casual Kramer sounds. He might as well be talking about some trivial subject. I still can't discern his motive in all of this. *What was his original plan?* Flawed logic aside, maybe part of him couldn't help but want to bring us all back together for a family reunion of sorts—albeit a twisted one.

"You're a monster," I say to him.

His demeanor changes immediately after the words leave my mouth.

"Pure evil," I add, fueling the nascent fire.

Kramer's composure rapidly gives way to something else— *someone* else. I watch as he turns away to leave.

"Perhaps I'll come back after you've had a chance to cool off," he says dourly.

"Wait!" I call after him, but it's no use. Kramer is gone.

* * *

The pain in my head starts to subside, but I can't shake the sleepy feeling buzzing through my body. I try to keep myself awake for as long as possible. I even stand up and do some stretching, though I don't make it very far before succumbing to the lassitude. Before I know it, I'm back on the mattress, falling unwillingly into a heavy slumber.

My recurring dream pulls me in even deeper. *The rabbit...* *I've lost it.* My plummeting body finally comes to a rocky halt. Both arms and legs ache from the impact, but I stand up and brush myself off. *No cuts or bruises.* I start to catch my breath while looking around the area. Suddenly, I don't recognize my woodland surroundings. The lofty trees loom over me like menacing foes, daring me to go back home.

I put one foot in front of the other and start walking. My shoeless one is cold and wet, sinking farther into the muddy earth with each step. Just then, I hear a sound across the forest. My head whirls around too quickly as my heavy braids hit me squarely in the face.

I see a figure in the distance: a man. I move towards him cautiously, careful not to make too much noise. It's not long until I'm standing a few feet from him. *Maybe closer.* Fear takes hold as I realize what I'm looking at. It's Kramer, raising his gun. But he's not pointing it at me. He's aiming for an animal—a deer.

"No!" I shout. "Don't!" But the gunshot drowns out my words.

Before I can stop it, a piercing bullet takes down the unsuspecting buck. I watch the creature hit the ground until the entire forest falls silent. Kramer approaches and pulls out a knife: the same one he used when we went hunting together.

"Stop! I yell at him, but nothing comes out. I open my mouth and try again. *Still no sound.* He can't hear me.

To my surprise, Kramer doesn't slit the animal's throat or cut off his head. He uses the knife to do something else. I watch in horror as he stabs it into the deer's chest. Blood spews in all directions, soaking his hands in crimson and guts.

My eyes expand as Kramer reaches inside the wound. His

arm disappears for a moment until he finds what he's searching for. I stop breathing when he pulls out a large heart—still beating—and examines it. Kramer holds it up high above his head, almost like an offering to the gods. Then he turns around and grins at me.

I wake up screaming at the top of my lungs. Sweat drips down my forehead as I roll over and gasp for breath. "Help!" I cry out. "Help me!" My panicked voice echoes through the cell as I slowly remember where I am: in a cage underneath Kramer's house. Tears pool inside my swollen eyes as I realize *what* I am. Trapped. Hopeless. Lost. *All the above*.

TWENTY-NINE

When Kramer finally returns, my only greeting is silence. He positions himself directly in front of the bars—even closer than last time. I feel his stare piercing my calm façade, shooting through the cell and threatening my self-control. I can't stand it.

"You know what, Fran?" He breaks the stillness. "I'll tell you everything you want to know."

I look at Kramer doubtfully.

"I figure I've got nothing to lose at this point," he continues, motioning to the prison. "So I might as well tell you the truth."

For some reason unbeknownst to me, I believe him.

"Go ahead," he urges. "Ask away."

I'm loaded with questions. "Where are we?"

"I should have expected you to lead with that." He smiles. "We're in Minnesota."

I'm unconvinced.

"I assure you, Fran." He lets out a strained laugh. "*Minnesota.* The good old U.S. of A."

"So this entire time, we've only been a short plane ride from my home?"

"Well," he clarifies, "technically speaking, this *is* your home."

"This is where I was born?"

"Yes. The truth is that Jane and I moved here before she got pregnant."

"You kept this place a secret for so many years—hid it from the media."

"Yes. We never revealed where we were moving."

"Why?"

"I prioritize privacy more than anything else. You should know that by now."

I raise an eyebrow. "So what, you just hate people bothering you?"

"I've never been very social." He shrugs. "Neither was Jane. She always preferred reading outside over engaging in surface-level conversations, anyway. This was—and is—the perfect location for a residence. Far enough off the beaten path that no one ever bothers coming here."

"But that would change if people realized where you lived."

"Exactly. That's why I keep it a secret. This way, no one knows I'm here."

I sit back down on the mattress. *Minnesota.* That's actually good news. If I make it over the gate, there's bound to be a small town nearby. I'll hitchhike if I have to. But first, I need to figure out how to open this cell.

"It's much safer out here than it is in any busy city. You used to love playing outside when you were little."

"If you're really my father, then why did you give me up?"

"It's complicated," he starts. "I didn't want to, you know. But Jane and I weren't able to take care of you the way we should have." His words are precise. "We could barely care for *one* baby, much less two."

"So you chose to keep Ramona? *Why?*"

Kramer doesn't speak.

"And you just gave me up?" I hear the bitterness in my own words. Before today, I didn't realize I was adopted. And now, the knowledge leaves me with an antipathy I can't deny. *The sting of years-old rejection.* "How could you do that?"

"As I told you before," he says defensively. "It was complicated—"

"Why did you even lie to me in the first place?"

"I didn't want to scare you off," he admits. "I wanted the chance to get to know you."

"You could have just told me the truth," I counter.

"Fran," he chuckles. "If I had started things off by telling you I was your father, would you really have believed me? You would have run off."

I'm still in disbelief.

"I wanted you to remember on your own. I wanted us to be close. I decided to wait until you warmed up to me—"

"A lot of good *that* did," I say derisively. "You really hit it out of the park."

Kramer sighs. "I just wanted to get to know you before I died," he says bluntly.

"You're dying?"

"Not at the moment," he says. "But I *am* getting older, and I'm not sure how much time I have left."

"How did you even find me?"

"I've been looking for you for a long time, Fran," he says. "But I didn't want to contact you while Mary was still alive."

The sound of my mom's name coming out of his mouth gives me chills.

"I finally found you after a lot of searching," he continues. "It was your byline in that magazine—SYNC."

Of course.

"I really enjoyed reading your articles," he adds.

I glare at him.

"Especially the piece about summer fitness routines. That one was great."

I can't tell if he's mocking me or being genuine.

"I liked the part about—"

"Next question," I cut him off. "Did you kill Jane?"

A pained expression takes hold of his face.

"Did you?"

"*No*," he says with conviction. "Of course not."

I still don't know whether or not to believe him. Kramer mumbles something to himself before I change the subject.

"Why do you keep Ramona locked up?" I ask.

"She's dangerous."

"What do you mean, dangerous?"

"That's exactly what I mean," he says evenly.

"But *how* is she dangerous?"

"Ramona can't be trusted."

"Oh, c'mon." I release an irritated sigh. "You're going to have to give me more than that."

"Fran," he starts. "The reality is that—"

I brace when I hear footsteps approaching. They sound like heels tapping on the icy floor.

"Here you go," says a familiar voice.

"Laurel!" I shout the second I see her face. "Please—you have to help me!"

She doesn't even bother turning her head, ignoring me instead.

"Help!" I try again, though it doesn't do any good. There's no way Laurel would help me. She works for Kramer.

She smiles and hands him a mug of something: coffee or tea.

"Thank you, Laurel. I was just about to ring you."

"Can I get you anything else?" she offers.

"No, no. This is perfect."

I watch Kramer take a long sip while she walks away.

"So she knows about this place too?" I ask.

He turns towards me and nods.

"Is she like your accomplice or something?"

"Well, Fran," he starts, "I really detest the term *accomplice*. It evokes an image of some sort of cheap Bond villain."

I roll my eyes.

"I prefer *confidante*. Laurel is my confidante."

"So she's been helping you this entire time?"

Kramer wrinkles his forehead.

"With the secret phone and the—"

"Secret phone?"

"I found it in your desk drawer," I tell him. "I know that you guys were texting about me. I read the messages!"

"Fran," he cuts in. "What are you talking about?"

"Don't even try to pretend like you have no idea what I'm saying. I found the damn phone!"

"A phone? I honestly don't know what you're—" He stops talking midsentence. Then his eyes close as his head rolls down towards his chest. *Did he fall asleep?*

"Kramer?" I say loudly, trying to rouse him. "Wake up!"

THIRTY

A long time passes—so long that I lose track—until I hear another noise. *A familiar one.* It's the same sound of footsteps as before: light clicks against the pavement. It's Laurel.

"Well," she muses. "That took a while."

I look at her in shock. She drugged him.

"Thank God for that wheelchair," she adds sarcastically. "He would have fallen smack on the ground. Might have cracked his skull, too."

"What are you doing?" I ask, voice unsteady.

But she just ignores me and chuckles. My mind files through possible explanations—reasons why she would do that. Up until this moment, I thought Laurel was Kramer's right-hand woman. *His trusted comrade.* I guess I was wrong.

"What are you doing?" I ask again.

"What does it look like?" she retorts. "I knocked him out."

I look from her to Kramer in disbelief.

"I couldn't exactly hit him like I did with you," she adds. "He's an old man. Fragile bones, and whatnot."

The shovel. It was her.

"Don't want to kill him just yet."

"But..."

"But, what?" She presses her thin lips together.

"I thought you two were working together," I say. "I thought—"

She turns her nose up before I can finish. "That's what he thinks."

Why is she turning on him like this?

"I never cared much for the man." She purses her lips. "All I ever was to him was *the help*." She shrugs. "Didn't care much for his wife, either."

I watch in disorientation as she pushes Kramer away. *Where is she taking him?*

"Now," Laurel says when she returns. "Are you going to cooperate, or am I going to have to hit you again?"

I bring a hand to my forehead and feel the tender bruise.

"Take this." She reaches through the cell bars and sets a tiny cup on the ground.

I look at the cup with uncertainty. *She wants me to willingly drug myself?*

"Now," she says firmly. "If you don't comply, I'm going to make things a lot more difficult for you."

I look at Laurel and wonder what she's really capable of. *I don't want to find out.* The mysterious liquid in the cup stares back at me, daring me to drink it. My better judgment tells me to avoid it at all costs. *But my fear.* My fear wins out.

"Take it," she repeats as I reach for the cup. "And swallow every last drop."

I have no idea what Laurel is going to do once I'm unconscious. But I can tell by her demeanor that the consequences of disobeying her will be a whole lot worse. With her eyes fixed on me, I bring the cup to my lips and drink.

* * *

I wake up easier this time. It's not so much a slow, hazy stirring as it is a jolt: rapid awareness shooting through my body. I'm sitting on the floor, back pressed against the cinderblock wall. It's the same room as before—this prison cell I'm trapped in. *This cage.* But my captor is different this time.

I look around and see Kramer sitting in the far corner of my cell. He's slumped over in his wheelchair, still unconscious. A million thoughts race around my head as I try to make sense of what just happened. He was keeping me in here, locked up underneath the house. *Was that his grand plan all along, or is he just paranoid now that I know his awful secret?* He's probably a murderer.

And now he's trapped inside here, just like me. Everything is happening so quickly—too fast for me to keep up. I still don't understand where Laurel comes into play. *Why does she want us both locked up?* I really thought they were working together, and apparently, so did Kramer.

I glance outside the cell and gasp. There's a metal chair sitting a few feet away from the bars, so close that I can almost touch it. But it's not the chair that makes my stomach swoop. *It's what's on top.* It's the doll.

Kramer wakes with a start. He squints around the room, recognition spreading across his face. I'm still shocked at the sudden change of events, but I have nothing to say to him. I turn back towards the front of the cell, eyes glued to the doll. *What is that thing?* Why does it keep popping up wherever I go?

Then I hear the faint sound of a door opening, followed by the lightest footsteps. They're coming this way. I stand up quickly and move further away from Kramer.

"What happened?" he asks hysterically.

I steady myself, ready to face Laurel. I'll figure out a way to get out this time. *I have to.* Maybe I can trick her into thinking I'm weak—unable to move—and lunge at her when she eventually opens the cell. I take a deep breath as the footsteps grow louder. But when she finally appears, it's not Laurel. *It's Ramona.*

THIRTY-ONE

Ramona approaches the cell and stands still. What is she doing here? How did she get out of her room? I stare at her in the shadowy light. *Am I imagining this?* I open my mouth in disbelief. But before I can speak, she starts banging on the cell bars. I jump at the suddenness of it.

"What happened, Ramona?" Kramer asks frantically. "What's going on?"

She stops hitting the bars.

"Tell me now."

She cocks her head at him.

"Tell me!"

"What are you doing?" I stop him. "She can't speak."

Then Ramona looks at me and starts to laugh. A shrill, bone-chilling, mind-numbing laugh.

"Of course she can," Kramer says. "What do you mean?"

I look back at her in disbelief.

Then Ramona speaks. "Hello, *Sis.*" Her voice is deep and gravelly: a sharp contrast to her petite frame.

"You—you can talk?"

She just smirks. *What kind of game is she playing?*

"I thought you couldn't speak."

"Oh, I can speak." She tilts her head at me. "Did you say hello to Mother?"

I flash her a confounded look.

Ramona gazes at the porcelain doll. "Sister is very happy to see you," she whispers. "She must have forgotten her manners."

My mind goes numb. She's talking to the doll.

She kneels down and caresses its porcelain face. "Aww," she coos loudly. "I love you too, Mother."

I'm so shocked that I turn towards Kramer, who avoids my burning stare.

Ramona pouts. "Mother says that she's mad at both of you." Her bottom lip quivers. "You've been very, very bad."

I can't believe what I'm seeing. *What I'm hearing.*

Kramer steals my attention. "I don't understand," he says to Ramona. "Laurel was helping you?"

She scoffs and stands back up. "She was always more of a mom to me than your beloved *Jane* ever was."

His eyes enlarge in shock.

"We both know it's true."

"Your mother may have struggled a bit with parenthood, but it was a big change. She loved you dearly—"

"Save it."

Kramer raises his sparse eyebrows.

"You really had no idea," she derides. "So oblivious."

He parts his lips to speak, but nothing comes out.

"Unlike you, I bothered to get to know Laurel," she says. "I'm the daughter she never had. We've been working behind your back for a while."

"But... how?"

"Various ways," Ramona simpers.

Kramer's jaw starts to drop. Clearly, he's just as confused as I am.

"We even text each other," she adds, holding up the black phone I found in the library.

I can't believe it. *The phone was hers.*

Kramer looks at me, recalling the end of our last conversation. "Is that the phone you were talking about?" he asks.

I nod. "I—I thought it was yours. I found it in your desk drawer..."

"I planted it there," Ramona interjects. "You're just so predictable."

"What are you up to?" Kramer demands. "Tell me!"

She fixes him with a steely gaze.

"*Ramona*," I plead. "You have to let me out."

She sighs before turning towards me.

"Please! Why am I still in here?"

Her answer is nothing but a devious smile.

"There's no point," Kramer mumbles. "She's insane, Fran."

"Oh, I'm insane?" Ramona sneers at him. "Try taking a look in the mirror."

"You're mentally unstable," he says definitively. "You have been for a while."

"You're the crazy one," she fires back. "You keep me locked up down here so you don't have to face the truth."

I look from Kramer to Ramona and back again. It's hard to know who—and what—to believe.

He sighs deeply. "It's for your own good."

"At least I was careful about it. No one would have ever known—"

"Careful?" He raises his voice. "You weren't careful! Your victims were from nearby towns. So close to home!"

"They were people who wouldn't be missed," she counters. "Only losers and loners."

He waves her off. "Still too risky. You should have known better."

I can't help myself anymore. "Will someone please tell me what the hell is going on?" I cut in.

The cell is suddenly silent. I hear my own heartbeat as Kramer and Ramona turn to face me.

Then she lets out a short laugh. "You didn't tell her, did you?"

Kramer looks away.

"Tell her the truth," Ramona commands. "Right now."

He doesn't say anything.

"What's she talking about?" I ask him.

"Tell her!" Ramona shouts. "I want to hear you say it."

"Your sister," he whispers. "She has an affliction..."

I wait for Kramer to continue, but he stops talking altogether.

"An *affliction*?" Ramona sounds amused. "You used to call it my *darkness*."

He shrugs. "What do you want me to say?"

"Oh, just spit it out," she says.

"Fine! You... you like to kill people."

Kramer looks stunned as the words leave his mouth, and Ramona looks satisfied.

* * *

Time seems to stand still for a while. Several moments pass before anyone speaks again.

"There we go," Ramona says with a smile on her face. She wears Kramer's remark like a badge of honor—a point of pride.

I can't believe what I'm hearing.

"It's an addiction," Kramer adds. "She can't help it."

"Addiction... affliction... darkness... whatever you want to call it," Ramona says flatly.

"I love her," he says. "Despite all that."

"You're ashamed," Ramona corrects him. "That's why you

don't turn me in. You can't stand the fact that your daughter is a—"

"Wait," I interject. "I don't understand." An image of the human heart encased in Kramer's sculpture flashes through my mind.

"It's not that complicated," Ramona says. "I like killing people. You know, cutting them up and slicing—"

"That's enough, Ramona!" Kramer's voice booms through the cell.

She flinches slightly, but appears otherwise unfazed. Then she walks straight up to the bars and sticks her face between them. "You know what, old man?" Her voice is taut. "You don't get to tell me what to do anymore. You're not in charge. *I* am."

Ramona's tone sends a chill down my spine.

"Anyway," she resumes. "I like to cut their hearts out."

Kramer looks down and grimaces.

"That's my signature, if you will. And you used to help me hide the evidence," Ramona says. "Didn't you, Dad?"

I wait for him to deny it, but he just keeps staring at the ground.

"What do you—"

"Just wait," she cuts me off. "There's more."

I swallow hard and watch her through the bars.

"He probably hasn't told you any of this, right?"

I shake my head. "He just told me that I was adopted."

She throws a hand through the air. "Tip of the iceberg."

"Ramona, please." Kramer moves his chair closer to her. "Fran doesn't—"

"*Fran*," she says. "What an interesting name. I'm guessing that your mom chose it?"

I nod.

"But did he tell you the important part?" she asks cynically. "The only part that really matters?"

I wait for her to explain.

"Did our lovely father explain why he gave you up?"

My eyes dart over to Kramer, who simply puts his head in his hands and sighs.

"You and me..." she whispers. "We were a team."

"That's not the whole story," he says.

"Well then." She shrugs. "By all means, please enlighten us."

After a moment, Kramer looks at me with sunken eyes. "You have to understand, Fran. It wasn't an easy choice. I still regret my decision immensely."

There's a sound coming from down the hallway. *A door swinging open.*

"Mona?" Laurel's voice calls. "Time for dinner."

The door closes.

"Well," Ramona says in a cheery voice. "I guess we'll press pause on this little chat for now."

"Wait!" I plead as she turns to leave. "*Please* let me out. I promise—"

"Save your breath, Sis," she stops me. "But how fun is this? The whole family is back together again! Well, almost." Ramona picks up her doll and holds it out toward us. "Say *bye-bye*, Mother."

As the sound of her footsteps fades away, the knot in my stomach tightens. I don't know who's worse: the monster keeping me locked up, or the monster inside this cell with me.

THIRTY-TWO

I'm sitting as far away from Kramer as physically possible. He's tried talking to me a few times, but I don't want to hear it. I'm too busy obsessing over how I'm going to escape. *I can't die in here.*

"God," he whispers. "You just remind me so much of her. Even now, while you're thinking. It's like looking at—"

"I get it," I cut him off. "I remind you of Ramona. We *are* twins, you know."

He looks at me with a bemused expression as I drag my eyes over to his corner of the cell.

"Yes," he continues. "She used to have episodes just like yours."

His words hit me like an avalanche.

"Exactly like yours. Watching you earlier today was unreal. You really are just like your sister."

"I'm nothing like her."

He stares intently at my face. "It's amazing that after all these years, you still have the same darkness inside of you. I thought that time and distance would have—"

"What did Ramona mean?" I ask suddenly. "What did she mean when she said we used to be a team?"

His mouth curves into a frown.

"You were both *interesting* children," he starts. "We noticed odd behaviors here and there... violent and destructive tendencies."

I sit enraptured, wondering what he means.

"Everything was dealt in extremes. You and Ramona were either the sweetest, most adorable kids, or you were the worst. If something upset you, you were vicious—spiteful and aggressive. It was horrifying."

I feel like he's talking about strangers.

"We didn't think there was much cause for concern until that day in the forest."

"What happened?"

"We thought you were just playing innocently." There's a distant look in his eyes. "But that couldn't have been further from the truth. You were killing rabbits."

I inhale sharply. *Rabbits.* The reason I liked to spend time in the woods—chasing animals and playing rough. The urge was ingrained, I just didn't realize it. *Ramona.* I didn't remember her. I didn't realize what we did.

"That's part of why I took you hunting the other day," he adds. "Thought it might jog your memory."

I'm completely lost for words, loath to believe any of it. "We were just children..."

"I know," he agrees. "Which is why we did everything we could to help. Jane researched and read the work of renowned therapists and specialists. Case studies and methodologies... we tried so many different treatments and regimens those first few years—exhausted all reasonable possibilities."

"And none of it worked?"

He shakes his head. "To no avail. You and Ramona actually

seemed to fuel each other... to intensify each other's emotions in a detrimental way."

"How?"

"I guess you sort of egged each other on."

"Did we fight with each other?"

"Not that I know of. But one of your therapists suggested that we separate the two of you. He was adamant that you would have a better chance living apart than staying together."

That's why they gave me up.

"It was an impossible decision."

I don't respond, though I'm left wondering why they chose *her*. Why not me? Was I even worse than Ramona? I want to ask, but part of me still refuses to believe it.

"We thought it would help both of you," he adds. "Maybe you could have bright futures if you were living away from each other."

"Why not give both of us up?" The question bursts out before I can stop it.

A pained expression twists its way across Kramer's face.

"Is that not something the therapists recommended?"

"We... considered it. But the idea of sending you to different families—the thought of not having contact with either of you..." He stops short.

"So you sent me away."

"We knew that Mary would be a phenomenal mother," he says. "The agency we used provided ample discretion, and—"

"And then what? You kept Ramona down here?"

"Not at first." He scratches his neck. "We exerted all our efforts toward getting her better. We ramped up the therapy sessions until they seemed to cause an adverse reaction. Her response was to rebel in any way she could."

I ball my shaky fingers into fists. "Isn't locking a rebellious child up a little extreme?"

Kramer raises his eyebrows. "It took so much more than that before we brought her down here. Ramona took one of my guns when she was a teenager. She went deep into the forest—farther than I'd ever gone before—and shot a man. A squatter, I think." He draws in a shaky breath. "She finished him off with a knife."

My face goes blank.

"After that, we just couldn't trust her."

"And the man? Didn't someone come looking for him?" I ask, the skepticism leaching through.

He shakes his head. "That's what we were afraid of, but no one ever did."

"She would have been—"

"Taken from us," he says. "No doubt about it."

"So you covered everything up for her?"

"We didn't even realize what had happened until Ramona ran back to the house screaming. She made up some story about how he was bothering her... didn't quite add up, but we trusted her every word. I even helped her destroy the evidence."

I swallow hard.

"The truth came out later when she killed again. That's when she told us everything." He pauses for a while. "It was the strangest thing, looking into her dark eyes. She didn't even have remorse. Not one shred of guilt."

A chill takes hold as he stares at me.

"Jane and I discussed our options. Every way we played it, Ramona would be taken from us—institutionalized, incarcerated, or worse. We just couldn't let that happen. We figured that locking her up here was better than anything else."

I have no words.

"I was in shock, Fran. *Disbelief.* By the time I came to my senses, it was too late. She had already killed several times at that point. Going to the police would have meant revealing that Jane and I knew everything. We would have been complicit."

He meets my shock with another attempted justification.

"I truly believed that she would get better, that she would—"

"So you just kept covering for her. You hid the truth."

"You don't understand. She's my child—my *blood*. As horrified as I was, I couldn't let her get hurt."

The starkness of this cell only serves to emphasize his insanity.

"You'll know what I mean when you have a baby of your own someday."

I can barely process this news, much less appreciate the irony of Kramer delivering it to me inside of a makeshift jail. Still, Ramona's words play back in my head. *Is Kramer just embarrassed?* Maybe that's why he keeps her down here: so nobody will ever know the truth.

* * *

The sedative that Laurel gave me continues to linger in my system. I find myself resorting to useless tactics in an unsuccessful attempt to stay awake—pinching my hand and rubbing my eyes until they water, among others. But after a while, the quiet is far too conducive to a reluctant nap. Silence pulls me under despite the unsettling information I just received.

Before I can fight it anymore, sleep wins out. No sooner do I drift off than a nightmare overcomes me. This one is brand new —completely different. It's eerie and unprecedented. This one is more haunting than all the rest.

I'm lying in a prison cell, much like this one, and chained to a table. The cold metal surface sends chills across the small of my back. I squirm around frenetically, struggling to break free from the chains. *But there's no use.* I'm stuck.

"Almost ready," says a woman's voice.

I turn my head as far as I can, but it's not enough. I don't see anyone.

"This will be my greatest work yet," she says.

I instantly recognize that gravelly tone and inhale sharply when she comes into view. It's *her*. It's Ramona.

"Please!" I beg. "Let me go."

She peers down at me, studying my face with a stunning pair of eyes.

"I don't think so," she says.

I strain harder against the chains as she moves closer.

"Please!"

Ramona puts a finger to her lips. "Hush now."

I watch in shock as she raises a knife—blade so sleek that I can see my own reflection in it. She brings the weapon towards me until it hovers directly above my chest. There are mere centimeters between my skin and the sharpest point.

"Hold still," Ramona tells me, eyes narrowing.

I do as I'm told. I don't even scream when the blade cuts into my flesh. *I don't feel it.*

"Incredible," she breathes.

I lie motionless as Ramona reaches inside and pulls out my heart. She clutches the blood-spattered organ between her fingers, admiring its steady beats. It isn't until the heart leaves my body that the pain sets in. It hits me all at once: the excruciating torture and pure, razor-sharp agony. I can't keep quiet anymore. My jaw snaps open to release a wild, all-consuming scream.

"Incredible," Ramona repeats.

Suddenly, something is yanking on my arm. *A firm grip.*

"Fran," says a man's voice. "Wake up."

I open my eyes and see Kramer above me. His wispy, cotton-white hair is disheveled as he leans down from his chair. I instantly jerk my arm away and draw in a rushed breath.

"You fell asleep," he says. "It's the medicine. There's a lasting narcotic effect."

"Stay the hell away from me." I sit up hurriedly and feel the cold ground beneath my legs.

"But, Fran—"

"No!" I stop him as I struggle to stand up. "Just stay away."

THIRTY-THREE

Ramona returns—sans doll—with a mischievous look on her face.

"You have to let us out of here at some point," Kramer says determinedly from across the cell.

"No, I don't."

He exhales and leans back in his chair.

I press myself further into the cold wall, trying to put as much distance between us as possible.

"By the way, Fran," she adds coyly. "Liam says hello."

She has my phone.

"He misses you, too."

Laurel must have taken it earlier and given it to her.

"Let's see," Ramona muses as she pulls the phone out of her pocket. "What should we write back?"

My jaw tenses as she types out a response. I'm surprised she's able to get service down here.

"The signal?" Ramona says, as if sensing my confusion. "I've been jamming it."

She's been controlling me this entire time.

"Hmm... what do we have here?" She taps my phone screen

with her nail. "Texts from an unknown sender. Let's see," she says. "Jonathan Kramer is lying to you..."

Kramer and I look up at the same time.

"Ooh!" She squeals. "How salacious! I wonder who sent these messages..."

Though I already worked it out, the realization hits me again as I stare back at her. "You."

Ramona beams with satisfaction.

"Why?" I ask. "Why did you send those?"

"Because messing with you is just too much fun!" She giggles, but there's nothing cute about the sound.

Is this an act, or is she genuinely enjoying herself? "What do you want?" I ask through clenched teeth.

She taps a finger to her lips. "Hmm, let's see. I want to know what you guys were talking about while I was having dinner."

I look away, and Kramer continues to stare at the floor.

"Aww." Ramona flicks a strand of jet-black hair away from her face. "Why the long faces?"

Neither of us says a word.

"I have an idea," Ramona chirps. "How about a story?"

I don't respond, knowing full well that she'll explain herself regardless.

"Let's begin," Ramona says playfully. Her eyes light up the way Kramer's did when he spoke about Jane. "Once upon a time there was an artist..."

I rack my brain for ideas as she continues. *Can I distract her or redirect her attention? Is this really as hopeless as it seems?*

"He met a brilliant woman," Ramona continues. "Almost immediately, he fell hard and plummeted into love headfirst. There was no going back." She glares at Kramer, who has a dismal look on his face.

"Ramona?" I ask gently. "Shouldn't we—"

She raises a hand to stop me. "She became his muse, his every inspiration. He couldn't create anything without her love and support. With the woman by his side, the artist became famous beyond his wildest dreams."

She's clearly telling the story of Kramer and Jane. I want to know everything, but I'd also prefer to listen outside of this cell. Preferably when my life isn't on the line.

"They got married, bought a plot of land in the country, and built their home in the middle of nowhere. The woman preferred remote locations to big cities."

"Ramona," Kramer objects.

She waves him off. "Before long, the woman got pregnant. Two baby girls—twins. She was overjoyed. The woman never pictured herself as a mother, but she eventually came around to the idea. She was excited to create a family of her own, and couldn't wait to raise her children with the artist."

I don't move a muscle as she continues.

"*But.*" Ramona's tone changes drastically. "The couple's daughters weren't the innocent little girls they imagined for themselves. The children had a darkness inside of them... something that no treatment or psychologist could cure. That didn't stop the artist, though. He obsessed over fixing the girls, trying to break them of their wildness." Her voice drips with disgust. "Eventually, the twins were torn apart. Rochelle left, and Ramona stayed."

"We wanted to give you each a better life," Kramer stammers. "One you deserved. When a specialist recommended it, we couldn't imagine going that far. But—"

She speaks over him. "Ramona finally learned that her darkness was a gift. She embraced it, chased it... one beautiful kill at a time."

I glance at Kramer, realizing that everything he said was true. My sister is a murderer.

Ramona gets even louder. "But she could never understand why the woman—her own *mother*—didn't love her."

"She loved you both," Kramer says.

"That's a lie!" Ramona screams, fisting around inside her pocket until she produces a tattered piece of paper.

"Don't," Kramer pleads before turning away.

Ramona mutters something under her breath and grips the page tighter.

"What is that?" I ask her.

She glares at me before slipping it through the bars. Kramer's face grows more aggrieved as I slowly open the paper. It's a suicide letter.

"Read the last line," Ramona says. "That's everything you need to know."

I can't believe it. This is Jane's suicide letter. My eyes skim the sheet before settling on the final sentence.

My last hope is that your sister turned out better than you.

Ramona taps her fingers rhythmically on the bars. "My *darkness*, as you like to call it," she says to Kramer. "That's what killed her."

"She suffered from severe depression," he interjects. "That's why your mother took her own life."

"And who do you think caused it?" she sneers.

I look at Kramer in shock. "You told me she had cancer."

"I thought it would be easier to digest." The creases in his forehead seem to multiply. "I didn't want you to know about any of this."

I take a deep breath and try to steel myself. "When do the lies end?"

His shoulders drop. "Unfortunately, there's nothing more I could possibly keep from you. You know everything now."

"Why did you even try to find me?" I demand.

"I told you," he says, voice unsteady. "I just... I wanted to get to know you. I wanted to see the person you grew up to be."

"Why now?" I press.

"I'm sick, Fran." He sighs. "I don't know how much longer I'll be alive, and I needed to meet you before it was too late."

"When I asked you earlier, you said you weren't dying..."

But he just shrugs.

In this moment, I can't even bring myself to ask more about his illness.

"I'm just a man, Fran. A flawed man with a litany of regrets. If I had another chance, of course I would do things differently."

The room is filled with a stiff silence as I process everything that's been said. Each disturbing truth and shocking revelation.

"You knew about me?" I finally ask Ramona. "All these years, and I never even remembered I had a sister."

"I didn't remember either," she says. "I had no idea you existed until I read *that*." She gestures to the letter still in my hand. "Mom's animosity started to make a whole lot more sense after that."

"The plan was never for you two to meet," Kramer cuts in again.

Ramona shoots him a pointed look. "Did you really think I would never find out?"

Clearly, her self-confidence knows no bounds.

Kramer mumbles something inaudible.

"Besides, Laurel keeps me updated on everything that goes on upstairs. She would have told me eventually."

Kramer shakes his head.

"She turned against you a while ago," Ramona clarifies. "We even had a plot to make you sick, little by little." Her tone is so cavalier, like it doesn't even matter. "I read about this woman who killed her husband with small doses of poison... so slowly that he didn't even realize what was happening. How ingenious is that?" She laughs sharply. "The guy just thought he was going crazy."

Kramer's face distorts as she continues.

"But then we found out that you contacted *her*." She points a finger in my direction. "My long-lost sister. And once I heard about your little plan, I devised one of my own."

My heart beats erratically until I get an idea. I can try to reason with Ramona and convince her that we're both on the same side. Maybe she'll even let me go. I walk to the front of the cell and place my hand on the bars. "I'm sorry about what happened," I venture. "What our parents did to you... it was unfair. It was cruel."

She's silent.

"You and I aren't so different, you know. We're *sisters*. We're both the product of—"

Ramona laughs. "Are you seriously trying to play to my emotions right now?"

I pull my hand back.

"That's rich, Sis. *Really*. But we're completely different, you and me."

"Listen," I say. "I'm not a happy, carefree person. I have these intense—"

"It doesn't matter," she cuts me off. "None of that matters."

I think of telling her about my episodes: the bewildering paroxysms of rage.

"You were raised by a nice, normal woman," Ramona says. "And I was raised by someone else. Someone who was ashamed of her own child."

I'm quiet as she continues.

"Our mother killed herself because of me. Right there," she says, pointing to a spot in the hall. "I'm the one who found her lying in a pool of crimson blood."

I feel the color drain from my cheeks.

"I sat in Mom's blood and read the letter. Every word."

Kramer protests as Ramona continues.

"That doll was my only comfort after it happened. I hugged her to my chest and stared at the heart... I swear it kept beating."

My mouth runs dry. I imagine Ramona clutching the doll,

smearing blood on it while reading our mother's suicide note. "*My last hope is that your sister turned out better than you.*" She quotes the pivotal line.

"She didn't mean it," Kramer cries. "Sh—she didn't."

Ramona ignores him and stares directly at me. "Don't you see? She died loving you and hating me."

"She didn't even know me!" I counter desperately.

"It doesn't matter, Sis. *Don't you see?* She loved you more." Ramona's eyes darken. "And for that, I just can't forgive you."

THIRTY-FOUR

What is Ramona going to do? The question clutches me like a held breath—sudden, sharp, and visceral. Fear blooms in my core as physical discomfort takes hold. My head still aches, I'm hungry, and the frigid temperature is wearing on me.

The inside of this cell is driving me mad. *Ramona has to let us out at some point, right?* We're going on several hours now. My stomach grumbles at the thought of food, and my throat has turned into sandpaper from all the yelling. I long for the familiarity of home. My humble apartment. My coworkers. *Liam.*

"What's she going to do?" I wonder again, this time out loud.

"She's unstable, Fran." Kramer turns his chair towards me and inches closer. "It's like I said before."

I lean away from him as he continues.

"Ramona likes to mess with her prey."

Prey. The word makes me stiffen.

"It's a little game she plays."

Are we really her prey?

"She always loved to hunt as a child, trying to outsmart the animals and chasing them through the woods."

My sister is a murderer. The words invade every corner of my mind. If she took innocent lives without any remorse, she won't hesitate to do the same to me. *She'll kill me.* Hot, boiling blood courses through my body until I can barely think. I'm half shocked, half furious. *Completely terrified.* The fear consumes me—pulses through my veins until it's all I feel. Frenetic energy with nowhere to go. It's only a matter of time until I black out.

* * *

The cell comes back into focus at a snail's pace. I widen my eyes as fractured light morphs into a kaleidoscope of shapes. Splinters of color. Everything moves together in one fluid motion, quivering back and forth. Glowing beams of gentle blue and gray. It's all muddled into a nebulous mess of vibrating sights.

I open my mouth and feel the stiffness in my jaw—pain from clenching my teeth so hard. Then I look down at my body and examine my limbs. They're dotted with bruises, and my knuckles are bloody and raw. *Did I punch something? Someone?*

Several minutes pass before I become aware of the rest of the space. I notice the wheels on Kramer's chair before I see him clearly. He sits in the far corner, nursing a wound on his arm. *Did I hurt him?* I must have.

"What happened?" I ask, eyes darting around the cell. I see Kramer look up at me, and I realize that Ramona is standing several feet away from the bars.

Neither one of them speaks.

"An episode," I say. "I—I blacked out again."

Ramona takes a few steps closer. "Fascinating," she says. "You have them too. So do I."

Our eyes lock for a moment before I pull mine away.

"I know," I whisper. "He told me."

Ramona nods slightly.

"I hurt you," I say to Kramer. I'm not sure if I'm asking or telling, because the answer is obvious.

"Yes." He motions to his left arm.

"I guess I set you off," Ramona says incisively.

"It was..." I bring a hand to my head. "It was just everything that built up."

"You can't control it," she realizes.

"I used to be able to."

"Well, clearly you can't anymore. I just watched you hurl your body against the iron bars and punch a cinderblock wall until your hands started bleeding."

I turn my palms over and glance down at my knuckles.

"So you call them blackouts?" She sounds intrigued. "Episodes?"

I don't respond.

"How exactly do you describe them?" she presses. "I'm curious."

I meet her stare. "I just... I've always had this force inside of me that I can't understand." I shrug. "Sometimes, it starts as a deep sadness for no apparent reason. Other times, it's irrepressible anger that morphs into aggression."

Her eyes sparkle as I speak.

"The outbursts are triggered by emotions—intense emotions." *That's all I tell her.* What I want to say is this: It's like there's this wild animal inside of me, trying to break free—a beast that's determined to claw its way out no matter what. *That's how it really feels.*

"The darkness will overwhelm you unless you learn to control it."

"Is that why you do it?" I ask her defensively. "Is that why you kill innocent people?"

She purses her lips. "Careful, *Sis.*"

I don't care. I'm done trying to win her over.

"But since you asked, *no.* That's not why I do it." She thinks for a moment. "It's the power—pure and undeniable power. There's nothing else like it."

She's depraved.

"Wow," she says to me. "I used to be jealous of you. I thought that you were so much luckier than I was." She shakes her head slowly. "But at least I can control my temper. I have a grasp over my emotions, my actions." She offers me a holier-than-thou smile.

I think Kramer would probably disagree.

"It's strange," Ramona says. "For the longest time, I just wanted to see you again. I wanted to live together like normal sisters... like friends. But there was never anything normal about us, was there?" Her gaze darkens. "The years I spent down here made that crystal clear."

I don't know what to say.

"Tell you what," Ramona says coyly. "I've changed my mind about you." She gestures to both of us.

I sit up straighter, bracing myself for what she's about to say.

"Let's play something." Her dark eyes light up once again. "How about a little game?"

I steal a glimpse of Kramer, who frowns at Ramona.

"I had other ideas at first." She taps a slender finger to her pale cheek. "But this will be so much more fun."

Kramer's frown has turned into a full-on grimace.

"Hmm... I know." Her voice is giddy now. "I'll give you a chance to escape."

What's she talking about?

"Yes!" Ramona squeals. "That's it."

I feel my shoulders tighten as she prances away. *What's she going to do?*

Just then, a double chime catches our collective attention. *My phone.*

"Well, well," she says as she pulls it out of her back pocket. "Someone is popular."

"Who is it?" I ask her.

"Someone named *Edna*. Wow, talk about bossy. She doesn't sound too pleased that you haven't gotten back to her." Ramona shakes her finger at me playfully. "Tsk, tsk. Someone's in *big* trouble."

I chew on my bottom lip and watch her stick the phone away.

"Now. Where was I?" she asks rhetorically. "Oh, of course!" She claps her hands together loudly and starts walking down the hall.

"Ramona!" I call after her, but it's no use.

"Don't go anywhere," she adds in a spine-tingling, saccharine tone. "I'll be back before you know it."

THIRTY-FIVE

Ramona returns with the same enthusiasm that she left with. The first thing she does is separate me and Kramer. *He stays, I go.* After handcuffing me through the bars, she unlocks the cell and leads me down the hall. I think about trying to escape—running away as fast as I can—but where would I go?

It's the first time I've seen anything beyond the cell. I initially assumed that it was the main attraction, but I was wrong. This place is so much larger than I realized. Ramona leads me down a long hallway with similar walls and lighting. Everything is cast in the same blue-gray.

She walks a few paces behind, ready to tackle me if I try to make a move. I steal glances on either side as we continue to move slowly. There are no more cells like the one I've been locked in for the past several hours—stark with iron bars. *Only a stretch of hallway.* Then we reach a set of white double doors.

"Keep going," Ramona snaps. "They're unlocked."

I use my shoulder to push the left door open before walking awkwardly through it. Then I stop moving. *What is this place?* Within a few feet, the ambiance changes completely. The dissonance is like night and day.

"Pretty cool, huh?" she says, sensing my shock.

I inch further inside and look around. My eyes widen as I take it all in: the lights, colors, and textures. I feel like I'm standing inside a chic urban apartment. There are distressed hardwood floors, mauve accent walls, and minimalist art prints showcased in elegant silver frames. My gaze lingers on a patch of exposed brick—probably a façade—that reminds me of the one in my own apartment. *Ramona lives here?*

"I've always loved interior design," she muses from behind me. "There's something so gratifying about creating a unique atmosphere, don't you think?"

I mumble something in agreement and peer into her glossy kitchen. There are sleek cabinets and a marble countertop, but the space is entirely bereft of appliances. A safety issue, perhaps?

"As you can imagine," Ramona continues, "I was forced to spend a lot of time down here over these past few years. I guess I have *Dad* to thank for that."

Hearing her refer to Jane and Kramer as *Mom* and *Dad* is still extremely unsettling.

"Now that I think about it," she says sarcastically, "I guess he was pretty darn generous. See, he could have let me rot in that desolate cage. But instead, he locked up me in this place." She gestures to the room and flashes an artificial smile.

Did Kramer build this himself?

"You won't find a secret basement on the home's original blueprints," she says, practically reading my mind. "Dad hired a contractor to do everything."

I scan the space and almost gasp when I see the doll. It's sitting in a little chair next to a tiny table. *Doll furniture.* There's even a plate on the table with fake food and mini utensils.

"My room didn't start out looking this way," Ramona says, moving past me. "But Dad agreed to a few minor renovations after Mom's suicide, and the rest is history. I even got to take care of the construction guy after he finished the job," she adds.

The visual of her slitting an innocent worker's throat while the doll watches is enough to make me gag.

"My style is much more elevated than the old-fashioned vibe Dad has going on upstairs—cluttered and outdated. This is pure sophistication," she says before doing a little twirl. "Still, being confined to an underground space starts to wear on you after a while. It's impossible not to go just a little bit *mad*." She exaggerates the last word and winds a strand of black hair around her finger.

My eyes are still fixed on Ramona, but it's hard not to look away.

"Dad barely ever came down here," she continues. "He couldn't even face me after what I did." She throws her hands up in the air. "*Coward*."

I want to ask her more about the past, but her emotions are unpredictable. *It's too risky.* I don't know how she'll react.

"He always made Laurel bring stuff down for me. I guess he couldn't bother to do it himself. Each week, she'd bring a case of nonperishable food and water. I didn't eat anything fresh for a while."

I wonder why Ramona is even bothering to explain this to me. *What's her motive?* Maybe she just needs someone to talk to. After all, she's been starved for attention her entire life.

"Then they finally wised up and converted this into a true home, kitchen and all." She bats her eyelashes and gestures to the fridge. "That's when I realized that they were planning to keep me down here for the long haul. That's when I knew that it wasn't just a phase."

I listen attentively as she goes on.

"Sometimes Laurel would sneak down here at night, but her visits were inconsistent. I think she felt bad for me—disapproved of the way our parents were treating their poor daughter. I taught myself how to cry on demand, which isn't actually as hard as it looks. I would always act miserable and bring out the waterworks when she was here." Ramona scrunches her face up and starts sobbing within seconds, tears streaming down her flushed cheeks.

The sight is nothing short of haunting.

"That's how I won her over. I played the victim. And after a while, it didn't even matter what I had done. Laurel was on my side. She would come visit me as often as possible. Not as frequently as she wanted, because she had to work around Dad's sporadic schedule. Couldn't have him knowing that she wasn't the *confidante* he thought she was."

"Did she let you out?" I finally ask.

She nods. "She never thought I should be locked up in the first place. And it took some convincing, but I finally got Laurel to slip Dad some medicine. Harmless, but effective. She'd put a little in his evening coffee, and he'd be out like a light within an hour."

Is that why Kramer has been sick on and off since I arrived? I picture Laurel brewing my coffee and wonder how many times she's tried to drug me these past several days.

"She wouldn't do it all the time," Ramona says. "Didn't want him to get suspicious. But those first few nights were the most liberating. I would walk around the house while he slept, free to roam to my heart's content." She has a far-off look in her eyes. "Over time, I got really good at sneaking around—learning to be light on my feet."

I think about how swiftly she moved when she came into my room.

"I even found some sneaky ways to get around the house. That's how I was able to visit you," she says with a wink.

Maybe I can keep her talking. The longer Ramona speaks, the longer I have to come up with a strategy. "If Laurel was on your side," I venture, "why didn't you guys just kill him?"

Her face lights up. "It's much more fun to watch someone suffer slowly."

Her plan to poison Kramer in small doses.

"Besides, Laurel took a while to come around. Leftover remnants of allegiance, I guess. She never cared for Mom all that much, but she worked here for so long that it was pretty impossible for her not to take Dad's side at first." She shrugs. "But she woke up eventually. Especially once she realized that Dad never really thought of her as anyone more than a house-keeper. Not that Laurel liked him romantically or anything— she definitely thought they were friends, though."

I follow along as Ramona snickers.

"But by the time Laurel finally agreed to more drastic measures, I found out about you. She told me that Dad wanted you to interview him for some magazine. She told me that you were coming all the way here, to our house."

I draw in a shallow breath as Ramona's eyes flicker. She looks keyed up for something I don't want to know about. *Something darker than I can imagine.*

"I've got big plans for you, Sis," she breathes.

THIRTY-SIX

Ramona's penetrating stare is glued to me. I feel her analyzing my every movement. I glance around the room, trying frantically to look for a way out—some sort of escape.

She senses this instantly. "Why don't you take a seat?" She points to a padded chair against the wall. Her voice is pleasant, even jovial. It almost sounds like she's hosting me in her apartment. But when I don't respond immediately, her tone changes.

"Now!" she barks.

I quickly do as I'm told, feeling the cuffs cut deeper into my wrists as I sit down. Ramona's volatility has me overwrought and on edge. She's impulsive, with an intense demeanor that changes like the weather.

"Mother." She pouts at the wall. "Sister is being bad."

I whip around and look at the doll. Ramona seems intelligent, but she's also talking to inanimate objects. Is it pure insanity, or something more? *Is she a sociopath?*

She paces back and forth as I struggle to find a decently comfortable position. I wonder if she's ever going to uncuff me, or if this is my new normal. Maybe she doesn't even have a plan.

"So." Ramona's voice rings through the room. "You can

probably imagine that growing up here was pretty lonely. Lots of land, but no one to play with. Dad was always busy with work, and Mom was... *withdrawn.*" She glares at the doll between words. "I never had any friends besides Laurel. And even then, she was more like a maternal figure."

Where's she going with this?

"Anyway, I had to find ways to entertain myself. You've already seen the library, right?"

She continues before I can answer.

"Well, that was where I spent most of my youth. Alone with books. I read everything I could get my hands on—novels, short stories, plays. You can learn a lot about the world by reading."

That might be the only thing we agree on.

"By the time I was fourteen, I had already devoured everything in there."

I imagine a young Ramona sitting in one of Kramer's armchairs, face buried in a fragile first edition.

"Have you ever heard of 'The Most Dangerous Game'?" she asks me.

I fidget in my chair. *Yes.*

"The story was also published under a different title, you know. 'The Hounds of Zaroff.'" Ramona's gaze darkens. "It's about a man who hunts humans."

I watch as her lips curl upward.

"I always thought that was so interesting—iconic, really."

My money is on sociopath.

"I mean, just think about it!" Her voice rises a few octaves. "Why hunt boring animals when you can hunt actual people?"

When Kramer said that Ramona loves messing with her prey, he wasn't kidding. My stomach is in more knots than I can count.

"Humans can reason in ways that animals can't. It's so much more exciting."

"You've done this before?" My voice is edgy and strained.

"Of course," she says with an unnerving laugh. "Does that scare you, Sis?"

I tense up as Ramona moves closer to me. She leans down so that our faces are just inches apart.

"I can see the fear dripping from your eyes."

"Please," I whisper. "You don't have to do this."

She doesn't respond.

"You can let me go, and I promise that I won't tell anyone about this. Not a soul."

"There's no way I'm letting you go," she says firmly. "I finally have someone to play with after all these years. A sister!"

"Ramona, please. If you want to play, we can do anything else. *Literally* anything else. How about—"

"Oh, Sis," she says admonishingly. "What were you going to suggest... sleepovers and nail-painting?"

I struggle for a response as she stands back up.

"That sounds like the most boring thing on the planet."

"I know," I say quickly. "I was going to suggest something else. How about we—"

"Don't waste your breath," she interrupts. "It's not worth it."

My pulse quickens as she walks over to the table.

"Besides, you should be saving your energy for our little game."

She's really going to do this, and there's no way to reason with her.

"This is going to be so much fun," she says eagerly. "I can't wait!"

She's going to kill me.

Ramona opens a cupboard and fishes around for something I can't make out. My heart sinks when I realize what it is: a vial. The same one Kramer and Laurel gave me earlier.

She walks back over to me. "I'm sure that by now, you're

becoming quite familiar with this liquid," she says in an impish tone. "The Kramer family potion, if you will."

I can't drink that. There's no way.

"I can't have you running off just yet. So you're going to swallow this willingly," she says, waving the vial in front of my face. "Or I'm going to make you swallow it."

If I do this, there's no chance I'll survive. *She's going to kill me.*

"So, what's it going to be?"

I have to do something. Now. *Think, Fran. Think.*

Ramona unscrews the vial and turns around to set the cap down. There's only a split second when she's vulnerable. A window of opportunity. I lunge forward and ram my head into her back, knocking her onto the ground.

"What the hell?"

I kick her a few times: once in the face, twice in the ribs. My hands are still cuffed behind my back, but there's no key in sight. I have to keep moving. Ramona writhes around and reaches for my leg, but I kick her again and again. I do this until she looks compromised enough—curled into a tiny ball on the floor.

I hurry away and I don't stop running. My body is pure adrenaline and panic. Fight *and* flight. I clear the double doors and sprint down the hallway as fast as I can. Everything morphs into a blur of bars and cinderblock as I go. My breath is erratic as I approach the cell where I was kept.

Kramer is still inside. Our eyes meet briefly before I pass him by.

"Fran!" he calls after me.

But I keep going. As fast as my feet can carry me. The rest of the hall is much longer than I expected—at least several hundred yards to go. I can barely see a door at the end of it. *Just keep running.* Kramer calls my name again, but I ignore him.

All of a sudden, I think I hear something else far behind me

—a distant sound. *Is it her?* I don't even let myself look back. I can't. My heart thuds against my chest as I approach a black door. It's closed and has a round silver handle. I turn around and fumble with the knob, trying desperately to turn it. It's locked.

I whip back around and notice a different corridor, leading somewhere unknown. The lighting is much dimmer than where I'm standing. There's almost no visibility at all. *Is this the way out?* I take my chances and try it. I have no choice.

My eyes have trouble adjusting to the darker space. I squint while making my way down the hallway, seeing nothing but cinderblock on both sides. Then I notice something up ahead. There's a row of doors—at least ten—staring back at me. I rush over to one of them and jiggle the knob the same way I did before. *Locked.*

I start going down the line and trying each one, but nothing works. My heart races even faster as I get to the last door. *Locked.* I feel my pulse in my eardrums, pounding through me like a beating drum. I can barely hear anything else.

I look down the dim corridor expecting more, but it ends here. *This is it.* I'm about to try kicking in the doors when something steals my attention. *Ramona.* I freeze when I hear her voice. It's faint, but clear enough to send chills through me.

"Where are you, Sis?" she calls.

I have no idea how close she is.

"Sis..." Her voice echoes through the space. "I'm going to find you!"

I want to keep trying the doors, but I can't afford to make a sound.

"There's nowhere else to run!" The rise in volume means she's getting closer. "Why don't you just come out now?"

I move quietly to the end of the hall and try to hide in the shadows. *What else can I do?* I press myself into the darkest corner and attempt to steady my breath. I don't hear anything—footsteps or otherwise—for the longest time. *Where is she?*

The sting around my wrists intensifies as I lean harder against the cement wall. I strain against the cuffs, only to recoil from the pain. Ramona appears suddenly, rounding the corner before I even realize she's so close.

"There you are," she says in a singsong tone.

I squirm against the wall with nowhere to go.

"I knew I would find you." She moves through the shadows slowly, pausing to really take her time. "You can't outrun me."

It isn't until Ramona gets closer that I realize she's holding a weapon. *A gun.* She raises it up and flashes me a toothy smile. Then she shoots without hesitation. The bullet whips towards me before I can even move, landing squarely in my left arm.

I wince at the impact and look down. She shot me. Then I feel my knees go weak as I begin sinking to the ground. A strange sensation overcomes me as I examine my arm. *But there's no bullet.* Instead, there is a dart. She used a tranquilizer gun.

My body hits the floor with a thud. I try to move, but everything feels sluggish and impossibly exhausted. I watch Ramona walk towards me through heavy lids. She stops right in front of my feet and looks down. There's an enormous grin covering the length of her face. *A twisted, childlike exhilaration.* It all blurs together as my eyes close against my will.

THIRTY-SEVEN

Conflicting sensations strike at the same time. The sharpness of
a twig stabbing the corner of my mouth. The hot, prickly feeling
plaguing my palms and sweeping the length of my fingers. The
pliable softness of a damp ground beneath my body.

I roll onto my back and squint at the sudden brightness. A
hazy sky hangs overhead, casting a pale gray light onto my
surroundings. Several verdant trees tower over me as I realize
where I am. *The forest bordering Kramer's property.* I sit up and
survey the landscape from my low-profile vantage point. Everything appears different from down here—giant, menacing, and
eerie.

I am abruptly made aware of the tension inside my body.
My shoulders are literally creeping up to my ears, and my hands
are balled into tight fists. *The handcuffs are gone.* I unclench my
fingers to reveal a white scrap of paper, crumpled up into a tiny
wad. I smooth it out until three inked words stare back at me.

Hide and seek.

I rub my eyes and stare at the cursive writing. It's definitely

Ramona's. This is the same writing that appeared on the mysterious note in my room a few days ago. *Check the library.* She has been messing with me this entire time. There is no doubt in my mind that she wrote this and left me out here to find it. Ramona wants to play a game.

I stuff the paper into my pocket and look up. A small flock of birds flies high above, gliding over the tallest oak with ease. This is the same place where Kramer and I went hunting last week. *Where I watched him slaughter a deer near the river.* The same forest Ramona and I played in as children. *Where we hurt animals.*

I stand up and take another glance around. Ramona is out there somewhere. I can sense her... feel her in my bones. *She's coming for me.* It isn't until I brush off my legs that I notice another message. This one isn't written on paper, but carved into a nearby trunk. One short word etched deep into the wood.

RUN

The word makes me stiffen. *Run.* Then it springs me into action. I take off sprinting through the woods, leaves crunching violently beneath my feet. All I can think about is escaping—getting away from Ramona before she finds me. I race through a profusion of trees until I start to tire out. The sharp air mounts in my lungs, rendering my breath ragged.

It occurs to me that I might be giving myself away. I'm being too loud, and she'll find me if I'm not careful. I slow down and try to be as quiet as my feet can manage. *Don't make a sound.* I step lightly over fallen branches and lichen-covered acorns. Then I start to reassess my options. I can run, or I can hide.

My feet carry me over a large clump of leaves as I consider each choice. *Run or hide.* If I keep running, I'll need to find a way out. The only opening I know of is the thick iron-gated entrance I saw from afar. It's locked, and I have no idea if I'll be able to climb over it. I'm already feeling exhausted, and adrenaline only goes so far.

If I don't find a way out, Ramona is going to kill me. The fact that I am probably going to die hasn't yet landed in my consciousness. *Not fully.* Panic courses through my body as I look around for a place to hide. There's nothing large enough to conceal me. Besides the oak trees, all I see is a bumpy forest floor with thick roots hugging the earth.

I'm about to keep looking when I hear a sound. A sudden crackle, loud enough to make me jump. The noise could be a bird or a small ground animal, but I don't wait long enough to find out. I don't even glance over my shoulder. *I run.*

The muscles in my legs cry out as I sprint past a pair of brown squirrels. They scurry up a wide branch, eyes and noses twitching simultaneously. I hurl my body between the trees and try desperately to think. *Where am I going?* I frantically vacillate between directions as I approach a fork in the forest. Both paths look the same: muddy clearings on either side of an enormous tree. Which way: left or right? Without more than a few seconds to think, I choose left.

I have a lingering feeling that I've been here before. *I have.* Not since I was a child, though, almost too young to remember. Kramer's words boom through my head. *We found you hurting wild animals. You were killing rabbits.* I still hear the dread in his voice as I keep running. The images of small, bloody creatures in my mind's eye are impossible to ignore. Are they real memories, or false ones? There's no way to know for sure.

THIRTY-EIGHT

I finally reach a large rocky crevice and slow down. This looks like some sort of cave. *A place to hide.* I approach it slowly, glancing over my shoulder as I go. The entrance is extremely small—low enough to the ground that I have to hunch. A twinge of pain shoots down my neck when I bend over.

Darkness begins to envelop me as I step into the cave. It's difficult to see clearly, but something immediately stops me in my tracks. *A startling pair of eyes.* They blink back at me until the realization registers. It's Kramer.

I step backwards and do a double take, wondering if I might be imagining things. *Is that really him?* My momentary hesitation is my kryptonite: my literal downfall. In those costly split seconds, Kramer is able to reach out and push me hard. It feels like he's hitting me with a large, sharp stick. I plummet downwards until my body smashes into the soft earth.

"Rochelle," I hear him say. *My birth name.*

I lie just inches away from the cave's entrance—so close to being hidden. I pull my head up slowly, still reeling from the impact.

Kramer emerges, still holding the stick out in front of him.

"What..." I am so shocked to see him out here that I can't even articulate my question. *Why is he in the forest?*

"Sorry, Rochelle." He sighs from his chair.

I strain my neck to look up at him.

"I thought you were *her*."

Kramer's face isn't fully visible from the ground, but his eyes are. I notice a sudden change in them as he moves closer. *Neutral to dark.*

"Then again," he says. "Maybe this is for the best."

His wheels crush the twigs near my feet. He's only about a foot away.

"I just can't have anyone spilling our little secret." Kramer's voice is embittered. "Your article... the interview."

Is he serious? "People deserve to know the truth."

"I'm sorry you feel that way," he deadpans.

"You're sick," I say, spitting the dirt out of my mouth.

"Someone has to make the hard decisions around here."

I wipe debris from my face and get a better look at him. The man is completely depraved.

"Someone has to protect the Kramer name." The subtle tilt of his head speaks of years-old acrimony.

"That's all you care about," I say under my breath. *Ramona was right.*

"It's more important than you give it credit for, Rochelle."

That's not my name. "*Fran*," I correct him.

Kramer ignores me, wholly wrapped up in his tangent. "You see," he says. "A man's legacy is really all he has. At the end of the day, after everything is gone... youth, possessions, people..." He pauses. "A legacy is the only thing that never goes away."

When the world knows the truth, Kramer's reputation will detonate—split wide open until all that's left is a disturbing skein of facts.

"My work is the most important thing I have left."

I hoist myself onto my forearms as pain shoots up my spine.

"I'm your child," I say to him. "Your *daughter.*" Verbalizing the fact doesn't make it any easier to accept.

"You're much more than that, Rochelle." Kramer looks at me with a soft gaze that contrasts the severity of his words. "You're my undoing."

I crawl onto my knees as he gets closer. The increasing ache makes it difficult to move, much less fight back or flee.

"I didn't expect it to come to this, you know." Kramer frowns, resting the stick on his lap. "Things were supposed to be a lot different."

I exhale through a clenched jaw as he speaks.

"Drastically different circumstances." He stares off into the distance. "Drastically different..." He stops speaking as his eyes shift again.

I watch cautiously while he mutters to himself. Kramer reminds me of Jekyll and Hyde, mood shifting with the flip of a switch. It's confusing and terrifying at the same time. His erratic behavior resembles Ramona's impulsivity.

"We shouldn't have—" Kramer starts before a remote sound steals his attention.

"Sister!" Ramona's distant voice calls. "Where are you?" She stretches each syllable out like pulled taffy. Even from afar, I can hear the eagerness in her tone.

"Ramona," Kramer whispers. "She's getting closer."

I instinctively reach across and cover his mouth. *Seal it shut.* There's no chance he's going to give me away. Then I grab the stick from his clutches, hurling it onto the ground before he can stop me. I half expect him to pull back or try to resist, but he just sits still.

"Don't make a sound," I command in a hushed whisper.

Again, Kramer remains still. *Then he smiles.* I feel his cracked lips move against my palm—a chilling sensation that forces me to pull my hand away.

"You're still so similar," he says with a dark glimmer in his eye.

I quickly look around the woods for any sign of Ramona.

"Just like your sister," he repeats.

"Shut up," I breathe. "Just be quiet."

"Jane would be aghast," he continues.

I glare at him. "I told you to be quiet—she'll hear us."

Kramer's face lights up even more.

He's going to get me killed. That's why he came looking for me in the first place, isn't it? He's trying to give me away and save himself in the process. My heart races at the thought. Why is he even out here? *Is Ramona hunting both of us?* I turn to ask Kramer, but he cuts me off.

"If only your mother could see you now," he says loudly. "Jane would—"

I slap my hand over his mouth again. "My mother," I say between gritted teeth, "was named *Mary*."

Beneath my palm, Kramer flashes me the same creepy smile.

"Your mother," he says, "was *Jane*."

My heart beats even harder, thudding against my chest as he speaks.

"Sister!" Ramona's voice calls out. The sound is still distant, but I can tell that she's getting closer.

Kramer stares at me from his chair. "I see it now," he says.

I don't respond, completely preoccupied with the growing threat moving towards me.

"We should never have given you up all those years ago."

I draw in a shaky breath as he continues. Thank God they *did* give me up.

"We should have kept you. *Only* you. You would have been able to control it..."

I hear Ramona's call again as my fingers start to shake. *She's going to find me.*

"It's my fault," Kramer says loudly. "It was—"

"Quiet!" I hiss. "*Please.*"

But he doesn't listen, continuing to raise his voice until I have to cover his mouth again. Kramer grabs my hand this time —yanks it away and digs his nails into my pale skin.

"You'll see!" he shouts. "You'll see that you're just like your sister. You're the same!"

On pure impulse, I lunge forward and throw my hands around his neck. *He won't stop.* He's going to get me killed. Thoughts of Kramer and Ramona and Jane swirl through my head as I squeeze. Hard at first, then even harder.

Somewhere in those early seconds, my fear morphs into anger. The emotion changes before I even realize it. *There's no going back.* Kramer manipulated me. He lied from the very beginning. Mary might have concealed the truth, but she was just trying to protect me. *It's all Kramer's fault.* He gave me up. He's the reason for all of this. The reason why I'm trapped in this forest, fighting for my life.

He struggles wildly against my grip, but I won't let up. I can't.

"*You,*" I fume. "You did this."

Kramer claws at my wrists as his face starts to turn red. I try to stop, but I can't. After a while, my body doesn't even feel like my own. *I cannot control it.* My arms are someone else's. These hands gripping his neck aren't mine. My conscious mind is in another place else entirely.

When I stare into Kramer's bulging eyes, all I see is darkness. It's like looking into a deep void—an expanse of nothingness. The rage courses through me as I squeeze with more force. *Harder and tighter.* My fingers are fixed and unyielding, refusing to let up while his limbs flail around me.

Images of my estranged family members continue to flash through my mind. A father who locked me in a cage... a mother

I never truly knew... a sister who's trying to kill me. *Estranged* doesn't even scratch the surface.

Tears threaten as a swirl of emotions takes over. Something brutal and vicious—an unyielding force. I'm so desperate to escape that I leave my body for a spell. I flee my physical form. Anything to halt the pain and pressure mounting inside of me.

Then suddenly, everything changes. It happens so rapidly: from one second to the next. *Kramer dies.* There's a pivotal moment right before the shift. Right before his body goes limp. I return, disoriented and shocked. Bewildered. I finally come back to myself and realize what I'm doing. I am strangling him— killing my own father.

The abrupt awareness is as awful as it sounds. But I don't stop. *I can't let go.* Although I've dropped back into my body, I still lack control. I glare into Kramer's half-opened eyes—heavy lids shutting slowly—and finish the job. I watch as the lights go out.

When I'm sure he's gone, I tear my fingers from his neck. They tremble as I look from my hands to Kramer, then back again. Sweaty palms and marks on my skin. A slack tongue and pink lacerations on his throat. *Murder.* A man cloaked in death.

I stand over Kramer's lifeless body, ground damp beneath my feet. *He's gone.* A strange feeling takes hold as I think about how little time we actually spent together. I barely knew him for more than a week. Less, if you factor in how late I was made aware of our biological connection. It wasn't a lot of time, but it was enough to gather that he was complicated: impassioned... artistic... unstable.

I didn't have a choice, did I? *I had to kill him.* My mind searches for any justification it can find. There was no way for both of us to make it out alive. Besides, Kramer was deceitful and unhinged. This is what I tell myself as I look up at the sky. A mass of clouds shifts overhead, revealing a bright patch of blue. I take a deep breath and shift my focus. *Ramona*. She's still out there.

THIRTY-NINE

She's coming for me. That's all I can think about while dragging Kramer's body back into the cave. *Why bother?* Ramona will find out soon anyway. There's no need to hide his corpse. Besides, she wanted him dead from the start. *Didn't she?* Maybe this was her grand plan from the very beginning. Maybe she wanted me to murder our father.

I have no idea what Ramona has in store for me. Hypothetical outcomes plague my mind until I reemerge from the rocky crevice. Wind stings my cheeks as I wonder how late it is. Daylight—or lack thereof—is starting to mess with me. Just minutes ago, I saw a blue sky. At least it felt like minutes ago. But now, the forest is overcast and dim.

A soft rustling sound steals my attention. I whip my head around, trying to identify it. *Where did that come from?* I look back and forth, above and behind me, but there's nothing in sight. The noise increases my sense of urgency, reminding me that Ramona could be anywhere. I need to move.

There are throngs of trees in every direction. I choose a path and start walking until I realize that I need a better strategy. I have to stop running and start thinking. I need to find a place to hide. There's no way to outrun Ramona, and it would be futile to even try. She has weapons and experience on her side. Not to mention lunacy.

I have no idea where I am in relation to anything: Kramer's house, gardens, or the thick iron gates sealing off his property. This place is larger than I could have ever imagined. These woods stretch on as far as the eye can see. *Farther.* The forest is deep and vast—dense with flora, fauna, and fear.

I look for a way to track my location: some sort of marker or North Star. But everything appears uniform, from the towering oaks to the shrubs beneath my feet. Patches of light break through the cracked clouds as I inhale and exhale, trying to steady myself. *Breathe, Fran. Breathe.* Then I keep going.

My quick pace eventually slows to a tired jog. I drag my shoes along the dirt until I step on something fragile. It juts out of the ground, partially buried beneath a mass of wild plants. I pause and kneel down to take a closer look. I uncover the camouflage of mud and weeds until I realize what it is. *Ramona's doll.* The sight of it scares me enough to keep running.

Everything continues to look the same—trees and otherwise —as I brush past a low-hanging branch. *Am I going in circles?* I really wonder if I'm just tiring myself out... maybe there's no chance of progress within reach. I keep moving until I see something that brings me to a sudden halt. It's one word carved into a tree trunk:

RUN

I don't even hesitate before taking off again. The message sets off raucous alarm bells in my head as I sprint deeper into the forest. *Unbridled terror.* I maintain a quick pace, but the dread courses through me faster than I can run.

The irony of these circumstances is not lost on me. My

fears, hopes, and motives have transformed dramatically during the time I've been here. It dawns on me how trivial my assignment seems right now. The stakes that previously had me in a chokehold have lost their grip.

When I make it out of here, life will be different. The things —and people—that terrified me before no longer hold the same power. I value my work, but I am so much more than my career. And while I still respect Edna, I refuse to cower behind my articles anymore.

These realizations run through my head as my body sprints across the forest. Feet striking the ground, step after step. These are the things that keep me going.

My vision starts to blur as I force myself to continue onwards. Before long, the trees blend into one incessant cloak of brown and green. A woodland maze. There are occasional flashes in the periphery: subtle movements from afar. I even think I sense Ramona a few times, but I never actually see her. She's too quick.

Still, I know she lurks beyond the fringe, maybe closer. Ramona is watching my every move, just waiting to strike. It's all a game to her. 'The Most Dangerous Game.' I can feel the fear blistering inside of me. I taste it on my tongue, melting slowly like a piece of candy, reminding me that my time is almost up. Ramona tastes it too. She can smell my fear.

There's that message again:

RUN

Either she has a penchant for carving words into trees, or I *am* in fact going in circles. My bet is on the latter. I ignore the tree and keep moving until I see something in the corner of my eye—a split-second dash. *Is it her?* Is it Ramona?

I don't have time to figure it out before I hear a strident sound. *Something is falling.* My eyes dart upward just in time to see a giant structure coming towards me. I hear myself scream, but the sound is somehow swallowed up. There's a loud bang as the object lands on the ground around me. Shock takes hold as I realize what it is. I'm standing inside a large camouflaged cage.

* * *

The structure is made of some sort of heavy material. It looks like wood, but feels like heavy metal. I've been trying to move this cage nonstop for the past half hour. *I can't.* I'm completely trapped.

"Sister."

I hear Ramona's gravelly voice before she even comes into view.

"I knew I'd find you eventually," she says from behind me.

I don't even turn my head around. *I can't face her.*

"It was only a matter of time."

I listen to the sound of her delicate footsteps outside the cage, holding my breath as she approaches.

"You put up a decent fight," she continues. "But there's something you should know."

Sweat drips into my eyes while Ramona speaks. I wipe the salty beads from my face as she steps in front of me. We're only two feet apart, with nothing but the cage between us.

"I *always* win." She holds a gun in her left hand, letting it hang casually at her side.

"Hide and seek," I whisper, remembering her little note.

Ramona's eyes glisten. "It's my favorite game."

I watch closely as she moves over to the nearest tree. She unwraps a thick rope from its trunk and tugs hard. No sooner do I wonder what the rope is for than I realize. *She's lifting up the cage.* I watch in awe as it rises slowly from the ground. Before long, it hangs high above my head, back where it started. I still can't believe I didn't see it in the first place. I was running too fast and not paying attention.

"Almost got it," Ramona says under her breath as she continues to pull.

I look around for an escape route, but it's pointless to run. *She'll shoot me.*

"Don't even think about running," she snaps, as if reading my mind.

I stand still while Ramona finishes securing her rope to the tree. She wears a bizarre look on her face: a combination of amusement and anticipation. My muscles tense as she walks back over to me.

"I'm actually surprised that I found you first," she says. "My money was on our father."

There's a hushed moment until I finally speak. "I killed him," I tell her. The words come out before I even consider their consequence.

Ramona fixes me with a hard stare. *Maybe she doesn't believe me.* But instead of asking questions, she smirks.

"I've got to hand it to you, Sis." Her grin widens. "I'm impressed."

My breaths are heavy as I picture Kramer's dead body.

"I didn't think you had it in you."

I flinch when Ramona takes a hasty step in my direction.

"How'd you do it?"

I press my lips together firmly, so hard that I feel my teeth cutting into them.

"C'mon," she urges.

I eschew her steady gaze and turn my eyes toward the ground.

"Just tell me."

The reality of what I did weighs heavy on me. *Heavier* now that Ramona knows the truth.

"Did you hit him with something?" she asks. "Push him over? Crack his skull with a rock?"

I remain silent, chary of her unrelenting questions.

"Tell me!" The eagerness springs from my sister's voice.

I drag my eyes from the dirt to look at her.

"Tell me," Ramona commands as she takes another step closer. Her tone is no longer fervent, but irritated. "Tell me!"

The words leave my mouth in a jumbled frenzy. "Choked! I —I strangled him!" Loaded emotions flood my shaky voice: pain, grief, anger, and shock. *Pain* from the truth about Kramer. *Grief* for what we never had. *Anger* at the person he really was. *Shock* from what I did. *What I was capable of.* I took someone's life. I killed my own father.

FORTY

"I strangled him," I repeat.

Ramona's laugh fills my ears with a hideous sound. It starts quietly, then ramps up into a loud chuckle. I can't repress my reaction, knitting my brows together in pure aggravation.

She doesn't even notice. "Wow," she says between laughs. "That's interesting. You *choked* him?" Her tone is a blend of astonishment and fascination. "I'm surprised. I would have pegged you as a sympathizer—too weak to hurt anyone."

I distance myself as she moves closer.

"Actually..." Ramona taps a finger to her lips. "I could imagine you killing somebody if you had no other choice. Sheer self-defense, of course." She leers. "But strangling your own father to death? That's just beyond."

I watch in horror as her eyes light up.

"I mean, not only did you kill him..." Ramona says. "But you made him suffer. Imagine how painful—"

"Stop!" I scream at her. My heart is beating loud enough that I can hear it. *I feel it in my ears.*

Ramona is unfazed. "Do you realize how painful that must

have been for him? Having the life squeezed out of his body, and—"

"Just stop!" I yell again. "Please just stop!"

This time, she complies. Ramona falls silent for the first time since she found me.

The next several moments are heavy, rife with realizations —tacit and vocalized. We stand in the stillness of the forest until I finally speak again.

"Are you going to kill me now?" I ask. My detached voice contrasts with how terrified I really am inside.

Ramona's face goes vacant. Completely expressionless. Even her eyes are unreadable.

"You're going to kill me," I whisper. I don't know if I am asking her, or simply preparing myself for what's to come.

Her lips curl into a subtle smile. "I haven't decided yet," she says cryptically.

I eye Ramona's gun and brace myself.

"But I've got all the time I need." She cocks her head at me. "There's no rush, is there, Sis?"

I don't react. She is nothing if not arrogant.

"On one hand, it might be fun to keep you around." Ramona shrugs nonchalantly. "But on the other, you're of little value to me."

Our father treated her like a failure her whole life, like she didn't even matter. And now she's doing the same to me.

"If they hadn't sent you away, maybe things could have been different. We could have been brilliant together."

I watch while she paces back and forth.

"But we didn't have that chance, did we, Sis?" she asks acerbically.

I shake my head.

Ramona throws a hand through the air. "I guess that's just how things go..."

I don't know what to say. The sky shifts above me, clouds looming like monsters.

She stops pacing and glares at me. "You don't even realize how lucky you are, do you?"

I've never wanted to fight back so badly.

"You have no idea."

I open my mouth to speak, but can't manage to get any words out. The atmosphere is buzzing with something dangerous—something electric.

"You got everything." She inhales quickly. "I got nothing."

"Ramona," I counter. "You have—"

"I don't even have a life!"

"That's not true," I say gently.

She scoffs. "Don't you get it?" Her words are biting. "Ramona Kramer never existed."

What's she talking about?

She takes another step towards me. "Mom gave birth to us in secret, and Dad never told a soul."

She's right. The world has no idea. Nobody realizes that Kramer and Jane ever had children. *Nobody knows about us.*

Ramona's voice raises several octaves. "*You,* on the other hand." She points a finger at me. "You were given a loving home and a different name. A brand-new life."

She's wrong. My childhood wasn't simple or carefree. I never had siblings or friends—no confidantes to share my thoughts with. No answers or explanations for my strange obsessions and nightmares. *Until now.* I never even grieved my mother's death properly. She was there, and then she was gone.

"You were given a better life." Her dark eyes betray her contrived smile. She's furious.

"Ramona," I start. "Things weren't easy for either of us. We both—"

"There's no *we*," she sneers. "Don't even pretend like you can relate to me!"

Her sudden change in tone is staggering.

"You have no idea how hard it was for me," she says sharply.

I swallow hard as she moves closer.

"You ruined my life!" Her words pierce through the forest.

There's so much hatred and misdirected anger in her heart. As much as I abhor Ramona, part of me also feels bad for her.

"You ruined it!" she rages.

I stay quiet and watch Ramona swing her gun wildly, stiffening every time the muzzle moves in my direction.

"It's all your fault!" She closes the gap between us until we're just inches apart. Then she points the weapon right between my eyes and lowers her voice. "Now it's time to pay."

Panic runs rampantly through me as she traces my face with the tip of her gun.

"Any last words, Sis?"

I stand still, immobile from fear.

"Isn't there anything you'd like to say?" The satisfaction glints in her eyes.

In the midst of these woods, I have an unexpected burst of clarity. I have spent far too long straitjacketing myself. Trying to compartmentalize, trying to conceal the ugliest bits of my psyche. *But not anymore.* I am done hiding. In this moment, I realize that I need the darkness just as much as I need the light.

I have attempted to resist what I previously deemed an evil force within me, shaming myself for each and every *episode.* I've carried around the guilt like a pile of bricks. An unyielding weight. I didn't even grasp how disconnected it made me feel. From myself, from Liam. From strangers.

These past couple of weeks have completely altered my perspective. I will no longer fight every urge so intensely, no longer resist my precious intuition. Especially regarding my feelings for Liam. Now that I accept—and embrace—the parts of myself that used to haunt me, I am ready for someone else to do that too.

Liam has always loved *me* for me. These events have placed front and center what I truly desire. I miss him terribly. I can't deny it anymore—I want to get back together. I know that now. As soon as this is over, I will tell him the truth. *All of it.*

"Time's almost up," Ramona says, pulling me back to the here and now.

I do not want to kill her. I don't even want to hurt her. But what I *want* is in the past. I have no choice anymore. It has all come down to this: my life or hers. There is no other option. I know what I have to do.

"This is it," she says. "Your final moment of life."

I have to flip the switch. A moment passes before I strike the weapon out of her hand. It flies through the air and lands several feet away from us.

"Wait—" Ramona starts, shock flooding the length of her face.

The anger begins to simmer inside of me. I don't fight it. I embrace the feeling, drawing in quick, jagged breaths to fuel it. Before long, my emotions are boiling hot and unrelenting.

Yes, I need the darkness just as much as I need the light. *I want both.* Every piece of myself—the good, the bad, and everything between. Dr. M's words play in my head as a virulent sensation courses through me. *You can learn to control it.* This isn't what he meant, but this is exactly what I have to do: succumb to it. So I lunge towards Ramona and let the rage take hold.

FORTY-ONE

I am guilty. I am innocent. Somewhere—deep within the confines of my mind—both statements are true.

"We're almost finished, Ms. Hendrix."

I hug my tepid coffee cup and meet Detective Khan's stare. Her gray eyes narrow, perhaps honing in on my poorly concealed uncertainty.

"Is there anything else you can tell me about your relationship with the deceased?"

"No," I say with a measured calm. "My assignment only lasted for a couple of weeks."

The words roll off too easily, each one more addicting than the last.

"Right." She nods.

"Honestly, I feel like I barely knew..." I trail off, but my tone is steady, stable, cogent. I placate the mounting urge to embellish my statement. People always say too much when they are trying to hide something. I am better off revealing less than more.

"Okay." She clears her throat with an audible *ahem*. "That about wraps it up."

Perhaps it is my imagination, but the suspicion seems to drain from her gaze the second she stuffs the warped pad of paper back into her coat pocket.

"Thanks for your time." Detective Khan hovers in the doorway of my shoebox hotel room, marionette lines underscored as she purses her ashen lips. "I'll be in touch with any further questions."

After she leaves, I throw our cups away and examine the chair she was sitting in. Detective Khan's imprint remains—marring the beige leather with a strange dent—despite my attempt to erase her presence from this room. Arms outstretched, I flick away the remnants of her looming specter.

An unwelcome ghost enters the foreground of my consciousness. Its face is taut, ivory, rife with anger. I see the bones beneath a thin stretch of skin, every minor shadow and curve. The most intriguing person I have ever met.

I think about what really transpired between us last month. The *deceased's* account would be dramatically different from mine—another story altogether. I consider each shade of gray involved, visualizing the color between stark veracities. I believe there might actually be one billion versions of the truth.

Memories of the incident weigh heavy—intangible burdens threaded through my every action, woven into my every thought. I am chained to their very existence, a prisoner of the repercussions. Time has only served as a cruel incubator. Each day that passes seems to deepen my paranoia, amplify my fear, swell my intractable anxiety.

An unyielding sensation takes hold of my chest, equal parts dread and fury. I sink into the mattress beneath me and exhale forcefully. My muscles are wrought with tension, straining against the dull pulse of each unforgiving spring. *There is nothing to do but remember*. I draw in a sharp breath, sweep my lids shut, and surrender.

* * *

After the investigation officially ends, I release the breath I have been holding since Detective Khan took my initial statement. I remember the sound of her pencil scratching against that tattered notebook as she vigorously documented everything I told her. The ragged breaths stemming from my chest only lent credibility to my words.

I revealed who Jonathan Kramer really was. The media will deify him regardless, lamenting the irreparable loss of his talent. I expect to see his face splashed across tabloids for the next several weeks. It does not matter, though, because I know the full story.

Three dead bodies. But as far as the police are concerned, there are only two: Laurel and Kramer. I chose not to even mention anything about Ramona. The name remained guarded between my teeth, a secret buried deep within the woods. The world will never even know she existed.

Three dead bodies. Their ghosts watch as I check out of the hotel, trail me while I ride to the airport, and hover nearby as I board my flight. Every set of stony eyes is fixed on me. Those frigid, brittle glares refuse to budge, even as I shrink into my seat and gaze out the window.

Once the plane takes off, though, each ghost begins to disappear. My memories of them fade to transparent fragments, thinning out like the cirrostratus clouds we are flying through. When the aircraft descends a few hours later, the ghosts are completely gone, along with any residual paranoia. I left it all behind.

Landing at JFK feels like a fresh start. *A blank canvas.* A chance to turn the page and rewrite my life. It all feels like a dream. I hail a cab and shut the car door behind me. Then I take a deep breath and exhale. *I am safe.* As I watch the city go by, I tell myself that everything is going to be all right.

FORTY-TWO

I wake up early, just as I normally do. *Right on cue.* I check my phone and turn off the 6 a.m. alarm. Nascent sunlight streams in through a corner window—thick double-paned glass to keep the noise out. Still, the muted sounds of traffic waft in from the busy street below. Fringe benefits of living in a city.

Fractured light blinds me momentarily when I open my eyes. Bits of brightness dance around the room like tiny ballerinas. I exhale and sink deeper into the spongy mattress beneath my body. It envelops me like a cocoon, wrapping my limbs in a blanket of warmth and relief. I am so relaxed that I drift back to sleep.

A loud knock on the door jolts me awake. *What time is it?*

"Fran?" calls a male voice.

I pull back the covers and sit up.

"It's me!"

I step out of bed, not even bothering to check my phone again. Another knock quickens my pace as I make my way towards the front door.

"Fran?"

I peer through the peephole and see him. *Liam.* My fingers instantly turn the lock and crack open my door. He stands about two feet away from me, grinning broadly.

"Hi," I whisper.

"Hey," he says between infectious smiles. "It's so good to see you."

I invite Liam in and lock up behind him.

"I was so worried when I didn't hear back from you," he tells me. "I didn't know what to think."

I inhale the incredible scent on his neck as we embrace. He feels warm against my cool, pallid skin.

"I missed you, Fran." Liam plants a soft kiss on my cheek. "So," he says. "Tell me everything."

If only. Poor Liam won't ever know what really happened. I will concoct some fake story to alleviate his fears—tell him that my utter love for him is what got me through. He is easy on the eyes, but he does not exactly strike me as a young Einstein. *Not even close.*

I will keep Liam around so nobody gets suspicious. Things will die down soon enough, but I cannot be too careful until then. Luckily, I fooled the police without much trouble. I think that detective even felt bad for me—an innocent reporter who endured shocking emotional and physical trauma. I played the part to an absolute T.

My work is not done just yet, though. *Far from it.* I still have a groundbreaking article to write. It should not be too difficult, seeing as how I collected all of Fran's notes before leaving Minnesota. Some of her writing is illegible, so I will have to improvise. *Not a problem.* While she had the pleasure of dragging information out of our father in meager bits, I already have everything I need. I know the truth about Jonathan Kramer.

For the time being, I have to reassure Liam that nothing has changed and convince him that I am Fran. Honestly, killing her was way easier than I thought it would be. *Murdering my only sister.* Fran was a fighter, but she was no match for me. No match for my anger... my indignation. In the end, I did what I had to do.

"Please, Fran. I want to know."

Fran. That name is really starting to grow on me. The fact that it is coming from his lips certainly does not hurt, either. My sister's name might actually be easy to get used to. I will have to remind myself for a while—commit her identity to memory like rehearsing lines for a play. But I have a sense that very soon, pretending to be *Fran* will feel like drawing in a breath or taking someone's life. It will become second nature.

Before Liam leaves, he regards me with a far-off expression.

"Something about you..." He trails off. Then he leans down and kisses the top of my head. "Your hair smells different."

"New shampoo," I say without missing a beat.

"Hmm," Liam muses. "I like it."

After he goes, I prance back into Fran's room. *My room.* Then I lift the lid on an old trunk at the end of the bed. It creaks upon opening: a shrill noise that sounds like a wicked orchestra. *A protracted scream.* I reach inside and pull out Mother. Her little porcelain mouth is chipped from the journey here, but I believe the look suits her. Scratches and fractures add character.

I hold her to my face and stare into those dark, beady eyes. Then I hug her close and whisper into her ear. "I have a feeling that we're going to like it here, Mother."

"Oh, Ramona," I hear her say. "Me too."

"Did I do good, Mother?"

"Yes, my precious girl," she tells me sweetly. "You've always been my favorite."

I beam at Mother—a large smile that stretches well beyond the edge of each cheek. My lips burn as they pull apart, chapped cracks splitting open like paper cuts. *But I don't care.* I think I will keep smiling forever. When I watched the last breath leave Fran's body, I felt like my life was finally starting. It's poetic in a way: her end becoming my beginning. Now the real story unfolds.

A LETTER FROM THE AUTHOR

Dear Reader,

Thank you very much for finishing *Tiny Wild Things*. I hope you relished the twists and turns of the story as much as I loved writing them! To hear about my upcoming releases and bonus content, please feel free to sign up for my author newsletter.

www.stormpublishing.co/danielle-m-wong

   If you enjoyed this novel, I would greatly appreciate you leaving a review. Even a few words can make all the difference in encouraging another reader to discover my books for the first time. Thank you so much!
   I have always been an ardent fan of psychological thrillers and mysteries. Whenever I begin writing a new manuscript, my goal is to give readers the same visceral high that keeps me returning to the genre. Thanks again for being part of this journey with me. I hope that you will keep in touch—connect with me on the platforms below and stay tuned for more!

All my best,

Danielle

KEEP IN TOUCH WITH THE AUTHOR

www.daniellemwong.com

facebook.com/daniellemwongauthor
x.com/DanielleMWong
instagram.com/daniellemwong_
bookbub.com/profile/danielle-m-wong

ACKNOWLEDGMENTS

Although writing is often a solitary act, bringing a novel to fruition requires an exceptional team. I am fortunate enough to collaborate with a brilliant group of steadfast and talented people. Without them, this book would simply not be possible.

To my friends and family—thank you for the continued love and encouragement. Your support means everything to me.

To my agent, Liza Fleissig—thank you for embarking on this journey with me. Your wisdom and positivity make a world of difference.

To my editor, Kate Smith—thank you for believing in this manuscript so strongly. Your experience and passion for the craft truly set you apart. It is an honor to work with you.

To Oliver Rhodes—thank you for giving *Tiny Wild Things* a wonderful home. It is a genuine pleasure to work with the outstanding team at Storm Publishing. From copyediting to cover design, every department is absolutely instrumental.

Thank you to the lovely network of authors I have gotten to know along the way. I count myself lucky to contribute to and learn from this literary community.

Finally, I want to thank you—the reader—for picking up this copy. I hope you enjoyed every thrill—minor and major—and I hope my characters get to meet you again in future stories.